# The Forgotten Duchess

# The Forgotten Duchess

by

Angela Petron

The Pentland Press Limited
Edinburgh Cambridge Durham

First Published in 1991 by
The Pentland Press Limited

All rights reserved. No part of this publication may be reproduced, stored in a retrieval system, or transmitted in any form or by any means, mechanical, photocopying, recording or otherwise, without the written permission of the publisher.

ISBN 1 872795 01 3

© Angela Petron

Typesetting by Print Origination (NW) Limited Formby, Liverpool L37 8EG
Printed and bound in Britain by Antony Rowe, Chippenham, Wilts
Jacket design by Ann Ross Paterson

*For Mabel and George Christie,*
*Bencraig*
*Fochabers*

I met a lady in the meads,
Full beautiful – a faery's child:
Her hair was long, her foot was light,
And her eyes were wild.

She found me roots of relish sweet,
And honey wild and manna dew;
And sure in language strange she said,
"I love thee true."

                        John Keats

## Author's Note

This story is based on events that occurred in the Highland village of Fochabers during the 18th and early 19th century. In 1776 the 4th Duke and Duchess of Gordon decided to move the entire village and rebuild it some distance from the castle. The beautiful Duchess who, at a later date, was to raise the Gordon Highlanders by giving a kiss with the King's shilling, had other plans too. She became a close friend of King George III and William Pitt. Her political gatherings in London and Edinburgh made her the most famous duchess of her day. But her restless ambition had an adverse effect on her relationship with the Duke.

When Alexander met Jean Chrystie, an attractive, warm hearted village girl, he fell in love and, when the Duchess died, married her. The marriage was deeply resented by close relatives and descendants of the Gordon family who took great pains to obliterate the memory of the 5th Duchess of Gordon. Jean is buried in Bellie churchyard under an imposing mausoleum with twelve slender pillars, but the marble slab which the Duke of Gordon had inscribed with her title is no longer to be seen, and few records remain to illuminate her life with Alexander. Jean Chrystie has indeed become The Forgotten Duchess.

William Marshall's famous clock is still in existence, and on show at the Fochabers museum. He was a man of many talents and was a prolific composer of strathspeys and reels. He was a great friend of Robert Burns and set to music his poem, "Of a' the Airts the Wind can Blaw".

In order to give continuity I have taken some liberty with the ages of Jean Chrystie and Robert Burns, who were in fact younger in the year 1776. Burns' visit to Gordon Castle began at a later date. John Ord was indeed the jolly inn-keeper of the Gordon Arms but Sheena is a fictitious character. No doubt Burns did find a bonnie lassie on his visits to Fochabers; it could well have been the Sheena of my story.

Milne's school still stands as a living tribute to the man who founded it 200 years ago. The Quarry Gardens have returned to nature, with here and there the relics of foundations and masonry and a few exotic shrubs as reminders of the garden's former splendour.

# Acknowledgement

The author wishes to express her appreciation to the staff of The British Museum Library, The Scottish Record Office, Elgin Library, The Highland Folk Museum, Kingussie, and in particular to the inhabitants of Fochabers, Scotland, who were more than willing to provide much background information for the book.
Special appreciation is expressed to the oldest inhabitant of Fochabers who, as a young boy, saw the destruction of the marble slab which had been on Jean Chrystie's tomb. The slab had been stored in a remote attic, possibly from the time after the 4th Duke's death.

# Chapter 1

"Are we going to sit here 'till morn trying to write one bliddy letter? Why don't one of ye go up to Gordon Castle and tell his Lordship that we're nae going to shift ourselves out of this village."

John Ord threw another log on the fire and looked across at Willie Robb who had spoken. "Awa' ye go yoursel' man. If the Duchess catches a sight of ye she'll be fair bowled over. She likes a good-looking buck. Maybe a word from you will end this whole business."

Willie Robb rose to his feet and gave a self-conscious laugh, then his eyes moved across the room to where John's niece, Jean Chrystie, sat doing her needlework. Jean felt his eyes on her and kept her head bent over the sewing. Gypsy Willie, as he was called because his mother had lain with a gypsy, could stir the heart of any girl in the village, but his flashy good looks did not appeal to her at all. "Let's get down to it, John," Ned Geddes, the butcher, said, "and maybe there'll be time to go across to your inn for a wee dram."

Jean tugged impatiently at the bodice she was trimming, irritated at the ineffective way the men were discussing the Shifting.

"Right, man," John replied, taking the quill in his hand. He had held the meeting in his old home because the kitchen was a good size. Anyway, he didn't want to mix business with pleasure, particularly a protest meeting. Apart from that, his wife Kitty might start girnin' and putting the men-folk's backs up before they had arrived at a solution. God almighty, it was a terrible thing that was going to happen to them; the entire village of Fochabers, every stick and stone, was being pulled to the ground and set up again over in the old pasturing ground near the burn. He had been told that the plans drawn up by Mr Baxter, architect of Edinburgh, were fine enough, but devil tak' the Gordons, you'd think we were a herd of cows needin' shifting to fresh pastures.

After chewing the quill for a moment, he said, "Maybe we should get the minister to write a few lines. I canna get my words together."

Rob Chalmers, the postmaster, spat in the fire. "Blatherskite! The minister will nae go against the Gordons for he's been promised a fine new kirk with a three acre glebe."

Jean rose swiftly to her feet. "Let me try to do it."

With a sigh of relief her uncle handed over the quill and a piece of poor man's parchment. "Aye, ye've got a fair hand, lassie."

Carefully, she wrote in the day of the month and the year: seventeen hundred and seventy-six. The men looked on in admiration as the quill moved, slowly at first, then faster as she condensed the gabble of words that had been flying around all evening.

Willie Robb stroked his chin. "I've been thinking, if the castle folk were to make it worth our while ... Ye ken?"

She jumped up and faced him. "You mean, bribed us out of our homes? What about the old folk? How do you think they'll feel when they're shifted from their corners?"

"Aye, ye're right there, lassie." A crackling voice came through the curtains drawn across the recess where Granny Chrystie lay in the box- bed.

"For God's sake," John muttered, "give your granny a dram and shut her gob. Once she starts..."

"But," old Meg went on, "I'm thinking if the Duchess of Gordon makes up her mind, we'll shift right enough. That one would make the wind fly if she set her mind to it!"

"Let the auld cratur be," Jean whispered. "She's had a good

sleep, for I put some honey and nutmeg into her glass of milk."

John rolled his eyes in exasperation. "A dram would have more effect."

"Well, I'm off now to find the factor and give him the letter," Willie Robb said, moving to the door. "Will you see me down the path, Jean?"

"You'll see your own way well enough, Willie. It's a fine night." Everyone began to laugh. Willie flushed. He had an impulse to drag her out by her long, golden-red hair.

"Ach, away to the door wi' Willie Robb," John said.

She looked at her uncle, hesitated, then smoothed the muslin apron over her gown and walked impatiently down the floor.

"Dinna be long," her granny shouted. "I want me pillow thumped." There was a sound of anxiety and craftiness in Meg's voice.

"No, Granny, I'll not pass the door. Goodnight, Willie."

He moved quickly, and putting his arm around her waist swung her outside against the rosemary bush.

"Will ye wed me, Jean? Say you'll wed me, lass." He was pulling her to him, bruising her body against the row of buttons on his waistcoat.

"I'm too young to wed, Willie."

"Too young," he groaned. "Eighteen, just ripe for the picking, my lovely."

"Jean—"

"There's me gran, she sounds in pain. You'd better go, Willie, and get that letter to the factor as fast as you can."

He muttered an obscenity under his breath. Jean rested her hand against the wall for a second as the sound of his footsteps faded away. The scent of the rosemary fell around her, its fragrance soothing the ache in her throat. Was this all there was to life? Trying to handle the likes of Gypsy Willie? She shut her eyes tightly to dispel the sudden rush of tears, then sniffed as the wind brought the smell of Bella Forbes' pigs. Maybe the wind was carrying the same smell into the castle drawing-room. Maybe the Gordons had more than one reason for wanting to move the village from their gates.

She walked down the garden path and looked about her. The cottages were straddled all over the place, many with their walls wrapped in arms of sweet-scented roses to bring a blessing of health and happiness to the home. The track that wound past the inn led to the pond which was used by ducks and where village lads were dooked before they wed. A high hedge, built by the Gordons' ancestors, gave the castle folk their bit of privacy when they went by in their carriages or on horseback. On one side of the village was the river Spey, and on the other, the Knowe of Tarryreach and Whiteash Hill Wood.

A rose-leaf fluttered against Jean's cheek like the touch of a butterfly's wing. She frowned. What was it that Doctor Johnston had been heard to say in the village? "Fochabers was a poor place with many ruinous buildings." A feeling of anger stirred in her. What did learned English folk know about life up here in the Highlands? From what she had heard of London the smell there was worse than any midden. And what about Edinburgh where they threw their slops out of the window, landing on folk's heads, likely enough. And the mannie going around in the evenings shouting, "Gardy loo." No wonder it was called Auld Reekie. Never mind how Fochabers looked, the cottages were kept spotlessly clean – well, apart from one or two. And you had only to lift your head to behold a sight fit for a king: the mountains over there smothered in purple and pink heather and jewelled by sunlight striking the late snow caught in the gullies.

Meg was getting anxious about Jean's absence. She had picked up her stick to strike the chamber pot to summon John, when her granddaughter's head appeared around the curtain. "You've been a whiley," the old woman complained.

"I had to get rid of Willie Robb."

"Did he fumble ye?"

"He didn't get a chance."

"That's my bairn."

"He'll try again, though. He's wild to wed me."

"You're no' to wed the likes o' him. He'll tak' to the road like his father afore him." Meg's eyes slid away from her granddaughter's gaze. "And if ye wed who'd look after your old granny?"

"Aunt Kitty," Jean said, teasingly, as she tidied the bedcovers.

Meg shifted her weight and rolled her eyes at the ceiling. "Lord preserve me! That one sours the milk the minute she sets foot in the house. My son must've been desperate to wed her."

"Hush!"

"But he didna wed her, lass, 'twas the inn he wed. Had his wee, canny eye on it since he was a bairn."

When the cottage door was opened, they heard a hail of welcome for the newcomer.

"Tis yoursel', Mr Milne. Come away in," John Ord said.

"Aye," a quiet voice replied.

"Sit down, man. You look as though you were in need of a dram."

Jean shook the little pot of scented herbs beside the bed and went to move into the kitchen. Meg caught her hand and whispered, "Dinna forget your old gran if there's a dram about."

Her granddaughter wasn't fond of whisky; besides, she was reluctant to spend their small income on the stuff, for it cost a shilling or two a bottle. Granny was a bit too fond of it. If there was a drop in the house she could smell it, even if it was buried twenty feet under the ground!

Alexander Milne, who was a lackey at the castle, sat by the fire looking pale and tense. "I've been dismissed from Gordon Castle," he said quietly.

"Why?" everyone asked simultaneously.

"Disobeyed the Duchess's orders."

"You didn't?"

"I did and I'd do it again," he said, his eyes fixed on the knives of rose-coloured flames leaping up the chimney, as though they were heralds and he wished them to proclaim his announcement. "The Duchess wouldn't let me speak to the Duke–said the staff at the castle were her responsibility and if I didn't cut my pigtail hair style I'd have to leave."

There was a droll laugh from behind the bed-curtains. "I mind Alexander Milne, when you were a bit of a lad, how the minister used to put ye on top of a tombstone to read the Bible to the folks who couldna get into the kirk. A right smart wee laddie, you were."

Lord, Ned the butcher thought, I wish old Meg wouldn't do that. It fair gives me the creeps.

"Good evening, Mistress Chrystie," Milne said formally.

Someone slipped out to the inn and returned with a bottle. John poured a generous tot of whisky into a mug for the unhappy lackey. Now I'll be stuck with them all evening until the bottle's empty, Jean thought impatiently. They'll blether on, forgetting the reason for their meeting. If only I could get their womenfolk together.

"Get that dram into ye, man," John said, "and maybe things will no' seem so bad."

Alexander Milne looked into the golden liquid as though consulting it before he uttered his next words. "I intend to go to the New World. I'll find a ship and work my passage."

There was a stunned silence. "Man," John said, "I wouldn't do anything in a hurry. We'll be needing the likes of you around to help us do something about this damnable thing the Gordons are inflicting on us."

Milne tossed the whisky down his throat and jumped to his feet. "Fight the Gordons, John Ord, and everyone of ye. Don't sit on your backsides and let the Cock o' the North hand out his orders. Ye ken what they say about the Gordons?

'The guile, the Gordons, the hoodie craw
Is the three worst things that Moray ever saw.' "

"We've just sent a letter off to the factor," someone told him.

"Factor Ross is the Gordons' pawn. He'll do their bidding. Aye, things have changed now, but times were when the big houses built the villages at their gates for the protection of the castle. Now we're just an eye-sore and they want rid of us." Alexander Milne sank down in his chair and sighed. "If we were educated we'd make a better stand against the gentry."

Every head turned in his direction. "We've got a fine wee school in this village," the postmaster protested.

"Aye," Milne replied curtly, "small heed the Master pays when bairns have to help their folks get the crops in or go up to the sheilings to herd the cattle."

"Ye didna do too badly yoursel', "Meg shouted. "Ye've got a fine brain in your head, laddie."

"Aye, Mistress Chrystie, but all it seems fit for is to wipe the boots of the Quality."

"You might've got some advancement like the Duke's clerk, Mr Marshall," Jean said thoughtfully.

"Well, I'm no' going to cut my hair and crawl back to the Gordons to find out," Milne said truculently. "I'm going to the New World to make a fortune—if I can. Then one day I'll return to Fochabers and build the finest school in Scotland, where bairns will learn every subject. Latin, Greek..."

The men began to laugh. Wasn't Milne the good turn.

Jean went over to the hearth and gazed into the fire. The pale blue smoke seemed to be mingling with a mist forming in her head. She turned to Milne and said quietly, as though the words were coming from a long way off.

"It'll be a fine school you'll build, Mr Milne. There'll be nothing like it in the length and breadth of Scotland, nor in England. Your name will never be forgotten in this village—not ever, down through the centuries."

# Chapter 2

Jean slipped behind the curtain and, leaving a stunned silence behind her, sank down on her grandmother's bed, feeling alarmed and confused by the words which seemed to have poured involuntarily from her lips. Meg was nodding off to sleep. She tucked the patchwork quilt around her, then picked up the chamber pot and placed it outside the window to take down to the midden. Unseen by the group of men huddled around the fire, she left the cottage.

Milne, with a far-away expression on his face, went towards the door too. In some strange way, the girl's vision had transferred itself to his mind. Already the hopeless futility of his life seemed to be slipping away. When the door shut behind him, someone remarked that Alexander Milne looked as though he were already searching out his fortune in foreign lands.

As she made her way down the road Jean Chrystie thought of the meeting and of the wives who had been left at home by their men. It'll be different next time, I'll see to that, she vowed. Where would the half of them be if their wives didn't bring in a few pennies every week from their needlework?

The women in the village always came to the Chrystie cottage to do their sewing, spinning and knitting. Meg, who had originally come from the West coast, had brought a lot of skills with her. The evenings were often gay with music and story-telling. She smiled, remembering the times when the fiddler had played a rousing tune and tempted them to throw down their needlework and dance.

The Duke's factor came out through the door of the inn. James Ross looked vexed. He must have read the letter she had written at the meeting, she thought, and now he's wondering how to tell the Gordons.

Too late, she saw Gypsy Willie. He came around the corner from the direction of the privy; by the look of him he had been drinking heavily.

"Jean," he shouted, and made a lurch at her.

"Let me pass, Willie. I'm just going in to see my aunt."

He grabbed her arm. "The devil take her, come awa' for a bit of a dander. You don't want to bother with auld greetin' Kitty."

At that moment the last person she wanted to see was her aunt; now there was no choice. Twisting away from the grabbing hands, she ran into the inn.

"Give's a hand," her aunt droned mournfully. "Your cousin Sheena is still working up at the castle and your uncle's over in the cottage stirring up trouble."

"What do you mean?" Jean said sharply, pushing a bench against the wall and picking up some dirty mugs. "You know we had to hold this meeting."

"There's them that thinks he'd do well to keep a still tongue."

"We're all of a mind in the village. None of us want to be pitched out of our homes."

"If they were pitched into a better place, who'd complain?" Kitty said slyly, giving her head a little shake and dislodging the wig she wore to keep up with the gentry.

"Has the factor been saying something to you?" Jean asked quickly.

"There'll be a fine new inn, I can tell ye that. I'm right 'shamed of this place. I'll never forget how reluctant that Doctor Johnston was to stay here when he came by the village a few years ago. Maybe he and wee bossy Boswell thought we had lice in the beds."

"Don't be silly, Aunt. All travellers say our Highland inns are a sight cleaner than the ones in the south. Anyway, I'm tired of hearing what Doctor Johnston said about Fochabers. Pity he wasn't good enough to stay at the castle."

"Aye, that was right queer, wasn't it? I heard tell that Boswell wrote to all the big houses on the way, letting them know that the great man was travelling in the Highlands and Islands."

"Free lodging," her niece said drily.

The smell of ale was in her nose and the sound of her aunt's voice in her ears as she went up towards the Peeps, the bank above the village. Kitty's attitude made her feel uneasy. Something must have been said between her and the factor this evening. It would be a crafty move to get the inn shifted first because it was the centre of life in Fochabers. Anger flared in her when she thought of the Gordons.

A startled pheasant rose out of the ground. It shot past, its brilliant plumage making a shower of colour. Something had disturbed it for she had been standing quietly in the same spot for a while. The delicate scent of heather was in the breeze. How she wished she could capture it, but every effort to make a scent from its flowers had been unsuccessful.

The sound of bracken being crushed by someone's feet made her turn around swiftly.

"Good evening." A man was standing some distance away under a larch tree. He was wearing nankeen breeches and short top boots. His left hand was thrust into the pocket of a pale grey waistcoat which he wore under a double-breasted frock coat. A gold-topped cane was held lightly in his right hand. From the sound of his voice and the appearance of his clothes, he looked as though he might be a guest at the castle. In profile, he seemed slightly familiar, but when he walked towards her, it was the face of a stranger. Never in her life had she seen a man with such fair hair and such clear blue eyes.

"And what are you doing here at this time of the day?" he asked pleasantly.

Because his words and sudden appearance had startled her, she said pertly: "Taking the air – it's free."

A smile moved the corner of his mouth. "I was not intending to charge you for it!"

Jean coloured slightly. "The Duke of Gordon doesn't mind if

the villagers come up here of an evening. Just as long as we keep our distance and don't taint the air they breathe."

He looked at her sharply and frowned. "I can assure you that the Gordons consider the villagers of Fochabers to be very worthy people."

"Oh aye, as long as we do their bidding. But I can tell ye, sir, we are not all that far removed from the serfs who served the grand houses in olden times."

Alexander, the fourth Duke of Gordon, stared at the girl before him and noticed the extraordinary green eyes and perfectly shaped features.

Jean stared back. The English folk staying at the castle often came by the village to gape at them—ever so discreetly, right enough. But they behaved as though the common folk had come from another planet. How her cousin Sheena could bear to work in that place, she couldn't imagine.

Alexander Gordon began to feel confused. Was this the same girl he had just seen running up the path? Now she seemed to have a dignity, an aloofness which he did not expect among the villagers. Perhaps she was the eldest of a large family, the mother a widow and they had to fend for themselves.

"What is your name?" he asked curiously.

A frown crossed her face at the abrupt question. Why should a guest from the castle want to know her name? Unless...She moved away slightly, knowing well enough how men of his class regarded village girls. She looked straight at him and saw that his expression was grave, and that there was a kindliness in his eyes that made her blush at the thoughts going through her head.

"My name is Jean Chrystie. I live with my grandmother in Rose Cottage. My uncle is John Ord who owns the inn. I must go, sir." She gave a slight curtsey and walked away gracefully.

As soon as she reached the top of the hill, Jean began to run with her arms outstretched. She always ran down the hill in this way because she felt part of the trees and plants, and of everything growing around her.

Alexander Gordon slapped the cane against his boot and began to laugh. The girl had kept her dignity until she thought she was out of sight, now she was running like a nymph through the dusk.

The men had all left the cottage by the time she returned. Meg drew the bed-curtain back and said: "I'm needin' a drink, lass–a drop of mint for I've got a touch of indigestion."

"Aye, Granny."

"Do I see a wee droppie left in the bottle o'er there?"

Her granddaughter picked up the whisky bottle and poured in what remained. "I wouldn't give that mixture to an auld sow!"

Meg smacked her lips. "'Tis right good. Where've you been this last whiley?"

"Up the Peeps."

"See anyone?"

Jean hesitated. "One of the guests from the castle, I think."

Meg rolled her eyes. "That Jane Maxwell canna bide with her own family, always crowding the place with visitors."

"Why do you call the Duchess that, Granny?"

"'Twas her name afore she wed the Duke. I knew her folks when I worked nearby in Edinburgh."

"You've travelled such a lot."

"When I'm gone, love, you'd do well to seek a job in service and maybe you'll see a bit o' the world too." Meg gave her a sly glance. "If you're no' goin' to marry Gypsy Willie."

"God forbid!"

"Well, there's many a fine man around. When I'm gone you'll be able to tak' your pick."

"Don't keep talking about when you're gone," her granddaughter said with mock severity. "You know fine you haven't a chance of going anywhere with all the fine potions I keep pouring into you."

"Aye, ye're a right clever wee lassie. You keep half the village in health."

"You taught me all I know, Granny."

"Nae." Meg looked at her thoughtfully. "You've got something special that I never had." The old woman's tone changed. "What about that mannie up the hill. Did ye speak to him?"

"Only a few words. He asked who I was."

Meg's face darkened. "He was making advances. That like would hae you on the grass afore you kenned."

Jean threw back her head and laughed when she thought of the tall, handsome man, years older than herself, and as remote as the stars in the heavens.

## Chapter 3

The following morning Jean rose early and set about kindling the fire and getting the pot on the boil to make the oats for breakfast. She filled the big iron kettle and hung it on the other hook on the crane for her granny who liked a good wash when she had eaten. After that, Meg usually took her daily walk around the bed, then sat on the chair by the open window and chatted to Jean while she tended the garden.

"Ye're movin' awfully fast this morning, lassie," the old woman complained. "I canna see my wee sachet of herbs in the water."

"You'll not die without them this once. I'm in a fearful hurry, granny. Tessa McDonald's youngest bairn has the croup and I want to get a few things together in my basket."

"Ye're nae goin' to that house?"

"I am, as you did before me."

"She couldn't name the father of one of them bairns if she tried, so Bella Forbes next door tells me."

"Och, never heed what Bella Forbes says. She's jealous because she can't manage to have a bairn herself for all the infusions of speedwell she's taken for her barren state."

"A pure wee lassie like you shouldna be mixin' with that besom. I hear she slips away when she sees the popish man comin' to pray o'er her. Leaves him lookin' like a jampot covered wi' wasps. Bairns clinging everywhere to get at the sweeties he brings in his pocket."

Jean put a poke of fudge in her basket with the medicine and smiled. "Och, I know, Granny, but she's not a bad mother."

"She's a wicked woman, lays wi' any man who gives her a penny, I hear."

Tessa McDonald's cottage was at the far end of the village near the road running down from the castle. It was a dilapidated looking building with a forest of weeds threatening to smother the walls. Tessa eased herself on the seat by the window. My, she was putting on weight. Sam Duncan, the kenner, said he liked a right good armful and was for aye telling her she had a bonny face, and that the flame of her hair warmed the cockles of his heart. Sam. What would she do without him? Tessa's eyes moved across the landscape and she felt the loneliness in her stretch out to the distant hills. What she'd give for a sight of Glasgow, the houses and the people–her ain folk. To think that she was only a bit of a wean, no more than fifteen years old, when she left the south with the Italian. Fine talk and promises, and all the time the bastard was wed. God knows what would have become of her if the priest hadn't taken pity on her when Bruno cleared off.

As Jean approached the cottage, she had the sudden impulse to climb on the hedge and take a quick look around the countryside and enjoy the smell of the sea which the wind carried from Spey Bay. Suddenly there was the sound of a carriage. Furious with herself for appearing to be gawping, she ignored the passengers, turned swiftly and jumped out of sight.

The Duchess of Gordon nudged her husband. "Did you see that Miss Impudence?"

Alexander Gordon was startled by the girl's sudden appearance. He smiled to himself, recalling their encounter on the previous evening and remembered how her elegance had seemed touched with a wildness, a freedom.

"Just wait, Alex," the Duchess said, "she'll not be flaunting her brazenness up there for long. Soon we'll have that ugly sprawl of cottages away from our gates." She sighed contentedly. "To think that this will soon be all parkland and the village out of sight and hearing."

"Yes," he said quietly. Alexander Gordon was heartily tired of the village and its problems. Why had they expected the people to move without a murmur? Now the factor was hinting that there might be trouble getting them to shift and that the estate would have to dig deeply into its coffers to make the scheme acceptable to the villagers.

Jean took Tessa McDonald's child in her arms, opened its mouth gently and applied the soothing honey balm. The little one looked up at her with wide, trusting eyes.

"It's a lovely bairn, Tessa."

"Aye, God spare it and you, Jean Chrystie, you've got a rare gift."

Jean pressed a piece of clean linen to the child's mouth.

"I mind well how old Meg used to tend folk around the village, but she never had your way, hen. Sit yoursel' down now and hae a wee dram afore you set out."

"No thanks, but I'll be back again to see how he's doing."

"Oh..." Tessa was taken aback. "'Tisn't every day I can offer folk a dram. I tell ye what, take a wee sup to old Meg."

"All right, I'll do that," Jean agreed. Whatever people said about Tessa, she was a good-natured soul.

"Fiona," Tessa called. "Fetch the whisky."

"Aye, ma."

"Hello, Fiona," Jean said when Tessa's eldest child came into the kitchen. "How tall you've grown."

Fiona smiled shyly and leant down to place the whisky bottle beside her mother. Jean drew back startled. "Good God, Tessa, Fiona's head is full of lice."

"You dinna say?"

"Did ye not see?"

"I didn't notice. The bairn's tall for her age."

Jean packed her things quickly into the basket. "Get the lye and black-oil and douse the girl's head right away."

Tessa poured a drop of whisky into a glass and said leisurely: "I'll see to it by and by. Take what's left in the bottle to your granny."

"See to it *now*. Them things hop ye know. The other bairns will get a dose as well." What was she talking about? The other heads were probably walking by now. Jean glanced at Fiona and saw the pale skin suffused with colour, and her eyes bright with tears.

"Don't worry, Fiona, we'll soon get it cleared up." She swung around on her mother, blazing with anger. "Will you get that oil, Tessa McDonald."

"Och," Tessa said easily, "dinna fash yoursel'," and heaved herself out of the chair to fetch a chipped, grey-beard jar.

"Pour some into a pan and get me a piece of flock, then go and fetch the other bairns."

Tessa shrugged at the impatience in Jean Chrystie's voice. 'Tis a wonder she comes here, the lofty wee body.

"You," Jean said in a low voice, "will not be popular with your men-friends."

Tessa looked at her in horror and flew out through the door.

"Thank you," Fiona whispered after Jean had soaked the girl's hair.

Though she smiled at her, Jean felt chilled with horror at the task she had taken on. However reluctant she felt at that moment, it had made a lasting impression on this girl who had known only the careless love of her wayward mother and the reluctant companionship of the other children in the village.

When Jean left Tessa's house, she tore down to the river with a lump of soft soap in her hand. Her hair would never feel clean again. After the children's heads had been cleaned, she and Tessa had soaked each other's with the black-oil. It was a pity though that they had had to use the shears on the bairns. By the time they had finished, the four heads had looked like little hedgehogs.

"That Tessa," she muttered, as she caught up her skirts and waded into the water. Then she smiled. There was something rather nice about the rough Glasgow woman.

Jean rubbed and scrubbed her head vigorously in the river, then went to a clear pool where her hair fanned out like a burnished silk wheel in the sunlight. When she raised herself, there was the sound of a man's voice somewhere nearby. She wrung out the strands of hair quickly, combed it through her fingers, then picked up the basket and walked across the shingle, feeling embarrassed and annoyed at being watched. There was something else; she had begun to feel guilty about polluting the river, a thought which had just occurred to her. Would traces of the black-oil in the water kill the trout and salmon? God, the smell of it was nearly killing her!

Alexander Gordon gazed after the girl feeling strangely disappointed that they had not spoken. It was odd, he owned every stick and stone of this land but some of his villagers didn't recognize him. He shrugged and kicked at a pebble. No wonder. When he passed the village in his carriage he was invariably wearing an elaborate wig and was formally dressed. He looked down at the simple clothes he wore around the estate. This was the way he liked to be dressed and this was the place, more than anywhere else in the world, where he preferred to be. He had done the Grand Tour in his youth, but no country had ever seemed so magnificent as the Highlands. The Duchess often said that he had no air at all about him and could be taken for one of his farmers. Alexander frowned when he thought of his wife who was becoming increasingly discontented with life at Gordon Castle. She approved of the fine new extension that Baxter had designed, but complained continuously about the delay in getting work started on the new village. Her developing interest in politics was her main preoccupation now. Their home in London, Buckingham House, was continually crowded with politically minded people. Even the King seemed to find her ideas worth listening to.

He looked bleakly into the distance. There seemed to be so little happiness and peace between them. Had there ever been any real happiness? In his youth, Jane's beauty and high spirits had attracted him. As the years passed, and despite their children, they were gradually growing apart. When the Duchess visited Fochabers she interfered with the management of the estates, and confused the factor when she demanded details about matters that were not her concern. Alexander smiled ruefully. The factor was also confused when her speech coarsened, which invariably occurred when she became irritated or excited.

Jean was walking in the direction of Burnside when she suddenly realized that the fine lace-edged handkerchief, which Meg had sewn for her birthday, was missing. She turned round, and with eyes on the ground, walked back along the river.

As she approached the spot where she had washed her hair, she became aware of dogs frisking among the trees. She glanced up and saw the man whom she had spoken to on the previous evening. He was standing with his back against a tree gazing thoughtfully in the direction of the Bog o' Gight where Gordon Castle stood. Though she recognized him immediately, he looked younger now than she had first imagined. You'd think that the fine folk hadn't a worry in the world. He gave the impression that he hadn't a friend in the world!

She waded into the water and immediately saw her handkerchief between two boulders. Anxious to retrieve it before it was swept out of sight, Jean moved too quickly and her foot slipped on a flat stone. She fell heavily on her side, crashing her head against a boulder. Dazed, she lay there for a moment then made an effort to pull herself to her feet, but the weight of her soaked skirt and the pain in her head made her lean helplessly against it.

The sound of footsteps came running across the shingle. Arms were drawing her out of the water and the next minute she was on the grass verge between the shore and the woods. "Good heavens," a voice said impatiently, "how did you manage to fall in there. You might have drowned. It is well the river is low."

In spite of her discomfort and aching head, Jean retorted: "I'm sorry I caused you to wet your boots, sir, but as they're in a bit of a state anyway maybe you'd be kind enough to go and find my hankie. It's over there by the boulder where I clouted my head."

Alexander Gordon looked down at the girl; it was the first time in his life that anyone of her station had ordered him to do anything. He smiled and said with mock severity: "Is the 'kerchief of such worth that I must go into the river again?"

"Don't bother yourself, then. I'll get it when my head is steady. We may not have the same idea about values, but if you could have seen my granny's old fingers working on that piece of linen, even you might put a bit of value on it."

"I'm sorry," he said quickly, and hurried over to the river.

Jean wrung out her soaking skirt and moved across the grass to a pool of sunshine. A wave of dizziness made her sit down abruptly.

Alexander pushed the wet handkerchief into his pocket and hurried towards her. Before she could stir he was on his knees beside her. "You've hurt yourself badly, I fear. Your forehead is cut. No wonder you were stunned." He put his hand under her chin and inspected the bruise. "You poor..." What was she? Child, girl?

She stared at him, and to her horror, tears began to fill her eyes.

No man had ever spoken or looked at her with such compassion before.

He couldn't take his eyes off her face; the girl's startling beauty overwhelmed him. To think that this lovely young woman had come out of one of those hovels over there in the village.

"You must get home quickly or you'll catch cold," he said.

She struggled to her feet. "I'm sorry to have detained you. I can't think what came over me. I've been leapin' the river since I was a bairn and I'm sorely tried to have flopped into it so stupidly, the way one of the grand ladies up at the castle might have done."

He saw her pride trying to overcome the weak moment, but he couldn't help laughing at her words. "I can assure you no grand lady has ever flopped so gracefully as you. Come on, or else you'll be abed for days. Is there somewhere near where you can go and dry yourself?"

"Yes, I'll go to Anderson's farm over yonder by the salmon fisheries."

"Let me help you."

"I've got two legs, sir."

"Not very steady ones."

"It would be best if I went alone, but... thank you."

They looked at each other for a second. Jean saw the strength and kindliness in his face and, something else. With a pounding heart she walked quickly across the shore.

## Chapter 4

Morag Fraser was standing at the table, knocking the devil out of a mountain of dough when Jean entered the farmhouse kitchen. Jean used to be frightened of the Anderson's skivvy when she was a bairn. "Loping Morag" the villagers called her because she never walked like other women but took great strides, clutching her skirts and staring ahead out of large, prominent eyes, as though she had witnessed some fearful incident in her infancy and the memory of it had left a permanent mark.

"There's nothing wrong with poor Morag," Meg always said. "Maybe her thatching's a wee bittie thin."

Whether Morag was weak in the head or not, she had made an impression on the villagers when cattle revellers came from the south one night to steal Anderson's cattle. When the revellers saw the screaming figure in a night-shift with staring eyes and long, black hair, they shouted: "Christ, it's a muckle black de'il" and ran off without the cattle.

Morag took one look at Jean's dripping skirt. Without a word she went to her room off the kitchen and returned with an old plaid.

"I saw ye down by the river. What were ye doing talking to the Duke of Gordon?"

Jean stumbled as she slipped out of the skirt. "Who did you say?" she asked, her eyes widening in alarm.

"His Grace the Duke of Gordon."

"I thought he was a castle visitor."

"The dog's ass. It was Himself. He canna be as high and mighty as folk say, talking to a wee lassie like yoursel'."

And I made so free with my tongue, Jean thought. If only I had stood up on the hedge gawping like everyone else when the carriages went by, I would have been wiser this day. "He was very kind."

Morag's eyes went through her. "I saw it all."

"Thank you for the dry gown, Morag," Jean said quickly as she bundled up her wet clothes. "I'll return it to you later."

"Aye," Morag replied vaguely. "Nae doubt ye will."

After Jean left the farmhouse, Morag put the bread on the girdle then went outside and flung a pile of sheep's wool under the elderberry tree. She sat down and began to pick out the bits of twigs and dirt before she set about washing it in boiling water. Afterwards, she would dye it with heather. Morag was proud of the skill she had to produce a clear yellow colour from the heather flowers. No one else in the village was able to do it so well, not even old Meg's granddaughter. That wee lass was too clever, too sure of hersel' for her years. The crafty way she had fallen into the river today, stealing Morag's dream.

Morag scrambled to her feet angrily and threw some wood on the smouldering fire in the centre of the field where she washed and dyed the wool. The times she had stood by the river, ready to take her chance when the water-horse emerged from the water transformed into a beautiful young man who would be the image of the Duke. The kelpie wouldna mind Morag's skelley eye for he'd know why she was disfigured, he'd know about her mother meeting the woman with the evil eye just before Morag was born.

She walked back thoughtfully to the elderberry tree, seeing in her mind the look that had passed between the pair by the river. Anger and dismay had made her creep away from her hiding place behind the whin bush and flee silently over the ground like a hare, until she reached the farm. Folk didn't know the Duke well for he never walked through the village when he came to the castle. But recently he had taken to coming down to the river sometimes wi' big Marshall. Perhaps he would like a chance to talk to Morag...

The skill at her fingertips began to make reality drop into her mind like drops of clear water. She tossed her head. It would be as well to forget about the kelpie, he had a habit of disappointing her. Morag bowed her head. She was covered in shame every time she remembered the excitement that had taken hold of her when a seeping figure had suddenly stepped out of the river last spring. The fine head and shoulders belied the body that followed: it was only an auld scallag ridding himself of a year's dirt – a right plaster, who settled himsel' in the bittie of ground at the top of the tattie field, expecting her to take his horn spoons and the like, to sell at the post office.

Usually Jean dallied in the field behind the cottage to look and talk to the livestock, and never went into the garden without running her hands through the herb-beds. Today she didn't notice anything.

"Flit the coo!" Meg's voice, sharp and impatient, reached her halfway down the garden. Jean turned back, untied the cow's rope from the tree and led the animal across to fresh pasturing ground. When she reached Meg's window she said cheekily: "Why didn't you do it yourself. Maybe you'd find your legs were as fit as your tongue. What's grieving you?"

Old Meg had a hard, wary look.

"And don't say you were lonely, for half the village bides in our house. Did Bella Forbes call?"

"Aye, and girnin' Kitty." Meg gave her granddaughter a piercing look. "Ye'll no' forget to be particular when you fancy a man to tak' him through the kirk afore he sets a foot in your bedroom?"

"Aye." So that was it, she had been seen down by the river and granny thought she had made a tryst with someone.

"Where'd ye get them auld duds you're wearing?"

"I had a fancy to fall in the Spey and I was rescued by a handsome stranger," Jean said tartly when she came indoors and began sorting out her wet clothes. "Who told you I was down by the Spey, Granny?"

"Your Aunt Kitty was in the woods pinching kindling and saw you. She didna ken who you were with because she's that short-sighted."

When the dinner dishes were washed Jean ran up the road to

see her cousin Sheena, who usually had a few hours off from the castle at this time of day. Uncle John was drawing a pint of ale when she entered the inn.

"I hear you were down courtin' by the river today," he said, his eyes dancing mischievously.

"I was not. It's a pity Aunt Kitty hasn't better eyesight."

"Well, lassie dear," he said with mock solemnity, "'tis a great sorrow to me too. I'd like fine to know what goes on in folks' houses when she takes a wee peep, passing by."

"Come away," Sheena called from the tap-room. "I was hoping you'd call. I've got something to show you." Sheena wrung the dishcloth, wiped the table and threw the water out through the door.

Jean loved watching her cousin work. Everything she did had a touch of quiet perfection. Although Sheena was two years older than herself they had always been good friends. "Have you got a news-sheet for me?" she asked.

Sheena pushed strands of fair hair from her brow. "Aye, I'll give it to you in a minute but the castle housekeeper wants it back. There's a piece in it about his lordship."

"The Duke of Gordon?" Jean said slowly.

"Aye."

John Ord came into the tap-room carrying an anker of whisky. "My, look at the pair o' ye with nae a man between ye. You'd need to take a wee trip to Clash-na-Bhan."

"Where's that?" they asked.

"Up by Braemar. Stone of Woman. They say it never fails to find a lover for a lassie."

Sheena threw back her head and laughed. "It'll have to be someone like that Doctor Johnson for me—a bit younger right enough. I'll never forget how he talked."

John gave his daughter an anxious look. "Oh, lassie, hauld your wish and look for your own like." He pushed the anker on the shelf and laughed. "I wonder, did Johnson meet Shakespeare's three witches o'er by Forres? Man alive, he was that keen to get to the place you'd think the witches were still sitting on yon heath, stirring their wee pottie." John dusted his hands and added drily, "I hope he found Forres more to his liking than he did Fochabers. Ah, well, wait until we get our fine new village then may be he'll come back and we'll gie him the Freedom like they did in Aberdeen. Now lassies, when are ye goin' to tak' that trip to Clash-na-Bhan?"

Much good it will do me, Jean found herself thinking as she followed Sheena to her bedroom. The Duke of Gordon had stirred the heart and soul of her in a way she had not thought possible. She shook her head impatiently. She would do well to remember her station in life.

A silk gown lay across her cousin's bed. It was a stream of pale, shimmering gold with tiny green flecks woven into the material. It had a round décolletage and tight-fitting sleeves trimmed with ruffles of lace that came to the elbow. A bergère hat covered with the same material lay beside the gown.

"It's far too big for me, Jean. You can have it if you'd like to alter it."

"Where'd it come from?" She had never seen anything so beautiful.

"It belonged to the Duchess of Gordon. Her woman, Mistress Tison—you know folk call her 'the wee Edinburgh body'—came to see me in the sewing-room. I nearly flopped on the floor with surprise. She said..." Sheena's grey eyes sparkled with fun as she tried to imitate a refined Edinburgh accent, "...that the gown did not fit her Grace and the Duchess would be *obleeged* if I would accept it."

Jean frowned. It didn't sound right, somehow. Why choose Sheena when there were servants of longer standing, and in higher positions working at the castle? Then she remembered her aunt's comments on the previous night; even a few minutes ago Uncle John had spoken about "the new village" as if he had accepted the fact that it was going to happen after all. He of all people, one of the first to rebel against it.

Sheena placed the gown in her cousin's hand. "Wait 'till I fetch a calico bag to put it in."

The material against Jean's skin felt cold and strangely unpleasant. Unnoticed, the gown slipped to the floor. She stumbled down on the bed, her head bent; one half of her mind was vague and clouded, the other half seemed to be trying to reveal something.

"Are you ill?" Sheena bent over her anxiously. "Whatever ails ye?"

"I think maybe it's the perfume on the gown," she said vaguely but the sudden sensation in her head alarmed her.

"You never get time to sew yourself a stitch," Sheena rambled on. "Your back's broken growing and picking herbs to tend the village; and there's your living to earn, knitting hosiery for the Aberdeen market. I've got plenty and soon there's to be a fine new inn."

Jean stiffened. "You know what people think about *that* idea?"

Her cousin looked troubled and uncomfortable. "The Gordons own the village. They say when the Duchess sets her mind on something, she gets what she wants."

Aye, and the Duchess is making a start by bribing the inn-keeper's daughter. What about the Duke? He doesn't seem to be giving much thought either to the wishes of the people. The devil's luck to them both, Jean thought angrily. Then she remembered his kindness, his concern, and the strange searching look which had caused such a tumult in her heart. Now she wished she had never met him. If I can help it, she vowed, I will never see him again.

# Chapter 5

Alexander Gordon and his factor, James Ross, were seated at the desk in the Duke's study at the castle, poring over a map of the estate. Alexander picked up a quill and sketched in a part. "Here James, in the hills just above the site for the village, we'll plant Scots pine and larch. Moving downwards towards the site–where it is warmer and the ground richer–we will plant oaks, elms, sycamores and beeches. It will give shelter to the village."

"Aye, Your Grace, it'll be a fine sight one day. I've been told that Doctor Johnson was very impressed by the number of trees you have growing on your estate compared to other parts of Scotland."

"Was he indeed? Well, I hope it will increase the number of wild-life and, very important, I hope to God I will have more time to spend at the castle to enjoy it all. For years I seem to have been coming and going. Wars, affairs of state."

"Now that the castle has been rebuilt, Your Grace, it should be a more comfortable dwelling."

The door burst open and Jane, Duchess of Gordon, walked into the room. "Ah, here you are, Mr Ross, I was needing a word with you."

The Duke rose to his feet. James Ross pushed back his chair and mumbled, "Good morning, Your Grace." He knew how much his lordship hated being interrupted during these sessions when he was working on plans for improving the estate.

"Sit down, my dear," the Duke said with strained politeness. He could see that his wife had an excited, impatient look about her. She had heard of the letter that had arrived from the villagers. It was pointless for Jane to try to harry the factor to speed matters. James Ross understood the people better than anyone and the Duke had every confidence in him. He moved the map aside and waited for the expected outburst.

"I understand a letter came from the villagers last night, Mr Ross."

"That is so. I was about to discuss the contents with his lordship when we had finished discussing another matter."

"I don't know what other matter could be more important at the moment," she interrupted. "I'm surprised you didn't send for me, Alexander."

"Well, you're here now," he said equably. "Perhaps you would like to read the letter to us, James?"

The factor went to reach across the desk when the Duchess pounced like a cat on a mouse and picked up Jean Chrystie's letter of protest. Her lips tightened as she took in the contents.

"Signed Jean Chrystie on behalf of the inhabitants of Fochabers." She drummed her hand furiously on the desk. "Jean Chrystie...an elderly woman? The writing looks youthful enough."

"She's only a bit of a lass," Ross told her.

The Duchess tossed her head. "One of her class in England would not have been able to write a letter like that. I don't know if educating the lower classes above their station is such a good idea."

Alexander Gordon looked pointedly at his wife. James Ross raised his chin and said stiffly: "Speakin' for mysel' Your Grace, I am very glad that there is a system in our country for educating ordinary folk."

Regretting her tactless words, the Duchess said: "Aye, you're right, Mr Ross. I'm sure it is only fair that everyone has a chance to learn."

The Duke picked up the letter and let his eyes move across the neatly written words. He felt startled and uneasy at the strongly worded protest but was amazed at the eloquence of the composition. For a second, the girl was before his eyes.

"Is that the girl living with old Meg Chrystie?" Jane Gordon asked.

"Aye, she's her granddaughter and niece of John Ord who runs the inn. John was the son of Meg's first husband. When you saw her last she would have been only a bit of a bairn."

"I remember, Mr Ross, you took me there some years ago to see the old woman when we were trying to get the villagers interested in sorting flax. Nothing much came of it, of course," she said drily.

"Ah yes, but Meg is feeble now and not around these days, though I'm told she has passed on all her skills to the young lassie." James Ross was a cautious man, and he always felt that he needed his wits about him when the Duchess began probing.

"James," the Duke said quietly. "You suggested offering the villagers a certain amount of money, or was that my suggestion?"

"Huh!" Jane Gordon interrupted. "They'll make the most of that."

"I think, Your Grace, we decided that an agreement should be drawn up with a financial inducement, and with the understanding that the people move by a certain date."

"Very well." Alexander Gordon made some notes.

The Duchess began to move about impatiently. To the factor's discomfort she tapped him on the shoulder and, ignoring her husband, said: "The Chrystie house–the one the old woman and girl live in–whose tenancy is it under? Who pays the rent?"

"It would be John Ord. He grew up in that house."

"I see. What right then has that girl taken on herself to rouse the people in her uncle's house?"

"Jane," the Duke said impatiently, "it is immaterial who pays the rent if the girl lives there."

"Well," Ross said cautiously, "I understand that the uncle was also present at the meeting." He gave a little smile. "In his absence, I had a word with his wife. She'll no' be too hard to persuade," he said sagely. "The thought of a fine new inn put a wee light in her eye, I can tell ye!"

"That's the way to go about it," Jane Gordon said promptly.

"The people have their point of view as well." Alexander

Gordon spoke curtly. "They must be given every consideration. After all, we are asking them to leave the houses which have been occupied by their families for generations."

"They don't give us much consideration with their hullabaloos. Like a pack of banshees at the castle gates sometimes. As you know, apart from the unsuccessful attempt at sorting flax, I worked hard to get some kind of cottage industry started. They all gathered in one cottage to save fuel and light...well, you know what happened then, the entire village made a party of it. It is always the same with unpolished people in the Highlands, a few of them get together and it ends up with drinking and rioting."

The Duke gathered his papers together. "I have seen some 'polished' people in our house in London behaving in a manner that would have shamed any Highlander." He rose abruptly. "Perhaps, James, we will continue our previous discussion later."

Mr Ross shot to his feet. "Very well, Your Grace."

"Come to my sitting-room a minute, Mr Ross," the Duchess said.

The factor's heart sank as he followed her down the corridor. Och dear, if only this woman would keep her own place, for aye nosing into the affairs of the estate. No wonder so many cross words passed between the pair of them at times.

Jane Gordon perched herself on the arm of a chair in her sitting-room and faced the factor. "My husband, as you know, Mr Ross, can be very easy-going. He's apt to have a bit too much sympathy with people. This girl, Chrystie, I want to put her in her place. I want no more interference from her. If she was clever enough to put that letter together, then she could be a great danger to our plans."

"What do you suggest, Your Grace?" he said carefully.

"I want her under my roof."

The factor's head shot up in surprise. "What exactly do you mean?"

"Give her a job in the castle where she will be subservient to me, and in my absence the housekeeper and yourself can keep an eye on her. First of all, I want you to write and tell her that the Gordons are displeased that she has taken it on herself to make trouble about the plans that have been made for the good of the people. Remind her that the house she lives in belongs to the Gordons and that the rent is paid by her uncle. You did say the inn people are keen to move?"

"Aye, the wife is very keen." And she's another bossy wee body like yourself. Tries to wear the trews... "About the job, Your Grace?"

"Tell the housekeeper to send word by the cousin, Sheena, but get that letter off first."

"Your Grace, there are no positions free at the moment. And there are other village girls who are waiting anxiously for a place, indeed who have been promised work at the castle." And what if the lassie doesn't want to come, the factor thought. A right canny wee thing she is as well. And there's old Meg to be cared for and the ailments in the village that the lassie seems to have a way with. Och dearie me, I wish this woman would leave well alone.

Jane Gordon stood up. "A job will have to be found for her. What about that sluttish girl in the kitchen, the one who hangs around the vegetable garden when... what's his name, is working there?"

"Gypsy Willie, as he's called. Aye, the housekeeper is finding her most unsatisfactory. Maybe..."

"See to it that she's got rid of and Chrystie can take her place. Thank you, Mr Ross. I will leave you to deal with these matters."

The following morning Jean was standing at the kitchen table using her pestle and mortar when Gypsy Willie came to the door. He had a letter in his hand.

"Factor told me to give ye that," he said authoritatively, and went to walk past her into the kitchen.

She pushed the door to. "Thank you Willie, I won't ask you in for granny's not well. I want her to have a bit of sleep."

"I won't make a sound," he said, his eyes roving over her lasciviously.

Her eyes sparkled with anger. "Clear off and find them that fancies your company, for I don't."

A sly look crept over his face. "Oh, so ordinary folk are no' good enough for ye now, only talk to dukes, my fine quine."

Och, she fumed, slamming the door in his face, you canna lift a finger in this village without everyone talking. The parchment crackled in her hand. For a second the grandeur of the paper stilled her curiosity, then she opened it. Incredulously, she read the letter from the factor.

'...and it would be unwise to hold any further meetings in your *uncle's house...*'

The final part of the letter alarmed her. She glanced at Meg who was sleeping and ran up the road to the inn.

"Uncle John, can I have a word with you?"

"Aye, lass, what ails ye?"

"Read this letter from the factor."

"You do it. It would tak me a whiley and by the look on your face, you'll no' want to wait."

John whistled softly and seemed put-out when his niece finished reading. She threw it on the table. "Where's everyone going to get together then? We've got the biggest kitchen in the village. Shall we ignore it?"

He looked embarrassed. "Well perhaps everyone had best stay in their own homes until this blows over."

"Stay in their own homes until what blows over? There's no time to waste."

She noticed that her uncle was looking increasingly uncomfortable. He picked up a mug and began to polish it.

"I'd better tell ye, lass, the factor's been around here and talked to the wife. I think we're going to be offered a right good proposition, and we've made up our minds to accept it. Face facts, lassie, in the end we'll have to shift whether we like it or not."

"I can see you're going to be well compensated," she said with bitterness, moving to the door. "Well, Uncle John, you can do as you like but that doesn't have to go for the rest of us." If a few more people gave in, all would be lost.

She hurried through the village until she reached Tessa McDonald's cottage. Fiona was outside hanging some rags over a whin bush.

"Fiona, I want you to do something for me."

The girl's eyes lit up. "I'd like that fine."

"I'm going to hold a meeting this evening on the green in front of the Pillar and Jougs. Will you go around the houses starting at the post office and tell everyone to be there about six o'clock. Tell them it's about the Shifting. I'll call at my neighbours and we'll check later that everyone knows."

"All right," Fiona said eagerly. "I'll just scoot in and tell me ma."

"Wish I was going too", Meg said wistfully, when her granddaughter was leaving the house that evening. "I can tell you one thing, love, the Gordons are in Elgin, so Bella next door told me."

"I don't care where they are, or auld James the factor, but I suppose he'll be snooping around as soon as a crowd gathers. Oh Granny, I do hope folk will turn up."

When she had called at some of the cottages about the meeting, she discovered that the factor had been there before her, trying to influence people to move peacefully. Several had been tempted to accept a money offer.

Tessa and Fiona were the first to arrive, then gradually women and children came with a few reluctant husbands dragging behind them. The men from the Quarters–the Duke's salmon hatchery and ice-house–all came together. Sam Duncan, the kenner–the leader of the river crew–was still wearing his leather apron. Tessa McDonald began to stroll in his direction. Sam was a good catch earning several pounds a year, plus a bit of bonus when it was a plentiful season.

When the kenner winked familiarly at Tessa, Jean said to Fiona: "Come and stand by me, I feel like a teacher with everyone staring." She was beginning to lose confidence, for she had noticed the expression in some of the men's eyes when they glanced in her direction. *They think they're going to have a right good laugh at my expense.*

As though Fiona had read her thoughts, she said: "Ma says, bad cess to them loons letting a wee cutty like yoursel' fight the Gordons for them."

"I'm not fighting the Gordons, Fiona. I'm fighting for our rights, if we've got any left."

The factor, well concealed behind a group of gorse bushes, bit his lip anxiously, waiting for the meeting to begin. What was he worrying about anyway? This very day he had made quite a few successful contacts in the village. John Ord was in the palm of his hand, and the post office folk were more than ready to shift too. It was fortunate that both premises were in a poor state of repair.

## The Forgotten Duchess

James Ross rubbed his hands. Man, they were right pleased when he told them that the Duke was prepared to build larger dwellings.

Some distance from the factor, the Duke of Gordon stood. He had found it necessary to return from Elgin before the Duchess. When the factor mentioned the meeting, Alexander decided to go and see for himself what the villagers thought of their plan. He watched Jean Chrystie intently. He noticed how she stood apart from the others.

"Why are we meeting out here, Jeannie?" someone called, "instead of roasting our legs by your fireside."

"The reason doesn't matter now. The thing that is important, the women in the village were able to come."

There was a good-natured cry of derision from the men.

"Because," she continued, "they will have to work twice as hard—*if we move.*"

"Right there, wee Jean," Big Annie, the butcher's wife, called.

Morag Frazer, with the look of disaster on her face, moved with her peculiar gait, and stood beside Jean.

"It's muckle black de'il," one of the men muttered, and there was a howl of laughter.

"Aye, some of ye are right smart wi' your tongues. A pity ye don't use them in the right direction. You loons are like a flock of sheep. If the Master in the big house says, away wi' ye, youse go off baaing wi' your tail between your legs."

There was a shriek of laughter from the women. Jean felt the tension inside her ease. She tried to point out the situation that they already knew and asked if anyone could offer any suggestion that might be presented to the Gordons.

Sam Duncan took the pipe out of his mouth and stabbed the air. "Right, you tell us what we're going to do for damned if I can. The Duke of Gordon has made a fine job of fixing up the castle, now he wants fine grounds to go wi' it, maybe for a wee dander o' an evening." Sam tucked his arm in Tessa's and the pair began to illustrate how the gentry walked, to roars of laughter. He pushed Tessa away from him. "They own Fochabers; if we're told to shift, I canna see what's to be done about it. And that's that!"

"Of course you canna see, Sam Duncan, an auld bachelor like yoursel' wi' no wife or bairns to hinder ye," Big Annie shouted.

Furious, Jean glared at the kenner. "Annie's right. You won't have the problem of shifting a family and all the possessions that have been gathered o'er many a year; or after a hard day's work start again on building a new home. But the rest of you...". Her eyes flashed over the men who were standing with their mouths wide open as though she were throwing the words between their lips, "...just think of it, the chimney corners where generations of your folk have worked and rested will have to be pulled to the ground to suit the Gordons. I'm not the only one who has an old granny lying a-bed for many a long year. Just imagine how they're going to feel about being moved."

"Aye, right there, lass," some of the women agreed.

"So what are we goin' to do about it?" she shouted. "Let our village be pulled down so that the Gordons can have a bit of parkland? The Duke doesn't know a thing about life in this village. I have never seen him around the place, nor in the hills above it." That is no longer true, she thought guiltily, then pushed it out of her mind.

Sam Duncan said in a surly voice: "Ye'll be seeing plenty of him in future, for he's got great plans to build up this estate, like the others he owns. So the factor was saying."

She felt irritated with their complacency. It was just like the meeting at the cottage; they complained but not one was prepared to raise a voice in protest. "Why don't we all march to the castle this very minute–every man, woman and child. Let the Gordons see how we feel," she raged at them. "Will you do that? Annie?"

Big Annie's eyes fell to the ground and there was a growl of dissent from the men. "Lassie dear," Annie said, "they would no' like that and we wouldn't have a bite to eat if the Gordons turned against us."

"But don't you see, if we all go, what action can they take? They're just as dependent on us as we are on them."

"They're not there," someone shouted.

"It doesn't matter. We'll talk to the factor or Mr Marshall, they can pass on our protest to the Gordons."

Everyone stared at their feet as though they had just discovered them. In exasperation Jean let her eyes move to the horizon where a burst of gold and vermilion was spilling across the sky.

The weaver said sheepishly: "There'll be a bit of money to help shift oursel's."

"Tell them to keep their money," she snapped. "It'll never make up for what we're going to lose."

"I, for one, need more space for my bairns," he said stubbornly, and walked away from the meeting.

A few others moved away too, mumbling under their breath. That's going to be the trouble, Jean thought dispiritedly, the offer of money will tempt them. To think that the Gordons are getting around people by bribing them out of their homes. She lifted her head angrily.

"If some of you are goin' to be tempted to make arrangements with the Duke's factor... Well, listen to me, demand as much money as you can get, refuse to budge if you don't get it. Maybe in the end the Gordons will have second thoughts about their plans and we'll not have to move after all."

## Chapter 6

"The lassie's right," the butcher said when Jean left the meeting and took the path leading to the hill. "He canna shift the whole damn lot of us against our will. But if he's prepared to gloss the path wi' a bittie o' gold?"

The factor strode away angrily. He was furious. So much for trying to stop the meetings in the Chrystie house. Alexander Gordon moved away too, his eyes cast thoughtfully on the ground. He looked up when he heard the factor's voice.

"Your Grace, I didn't know you were thinking of coming down here." James Ross was startled. Imagine the Duke listening to the lower orders criticising him. If only he had stayed in Elgin. Apparently he came riding back hell for leather. Some trouble with the Duchess, likely. That one would stir the dead in Bellie churchyard!

"Can I accompany you back to the castle?" the factor offered, glancing anxiously at the Duke's face.

"No, thank you, James. I think I'll go for a short walk." He frowned. "That girl..."

"Jean Chrystie?"

"Yes. She's quite... unusual, isn't she?"

"Aye" the factor said drily. "An old head on young shoulders, that one. I'm sorry you heard what was going on, Your Grace."

"I have the right to know what's going on," Alexander said shortly.

As Jean walked away, she felt ashamed and disloyal when she recalled the feeling that the Duke had aroused in her on the previous day. She stood for a moment on the top of the hill and looked down towards the Spey. The quietness of evening had settled over the valley but she could see people still standing around in groups at the meeting place.

Alexander Gordon was coming up through the woods when he saw her. He stopped. For the first time in his life he hesitated, unsure of what to do. He felt annoyed and alarmed at the way this girl had tried to arouse the villagers, and particularly when the factor said that many would be prepared to fit in with their plans to transplant them. Well, James, he thought grimly, I believe our problems have just begun.

He settled his feet in a bed of roses and watched her. The plaid shawl had fallen from her shoulders and lay in the crook of her arm. A minute ago he had been furious with Jean Chrystie for trying to thwart their plans but now, as he gazed at her, he felt confused. She was intelligent as well as beautiful. It was amazing how one of her class had so much authority in her bearing.

The Duke took a step forward, then exclaimed in pain as he felt a vice tightening on his foot and heard the snap of steel. His involuntary cry reached Jean's ears just as she was about to move away. She ran in the direction of the lower woods and almost immediately saw the figure of a man leaning against the trunk of a tree. That snapping sound...someone's got caught in a snare. God damn that sneaky Willie Robb, it would be the sort of thing he'd get up to.

"Wait a minute," she called as she ran. "Don't struggle. I'll release it."

He lifted his head. She stopped. "Your Grace."

"My foot seems to have got caught in a snare. It has bitten into the boot."

She rushed to his side. "Ease yourself down on the ground. I'll get at it better there. Slowly now. Don't be feared to lean on me. I can take the weight."

Swiftly her fingers moved across the ugly gadget and began to work on the spring. The sharp metal pierced her finger and the blood trickled over her hand unnoticed.

In a dazed sense, Alexander had the strange feeling that his wound had caused her blood to flow too. He shook his head impatiently at the thought.

"Keep your leg still," she said authoritatively, then added grimly in an undertone: "This contraption was one of *his* making, I'll be bound."

"Whose?" he said between clenched teeth.

She didn't reply. He watched her slender fingers working with the snare. For some reason, he knew she was capable of releasing the damnable thing, and didn't suggest that she should run for help. When it sprang open, Jean threw it aside, picked up a heavy stone and tried to smash it, then went down on her knees and began to undo his boot.

"No," he said, protestingly, "I'll have it seen to when I return to the castle."

She raised her head and for the first time, looked straight at him while her fingers worked away. "It would be better to give it some attention immediately, Your Grace. That thing was very rusty; you don't want foreign devils in your blood."

He smiled at her and said: "I am completely at your mercy, am I not?"

The severe look of concentration left her face and she replied: "I'm afraid you are. I never leave a job half done."

His fine sock was saturated with blood. She jumped to her feet, turned her back and lifted the edge of her skirt and ripped a length of her petticoat.

"Will you remove your sock while I soak this in the stream. I'll pick some comfrey."

"Comfrey?" he said, bewildered.

"It will clean and heal the wound."

"Attend to yourself," he suggested gently.

"It's only a scratch."

"You don't want to get foreign devils in your blood, do you?" he said smiling.

She ran across to the stream, and after a few minutes returned with bruised comfrey leaves in a piece of linen, also a wad of moss to cushion the wound from the pressure of his boot. Though the Duke was sceptical of herbal medicines, he felt strangely happy and relaxed. Jean was just about to apply the compress when the scratch on her finger began to bleed again. Horrified, she watched blood drip on to his injured foot. For a second their eyes met, then he said lightly:

"A gypsy wedding."

She bent her head quickly, her face flushing. He felt the gentle movement of her hands and smelt the delicate scent of rosewater from her skin. If only the factor could see him now!

When his sock and boot were on again, she said, "It won't be comfortable to walk on but it won't kill you either."

The girl's like a tonic, he thought as he stumbled to his feet.

"Lean on me, Your Grace. The path through the woods is the shortest route to the castle."

"I know."

"I'm surprised, considering the length of time you spend around the place." She bit her lip in annoyance. She had no right to make such a comment. Indeed, she had been chattering a bit too much, forgetting who he was. Yesterday was different; today she knew that he was the Duke of Gordon. For all his friendliness, he would pass her tomorrow without a second glance. Such were the ways of the nobility.

He saw the change in her mood and said gently, "Your medicament is already doing me good."

She nodded her head gravely.

"You know who set that trap, don't you?"

"He won't do it again."

"I see."

"I think you misunderstand," she said quickly. "He's no kin or like to me. I can't reveal his name for if the factor knew he would dismiss him and he'd lose the cottage. There's an elderly mother."

"I understand. But one of my children...even you might have been caught in that vile contraption."

"I'll go and see the man this very evening. I give you my word."

At the end of the path they stopped. "I hope the wound will soon heal."

"Thank you for your attention," he replied gravely.

She curtsied and was about to walk away when he spoke again.

"There is something I want to say to you." He hesitated. "I

want you to know that there's no need for you to worry about your home when the village is moved. I will make sure — "

Jean stiffened and turned to face him, her eyes flashing with anger. "I don't wish to discuss that now. There are dozens like me in the village, worried about their elderly folk. What can *you* do to replace what you intend to take from them?"

The Duke watched her until she was out of sight. He wanted to call her back to try and make her understand that the reason for transplanting the village was not only for his own benefit but for all their good. There was the economic reason. Also, there would be a great improvement in the houses in which they lived. He began to wonder if they had failed to make these facts clear to the people—indeed, had taken the people for granted.

"God dammit," he swore as he limped up the castle drive, "what is the matter with me? I must be mad to feel so disconcerted by one of the villagers."

John Ord swung his fishing line into the river. Further down, the postmaster was fixing bait on his hook.

"Do you think there's anything in it, John, about a wee spot of whisky catching the salmon?" Rob Chalmers didn't wait for a reply, he took out his flask and sprinkled a drop on the bait.

"Man," John said impatiently, "if ye let any more whisky spill into the water, you'll nae catch fishies but every gillie along the river." John shook his head. The postmaster was sensible enough but he had the head and hands o' a silly loon when he came near the Spey. Och, well, maybe he was talkin' daft to hide his feelings.

The two men had taken themselves away from the village when they heard about the meeting being held. As things stood, it could have been a bit awkward for they had both kicked up a fuss in the beginning. The factor's offer had made all the difference and they had changed their minds.

"John, one of the gillies was telling me that he heard the sound of horses crossing the river again last night down by the Boat o' Brig, and not a body in sight. What do you make of that?"

"Is that so?" John gave an impatient shrug and wished he'd stop blethering.

"Elsie says it's the ghost of Cumberland's troops when they

were chasing Charles Stewart. Ye know they raided the village and helped themselves to all the horses? The men in the village might've gone after them and throttled the bastards in the river."

"More likely the women did," John Ord said shortly. "If there were a few lassies around like my niece!"

The postmaster sighed deeply. "Are ye feeling as guilty as I am about the Shifting?"

"Aye, guilty enough. However, it means I'm going to get the wifie away from under my feet. The factor has made a certain offer; it will give me a new lease of life," John said briskly.

"Ye tell me that? Elsie got a few ideas too, when she realized how anxious the factor was to move us. He was taken aback but she held out. A man has to think of the future, ye ken?" the postmaster added uncomfortably.

"Right enough, now stop blethering, the Gudeman o' the Bog might come along. We're right below the castle. I hear he's taking a great interest in the river since he's been back." John rose and moved further along the bank.

Some time later, he noticed the girl on the opposite side, who was herding cows, give her head a warning shake. He looked about him; there was no one in sight. A funny wee lassie that, the accidental daughter of one of the local landowning families.

"Aye, aye." The postmaster, looking pleased, joined him.

"Any luck?" John asked.

"I hooked an eel about ten feet long. What about yourself?"

"I got nae bites but I hooked a lamp which must've belonged to Cumberland's troops; the light was still burning."

"Och, rubbish," the postmaster said impatiently.

"Well, if you cut a few yards off your eel, I'll blow the light out!"

The two men looked at each other and began to roar with laughter. On the ground above them, stood the factor. He had come down to the river to cool his anger after what he had heard at the meeting by the pillar. And now he was confronted by the inn-keeper and the postmaster fishing on the Gordons' special part of the Spey, if you please. The cheek of it. He had a mind to go down and give them a good telling off. After what he heard at the meeting perhaps he'd be as well to keep a still tongue.

These were his prize catches. Get this pair moved and the others would follow soon enough.

The cottage where Gypsy Willie lived was on the outskirts of the village, close to the Knowe of Tarryreach. A thatch of turf and heather covered the roof and the broken-down out-houses which leaned against the living quarters. Hens were housed in one outhouse, in the other, a few pigs. Willie's mother, Sarah Robb, was sitting by the fire where a pot of animal swill was cooking, when Jean entered.

" 'Tis yoursel', lass."

"Is Willie at home, Sarah?"

The elderly woman gave a cackle of laughter, picked up a short clay pipe and plunged the tongs into the heart of the fire to extract a small red coal with which she proceeded to light her pipe.

"Och, all the lassies are after my Willie. You're nae the first around here this evening."

"Where is he?"

"He's awa' courtin'. Sit down, lassie, and give's a bit of crack. I hear you're taking on yourself to fight the castle folk. The factor will be after ye. I mind when he hadna a seat on his trews."

She'd need to soak in suds and lye for a week to get rid of her dirt, Jean thought. And the smell of the place... There was an angry looking bruise down the side of Sarah's face. When she went over to look at it, Jean caught a whiff of raw spirits on the woman's breath. It was said that Willie kept a whisky still up behind the pig house.

"How did you get that bruise, Sarah?"

"Slipped on me backside chasing the wee pig out."

"I'm glad to see you've got it out now, and not in the corner."

To think that this was the cottage Doctor Johnson called at to ask for a glass of milk. He must have been jumping over every hedge from here to Elgin. Anything Sarah gave you was as good as a physic!

"I'll bring you a pot of ointment later. You'd be better to take a drop of swill out of the pot instead of whatever you've been drinking," she added, walking towards the door. Sarah's laughter followed her down the road.

Willie was at the inn with a swarthy looking companion, a member of the tinker family who had moved to Lhanbryd. Irish tinkers at that, Jean decided, when the girl opened her mouth. Willie jumped to his feet and gave a mock bow.

"I'm honoured, Mistress Chrystie, meet my friend, Eileen O'Hara."

"You'll take the smirk off your face, Willie Robb, when I tell you that the Duke of Gordon was injured this evening up in the woods. His foot got caught in a rabbit snare. All the castle staff are now out looking for the man who put it under the rowan tree."

Alarm raced across his face, then he tried to give a nonchalent shrug. "And what has that got to do wi' me?"

"I know what it's got to do with you. I've seen you making them outside your house."

His hand shot out and gripped her wrist. "You didn't say that to anyone, did ye?"

"No, because you'd be thrown out of the village and your mother wouldn't have a roof o'er her head. I'm warning you, Willie Robb, if you set one of them things again, I'll go to the factor."

"Jean..." her uncle John called, with a disapproving look on his face. "What's all this about you holding a meeting?"

"It was all right for you to hold one over in the house before you knew which side your bread was buttered on," she snapped angrily.

"Come inside," he said abruptly. "Sheena has something to tell ye."

Her cousin was polishing pewter mugs in the snug-room where special customers drank their ale. "Hello," she said warmly, wiping her hands.

Jean smiled and sat on the edge of the table, feeling weary now after such an eventful day. When she lifted her head, Uncle John was giving her cousin a shrewd nod. "What is it?" she asked frowning, looking from one to the other.

Sheena said in her soft voice, "The Gordons' housekeeper sent for me today and said there's a job for you at the castle. Isn't that grand? I explained how you had to care for Granny. She said you can have time off."

"Doing what kind of work?" Jean interrupted. "And why is she offering me a job?"

"I dinna ken why, but there's a scullery maid's job going by the end of the week."

The tiredness left Jean's body. She was too stunned to speak for a moment. "I don't want to work there," she said dully. The very thought of it appalled her, though she didn't understand why.

"Ye'll have to think about the future, lassie," her uncle said quickly.

"The future?"

He came over, placed a hand around her shoulders, and said kindly: "Your granny's eighty-five years old. She canna have much longer on this earth. What are ye going to do then? You'd hardly like to go and live wi' your mother down Spey Bay for I doubt if your step-father would want ye. You'll need to make your own way."

"I earn good money from knitting hosiery and spinning, and there's my other work."

"It's where you're going to live, lassie. Your aunt has the idea of retiring from the business and when your granny has passed on—"

"You mean," Jean said, horrified, "Aunt Kitty will move to the cottage when granny dies?"

"Aye, she wants to leave the inn and have a wee place away from here, and as you've had the honour of being offered a job at the castle... well," he shrugged, "you'll be able to live in, if ye wish."

"Come up tomorrow after dinner and see the housekeeper," Sheena suggested. "Someone like you, Jean, will be able to improve herself. Look at me. Remember I started in the kitchen and now see how well I'm doing."

Aye, Jean thought, upstairs mending shifts and sheets. She sprang to her feet. "I'll think about it."

Meg was asleep when she returned to the cottage. She shovelled white ash over the live embers for easy lighting in the morning, then pulled out the crane, lifted off the heavy iron kettle and filled it from the bucket of spring-water. The sod-peats would smoulder all night and heat the water for cooking oats for breakfast.

When all the night tasks were completed, Jean drank a mugful then poured the rest into a basin to wash herself. In her room she took a flask of rose-water from the press where the herbs were stored, and added some to the basin. She stripped off her clothes, washed thoroughly and put on a clean shift. This little ritual every night was one luxury she looked forward to at the end of each day.

In bed, Jean tried unsuccessfully to put everything out of her mind; she felt restless and was unable to sleep. Getting out of bed again, she pulled on a skirt over her night-shift, tied a shawl around her shoulders and slipped through the window to the garden.

## Chapter 7

The Lochan was in Whitash wood. Tall conifers that surrounded it gave the loch an air of secretiveness. Here, Bonnie Prince Charlie's followers camped when the Prince lay at Thunderton House, while Cumberland was no distance away resting at Speymouth. Jean loved this place and thought of it as An Lochan Uaine – the green lochan. When she was a bairn, Meg had often taken her walking this way. While her grandmother had sat knitting, she had blown dandelion heads on the water and watched them sail away like gossamer fleets. Then there were the birds, the one with beating wings and a fanned tail, chasing its mate through the trees in a corkscrew flight. The old Master, who had come by, had told Jean that it was a siskin and pointed out how the hen chose the nest high in the conifers and built it while the cock sang nearby. Her interest in birdlife had begun from that time and had become as fascinating to her as the herbs she had been taught to coax out of the light sandy loam in the garden.

It was to Lochan Uaine that Jean had taken her restless thoughts. Instead of considering what she must do with her life, she stretched out on the long grass and let everything drift away as she gazed at the star-studded sky, reflected in the water. The sound of a horse cantering through the woods made her jump to her feet; before she could slip out of sight, the animal and its rider came through the trees and down to the water's edge where it drank thirstily.

Alexander Gordon tugged gently on the reins and they moved towards her. She looked up at him, her heart thumping uncomfortably. For a second neither spoke, then he smiled and seemed to look young and carefree. "This is a strange hour to meet you." He looked about him. "I have not been here since I was a boy. I remember the water lobelia and lilies."

"It is strange that you should come here this evening," she said impulsively.

He hesitated and smiled. "A tree has been cut down over there; I saw you."

She pulled the shawl across her bare throat and as she did so, a piece of rosemary, pulled absent-mindedly in the garden, fell at her feet. The Duke swung his leg across the animal's back and dismounted slowly. Immediately, the horse moved to the water again. He picked up the rosemary. "In spite of your good attention my foot still aches a little."

"You should be in bed resting that foot."

"And you, Mistress Chrystie, should not be so far from home".

"I feel at home here, I love the peace and stillness."

He held the spray of rosemary to his nose. "How delicate the scent is. Has it really got all the powers attributed to it?"

"I think so."

He handed it to her and said: "It would seem it had some importance to Shakespeare too:

'There's rosemary, that's for remembrance;
pray, love, remember...'"

Moved by his words, Jean was silent for a moment, then she said, "I must be getting back."

"You must ride with me. I cannot allow you to walk that distance alone especially as I'm passing the village."

She hesitated. All this was like a fantasy, as though her head was still on the pillow and she was dreaming. They travelled through the woods in silence. She wondered at her feeling of happiness and joy, and wished that their journey could go on for ever. Her eyes were riveted on his hands holding the reins; she noticed their strength and beauty, then smiled at such a thought.

"You are amused at something?" he said inquiringly.

"I've always thought that men's hands were the ugliest things on God's earth."

He began to laugh. "What has made you change your mind?"

"Yours are very fine," she replied shyly.

"A few weeks working on one of my estates and they can be as calloused as the next. Ask my clerk, Mr Marshall, or the factor. I am happiest when I'm working out of doors."

She turned and looked up at him. "Really? I didn't think the gentry liked using their hands."

He stared at her for a moment. "Yes... really," he replied slowly.

They didn't speak again until they reached the field near the village. "I can take a short cut from here," she told him. "It leads to the back of the cottage."

He went to dismount. "No... please. Mind your foot. I'll just slip down and be off."

On the ground, she glanced up at him, about to give her thanks, but his look silenced her. They stared at each other for a moment, their eyes holding in a way which revealed the feeling that was beginning to grow between them. She broke off a piece of the rosemary, handed it to him, then hurried away.

The Duke watched her as she crossed the path and disappeared behind the trees. Abruptly he turned his horse and rode furiously in the opposite direction.

The minute the Duchess arrived from Elgin the following day she sent for Alexander with the imperious manner she always adopted after one of their quarrels. The message was brought by his daughter, Charlotte. "I'll come in a minute, darling," he told her.

"Come now, Papa. Mama is in quite a state."

He rose immediately because he could see Charlotte looked distressed. "I'll race you and shock the household," he said with an affected soberness.

She burst out laughing and, tucking her hand in his, they ran down the corridor past flunkeys and servants.

"Alex," the Duchess said, "I hear the Chrystie girl has been making trouble again. She got a rabble together down by the old pillar and told them to take every penny from you that they can. That young madam," she said, her voice growing harsh, "is trying to make us dance to her tune."

Alexander lowered his eyes. If he met Jean again he would try and explain some of the more serious aspects of the situation. When they met again... He tried to turn his attention to the woman who had every claim on his time and affection, and who had too often rejected both.

"Wait 'till I get her under my roof, then she won't be so free with her tongue."

"What do you mean?"

"She'll be coming here to work. There's a place for her in the kitchen, in the back scullery where the lowest skivvy spends her time. That'll cool her tongue!"

Alexander looked across the room letting his eyes rest on the Angelica Kauffman paintings at each side of the fireplace: Ulysses, Calypso, Bacchus and Ariadne. Then his eyes travelled to the full length painting of himself by Pompeyo Battoni, leaning against a horse, with a gun in his hand and dead game at his feet. The thought of Jean Chrystie working at the castle in such a capacity filled him with repugnance.

Jane Gordon turned in her chair and followed her husband's gaze. "Is there something wrong with those pictures?" she asked impatiently. "I wish you'd take more interest, Alex, in what this Chrystie girl is trying to do. She may not have much sense in her head but when she opens her mouth, she needs watching."

He said quickly without thinking: "That is not the impression I had. I believe she spoke with some authority and... sincerity."

His wife was too occupied with her own thoughts to take in what he was saying. "Sincerity? What rubbish!" She jumped up impatiently. "Never mind how she spoke; it's what she gabbed we should be concerned about."

Alexander couldn't help smiling at her choice of words. At times her tongue was as sharp as a whip, and equally amusing. The King had been heard to say that the Duchess of Gordon was the only woman who could deal with a serious matter in an entertaining manner. When Alexander was a young man of twenty years old, Jane had seemed so refreshing compared to other young ladies. Sadly, her outspoken, blunt manner often lacked refinement and was so coarse at times that her jests were more suited to male company. He recalled the last banquet at Buckingham Palace where Wraxall, who liked the Duchess well, had been heard to say that her good nature and ready wit were marred by a singular coarseness of speech. It irritated Alexander when those who continually sought his wife's company because of her friendship with the King, were capable of criticising her behind her back.

"I'm told that the noise at that meeting was awful," the Duchess continued.

"Well, my dear, we would be foolish to expect the people of Fochabers to accept our decision without protest. The Highlanders are a strong-minded people."

"They're a thrawn lot," she replied, dismissing the subject and turning to a pile of material samples which had just arrived.

"You're awful pale this morning, lassie," Meg said. "Have ye the flux?"

"Indeed no, Granny. I didn't sleep too well."

"I told ye to put more hops into your pillow."

"Aye, well..." Jean knew by the look in Meg's eyes that she was probing. God forbid that she should have an inkling of what was going on in her mind. Her thoughts were tormenting her; one minute she was filled with joy, the next with a terrible feeling of guilt. A short time ago she had felt a deep resentment against the Duke of Gordon. Now she was confused.

After working for an hour in the vegetable garden, she folded the piece of sacking tied around her waist, and washed her hands in the rain tub.

"Granny, that job I was telling you about, I think I'd better accept it."

Meg was silent for a moment. "I think ye'd be wise. It's no' every day that the castle housekeeper sends for folks. I hear there's a fine still-room o'er there. Maybe that'll be your work looking after it."

"Maybe. Well, I'd better clear up all my other work. There's a pile of oat bags in the loft which needs washing before I make them into pillow-cases."

When Jean was leaving the cottage with the bags, she said to Meg "Don't forget that the minister will be coming this morning. Keep the curtains drawn back, hide your pipe and leave the window wide open."

"If I keep the screen around my bed he'll think I'm no' well and need a bit o' quiet," Meg said with a crafty look.

"Granny!"

"What do I want to hear all that blethering about auld Job? Sure I know all about patience sitting here on my backside from morn 'till night. And that Jeremiah... A right queer loon he was. Jean, listen, d'ye know what Bella next door told me? She says the Popish minister doesn't rave out of the Bible and that he's no' past filling a body's pipe and slipping a wee dram into folk. Och, I'd like fine to be Popish at times."

"What?" Jean said horrified, then she put her arms around Meg and hugged her. "Wait 'till the fair comes to the village green. I'm going to set you up in a wee booth so that folk can pay just to hear you talking!"

Down by the burn, she ripped open the oat bags, shook them and threw them into the water where they were trodden with her feet. The decision she had made that morning was foremost in her mind: if she became a castle servant that would soon end any further friendship with the Duke, for he would not dare speak to her when she was under his roof. You need bringing down to earth, Jean Chrystie, she told herself. And what better way than becoming a skivvy in his home?

Dusk was falling when she set out for Gordon Castle. She was supposed to have been there earlier but it had suddenly occurred to her that Gypsy Willie's mother needed ointment for the bruise on her face. When she arrived at the Robbs' cottage, Sarah was ill in bed and Jean had set about making some brose. The gloaming cast a comforting and protective veil around her as she approached the castle. She was turning the corner towards the back area of the house when the sound of music came from one of the rooms. Edging near the window, she peeped in cautiously.

The sight that met her eyes seemed to belong to another world. Men and women were standing in little groups wearing the most magnificent clothes she had ever laid eyes on. She searched

## The Forgotten Duchess

through the crowd in the room, then suddenly realised that her glance had passed over the Duke without recognising him. Scarce wonder, for his clothes were as fine as the ladies and he wore an elaborate wig.

The Duke's face seemed to be a mask of politeness—a slight smile, but little warmth in his expression. She hurried away feeling as though the hand of God had made her witness something that showed how presumptuous it was for her even to think about this man. Had she remained a minute longer, she would have seen his daughter whisper something to her father, his mischievous wink and their suppressed giggles as the pair of them slipped out of the room.

There was a silence when she entered the kitchen. Her first impression, when she looked in the window, had been of flunkeys and maids dashing around. Now everyone was standing still and staring as her as though she had two heads.

The cook waddled over. "Ye've come then? What time of day is this, miss?"

"I'm sorry to be late."

"Housekeeper's nae pleased wi' ye, lassie, and I'll tell ye something, I'll nae be pleased either if you turn up late for work when the pantry's all amucket when you should be cleaning it."

James Ross, the factor, came through the kitchen on his way to the inner region of the house. Everyone moved, obsequiously, to make way for him. He gave Jean a piercing stare and walked on briskly. The interruption released her from the others' scrutiny. She took a deep breath and felt better.

"Eileen O'Hara," the cook shrieked at the top of her voice. "Come awa' and show this wan the work."

Gypsy Willie's girlfriend appeared at the scullery door with a sullen expression on her face. Jean followed her into a dark room which had a smell of stale food, and piles of greasy dishes on two long tables. There was a pair of double sinks, one of wood, lined with copper, and one of porcelain. An old wooden milk-churn, filled with washing soda, stood in the corner. She looked at the dishes with distaste. "Is that what I'll have to do, wash these all the time?"

"Are ye too grand, begod? Did ye think the Duchess was wanting ye for a personal maid? This is what ye'll do from morn till night, as well as peeling spuds. And I'll tell ye something my fine lady," Eileen O'Hara whined, "you're taking the bread out of me mouth. I don't know where I'll lay me head and that's the God's honest truth."

Jean looked at the mess in the scullery and the bitter-faced girl; her one instinct was to take to her heels and get away from all these people to her own cottage where the air was always fresh and scented with herbs. Her eyes moved to the girl's hands which were rough and grimy with labour. Mine will be like that too in a few weeks time, she thought with horror.

"You can keep your job, Eileen, for I don't want it," she said, moving towards the door again.

The Irish girl looked at her disbelievingly, then a cunning look came to her eyes. "Sure aren't ye the wise one. Mother of God, what would the likes of you be doing a skivvy's work for? A fine girleen who can talk to anyone, God love ye."

The sweet words fell sourly on Jean's ears. Eileen O'Hara had the tinkers gift o' the gab. The housekeeper was waiting when she returned to the kitchen. She looked her up and down, sniffed and said, "Weel, I hope you're not going to make a habit of turning up late." The grand accent collapsed, and the woman's face grew angry. "It'll no' do, Chrystie, it'll no' do at all, you walking in here when you take the fancy."

"The job will no' do for me either, mam, for I don't fancy it."

The woman's face went crimson with anger. Before she could utter another word, Jean turned and was out of the door in a flash. She ran faster than she had ever run in her life, and all the time, the dark cloud of depression that had been building up since she approached the castle earlier on, began to fade. To be a skivvy under his roof... to be ignored by him for the rest of her life. It was unthinkable.

"God save us, lassie, what ails ye?" Meg said, looking up from the piece of crochet work in her hands when Jean dashed in and hugged her.

"Would you like a wee dram, Granny dear?"

"I wouldna say no but where would ye get it?" she asked craftily.

Jean went into her room, climbed to the top shelf of the press and brought down a flask. To Meg's surprise, her granddaughter poured two tots.

"Ye'll be celebrating, then? Ye've got the job? My, that was lucky."

"No," Jean said slowly. "I don't want the job. You know, Granny, I've only just realised how sweet my freedom is." There was something else; she was recalling the feeling she had experienced when approaching the castle. Every instinct in her body had seemed to be drawing her away from the building, as though some force was trying to prevent her from going there.

Meg took a sip of the whisky and said cautiously; "You canna live on fresh air, lassie dear." As the old woman bent her head, she gave Jean a long, searching look.

The Duchess of Gordon was furious the following morning when her companion, Mistress Tison, came and told her that the housekeeper had not been able to secure the services of Jean Chrystie.

"You'll never believe it," she said, storming into the Duke's study. "That brazen Chrystie girl has refused to accept employment in the castle. She walked out of the kitchen last evening without a by your leave."

Alexander began to laugh. The Duchess swept a pile of papers out of her way, leaned across the desk and glared at him.

"What is so amusing about it?"

"I'm sorry, Jane. How would you like to be ordered at a minute's notice to go and scour someone's kitchen?"

"If need be, I'd do it like the next."

He glanced at her and said with fairness: "Yes, I believe you would. But the girl has not expressed a need to work at the castle. Mr Marshall tells me that she is extremely knowledgable in herbal medicine and tends the sick in the village."

While the Duchess drummed her fingers impatiently on the desk, Alexander thought: my wife is said to be the most spirited and independent woman of this age, yet when she meets this quality in another woman, she resents it.

"If she stirs up more trouble—" The threatening words ended in a gesture as Jane Gordon strode to the window and pointed angrily at the village. "Just look at that mess, Alex. Devils' brooms, I can't get it shifted fast enough."

Alexander drew a line across a row of figures. "Their ancestors used to guard the castle gates when an enemy was sighted." He frowned. "When you consider, it is only about thirty years since the battle of Culloden."

"Aye, Culloden," she said soberly. "And to think I've got to eat and sup sometimes with that banshee mistress of Butcher Cumberland. God's blood," Jane Gordon said vehemently, "there are times when I've looked at that crowd of Sassenachs in our house in London filling their bellies at our expense and I've felt like jumping on the table and shooting every damn one of them."

"Hush!" the Duke said, laughing at her inconsistency. "If you talk like that you'll be thrown out of Buckingham Palace the next time you go to visit the King."

The Duchess looked away from her husband's gaze. London was her lifeline, where the most powerful men in the kingdom were her closest friends. But first things first. Gordon Castle would have to be made fit to entertain King George. That sprawl of hovels would be no sight for a king to view from his bedroom window.

When the Duchess returned to her apartment, she called impatiently: "Tissy, get my bonnet, we've got a call to make."

"Yes, Your Grace?"

"We're going to the village to make a call."

Her companion looked confused. "The village? Shall I summon the footman, the carriage?"

"The carriage? Are you daft? I said the village, not Elgin. And there'll be no danger of footpads either."

The Duchess swept along in her usual brisk manner. "Tissy," she said impatiently, "you'd think there was ice on the ground and you were in danger of landing on your backside. Lift your head, woman, every eye in Fochabers is on us."

Mistress Tison caught up her skirts. Castle dirt was one thing, but she wasn't going to take any chances among the lower orders.

The post office, which was also the village shop, was crowded. Elsie Chalmers, the postmistress, made everyone welcome and the place was the heart of the village.

## The Forgotten Duchess

"Don't look now," Elsie shouted above the chattering, "the Duchess and her woman are coming down the wee path from the castle."

Immediately all eyes flew to the window and there was a rush forward to get a good view.

"Tissy," the Duchess murmured, "will you take a look at that window, every orb in the village is on us."

Her companion gave an exclamation of disgust.

"I'll soon scatter them." And at that Jane Gordon changed her direction.

There was a mad scramble in the post office, everyone making for the back door. Jean Chrystie moved first and Big Annie followed. Bella Forbes tripped over Annie and the others all fell in a heap, helpless with laughter. The postmistress slammed the door on them and they heard her fluttering welcome to the Duchess of Gordon.

"Hush!" Annie said. "Be quiet, let's hear what the Duchess has to say."

They heard her congratulating Elsie Chalmers on being one of the first to be moved to the new site. "The factor tells me," the Duchess said, "that your out-houses are built of good stone. I advise you, Mistress Chalmers, to empty them and the stone will be taken over to the site where work will begin immediately."

The words silenced the women's laughter. Jean eased herself into a sitting position and they all whispered together for a few minutes, then they slipped out through the scullery and made their way home.

A short time after this, Jean was standing at the kitchen table working with a pile of lavender and rose leaves when there was a knock on the cottage door. Meg was dozing so she drew the curtain across the recess.

The smell of musk, after the scent of the garden flowers, made her draw back for a second. She quickly recovered, and hiding her surprise, made a quick curtsey and invited the Duchess of Gordon and Mistress Tison to enter.

The Duchess walked in looking about her curiously. Jean noticed how her companion lifted her skirt off the floor and felt angry. Thank goodness the hearth was swept and the place tidy. Let them see what a fine wee house they were planning to pull down.

She moved the bench and invited the ladies to sit, then said quietly: "Can I offer you some refreshment, Your Grace?"

Jane Gordon looked at her in surprise and Mistress Tison raised her eyebrows in a supercilious manner. Jean didn't wait for a reply but hurried down to the room, took out two silver goblets and a bottle of blackberry wine, then went over to the pot of mint on the window ledge kept for deterring flies and pressed her face into it. Immediately she felt calmer.

"Those are fine bits you've got there," the Duchess commented curiously, when Jean laid down the tray.

"My great-grandfather found them in the Roman site over at Boghead," Jean told her, as she offered the ladies a plate of honey biscuits. She looked directly at Mistress Tison. "They have been carefully washed."

The Duchess threw her head back and shouted with laughter. She took a sip of the wine. "This is quite pleasant. You made it yourself?"

"We make everything for ourselves, Your Grace." Despite her quiet words, Jean began to feel nervous. She had refused an offer to work at the castle, but why had the sudden offer been made anyway? And why had the Duchess of Gordon called? If only Granny would wake up.

At that moment Meg began to snore and give little snorts in her sleep.

Mistress Tison said in her high-faluting accent: "Haave you got piglets in the house?" She twitched her skirts higher as though she were expecting a stream to rush through the kitchen.

Jean felt mortified, and to make matters worse, the Duchess kept staring hard at her. With sudden anger, she said: "Does it look as though pigs are kept in the house?"

At that moment, Meg spoke. "Who's out there, lass? Will ye open up all the windows, for the midden smells sweeter."

There was a shattered silence. "Where did that voice come from?" Jane Gordon asked. "Is it your grandmother? I thought she was in the bedroom, ill."

"Her bed is down there in the recess, Your Grace."

"Well, pull the curtain back," she ordered impatiently.

"If she's willing. Granny is very old and it's her wish that they are never drawn unless she agrees." Jean's eyes went to the

Edinburgh woman. "She finds some folk right trying."

Impertinent baggage, the Duchess thought. No wonder there's trouble with this one. It was a wasted effort my coming here. I was expecting a simple village girl with a bit of spirit. There's something quite different here.

Jean crossed the kitchen. "Granny, the Duchess of Gordon has called and would like to see you."

"Ye dinna say?" Meg sounded pleased and not a bit put out.

Jean placed another pillow behind her back, and sprinkled lavender-water on a handkerchief which Meg dabbed on her face. Then the curtain was drawn.

Jane Gordon rose to her feet. "Well, Meg, I am sorry to see you in bed," she said kindly.

"Ah, well, Your Grace, I reckon I've had a long enough run and it's time to put me feet up. But m' fingers are active enough and I can still earn a shilling."

"Your granddaughter doesn't seem anxious to earn a shilling." The Duchess swung round and looked angrily at Jean. "My housekeeper tells me you refused an offer of work."

"I didn't ask for the work," she replied quietly, and drawing herself up to her full height she had the satisfaction of looking down slightly on the other woman. "Anyone, Your Grace, can wash dishes, but it takes a bit of knowledge and time to go out to the hedgerows and pick herbs to help folk's aches and pains."

Jane Gordon hid her irritation. She turned to Meg. "Hadn't you that kind of gift, I seem to remember?"

"Aye, and I passed it on to the lassie."

"Surely it doesn't give you an income," she said severely, glaring at Jean again.

"No, Your Grace," she agreed. "But folk pay in kind." She stopped. Most of the fish and meat brought to the cottage were poached from the Gordon estate. And there was the firewood. When the factor was at one end of the estate someone cut down a tree or two at the other end.

"Do the village women still gather here to sew?" the Duchess asked abruptly. "As you know, I am anxious to get the Cottage Industry started in earnest. When the new village is built I'm bringing someone from Aberdeen to see if some worthwhile work can be organised."

And we'll do it in our own way in the end, Jean thought. How these gentry looked down their noses, as if they owned you.

"Are ye no' going to let an old body die in her own bed?" Meg said with a deliberate whine in her voice. "If they flit me out o' this corner, I'll tak' wings if the good Lord will have me."

The Duchess of Gordon turned away; she had no intention of discussing *that* business here. She had made her point.

Meg began to peer at Mistress Tison. "Who's that wee body you've got wi' ye, Your Grace? For a moment I thought it was your sister, Betty–och, I'm forgetting, she's Lady Wallace of Cragie now, isn't she?"

Mistress Tison stiffened in her seat at being referred to as "a wee body". Meg's memory went drifting back. "Och, I'll never forget when ye used to ride on the pig's back down the wynd into the High Street in Edinburgh."

Jean looked at her granny in horror and the companion's face blazed with indignation. The Duchess was laughing. "Well, fancy you remembering that. I was a right hoyden in those days, and so was my sister."

"Isn't it time we were going, Your Grace?" Mistress Tison said coldly. The way Jane Gordon hob-nobbed with common people was quite unbecoming. She should remember her station. She had done her best to get up in the world; now that she was there, she should behave as though she belonged.

When the two women left the cottage, Meg complained, "I canna abide that wee body the Duchess had wi' her. And did ye see yon hair? Like a thatch gone wild in the wind. God knows what was nesting in yon..."

As Jean made preparations to distill her collection of flowers, she felt uneasy and disturbed by the Duchess's visit. One thing the woman had made quite clear anyway, they would all have to move out of the village whether they liked it or not.

## Chapter 8

Two evenings later the village was sleeping peacefully as several shadowy figures met near the Green Cairn. Silently, and in pairs, the women went across to the field where they had hidden their wheelbarrows, then they proceeded to the building site. The stones from the post office had been piled like a pyramid.

"Bad luck to them," Big Annie said, "we'll not get on so fast with them in that order. Two of us had better stand on our barrows and pass the top ones down. Not you, Jean, me and another big lass."

The minute Annie stepped into the wheelbarrow, her foot went right through the bottom. She fell against the stones, dislodging the top ones which fell to the ground with a loud rattle. Alarmed, they all crouched behind the pile, terrified that someone had heard.

After a while, Annie whispered: "I'm stuck, I canna get me foot out."

Apart from a few rabbits, the noise had not apparently reached anyone's ears. They crawled around the wheelbarrow and, convulsed with laughter, tried to release Annie. The barrows were then loaded and pushed away from the site.

One hour later when the task was completed, Jean stretched out on the rough grass, completely exhausted. It had been a silent protest, all that they were capable of doing. Overhead, clusters of berries on the rowan tree hung down like red jewels. From the hills a soft breeze brought the scent of pine, juniper and bog myrtle. Suddenly and quite unexpectedly, a feeling of deep happiness came, and her fingers, pressing into the earth, seemed to be drawing out its precious minerals. She sat up slowly and listened to the murmur of water in the burn. Gradually, each thought that went through her mind seemed to be building a chain of awareness. For the first time, it occurred to her that it would be foolish not to see the advantages of living in the new site for the village. The ground was higher and drier, and the air purer. Then there was the road that had been mentioned, a road that would go through the new village, straight to Aberdeen. Perhaps in time, the women would be able to travel to Aberdeen and sell their own work, instead of waiting for the dealers who paid what they pleased.

She jumped to her feet and ran towards the brae. Though the land was enveloped in a deep blue haze, she could see in her mind's eye across the Spey to Lochnabo and the lovely plains of Urquhart which were no distance from the town of Elgin. She sat down on a tree trunk letting her thoughts wander on, guided by the knowledge from the books which the old Master had loaned her. It was strange to think that at one time there had been elk, bear and wild boar roaming around this countryside. Now there were deer and wild cat, and the king of birds–the *iolaire,* or golden eagle.

A rustle in the bushes made her turn round quickly. For a second she thought it was a *fiadh*. But as the animal came closer, she realized that it was not a red deer but a highland greyhound with long, rough hair. Before she could move, Alexander Gordon came into sight. In a second he had seated himself a short distance from her.

"Were you not able to sleep either?' he asked.

The glimmer of a smile touched her eyes.

"Or," he continued, smiling broadly, "did you even try?"

Her eyes widened. "You know?"

"I know!" And to her surprise, he laughed outright.

Jean lifted her chin defiantly. "It was meant to be a protest."

He looked at her, his head to one side. "An admirable one, if I may say so—even though I realize it was at my expense."

She gave him a cautious glance. He went on: 'I don't think I have ever seen such a striking little procession in all my life."

"Most of the women's husbands work for you; if the factor..."

"Don't worry," was his immediate response. "I have no intention of revealing to my factor how the postmaster's stones re-appeared so strangely back in the post office yard."

The dimple in Jean's cheek deepened, and suddenly they were both laughing.

"Tell me, who was the giant leading the procession?"

"That was Big Annie, the butcher's wife." She found herself giving him all the details about what had happened at the site.

He stretched out on the grass and said, "How good it is to relax with laughter."

She looked at him shyly. She had chatted away as though he were just anyone. "I must go."

He sat up. "Not yet Jean, I have something for you."

Her heart took a wild leap when he spoke her name so naturally.

"You were kind and helpful the other evening, attending to my wound," he told her, putting his hand in his pocket.

"Has your foot healed all right?"

"Quite healed." He smiled and handed her a silver-wrapped package.

She opened it with a quick, excited breath and took out a pair of exquisite kid gloves. Jean touched them reverently. "For me?"

"Yes, of course. You can't see the colour in this light but they are a deep, golden shade."

"How did you know you'd meet me this evening? It is only by chance that I came here."

"We always seem to be meeting in the wee sma' hours, don't we?"

She smiled. "You sound strange talking like that."

"Ah, but I, too, am bilingual. I must confess I was hoping I'd meet you, for I feel we are both what is called night-birds. It has been a habit of mine since I was a young lad to roam around late at night."

She slipped on one of the gloves and held her hand to her face, inhaling the delicate scent of fine leather.

"You have very beautiful hands," he said and, folding back the rim of the glove, laid his lips on her wrist.

Jean drew back as the shock went through her body, then sprang to her feet. "I must go now."

"Of course. I will stand here and watch while you go down the hill and across the site. If you meet a muckle black de'il before you reach your garden, shout and my dogs and I will come to your rescue! Goodbye, and...God bless you."

Goodbye. It sounded so final.

"Are you going away?"

"Yes. I must leave for the south sooner than I planned. There's trouble brewing in the American Colonies and I may have to form a regiment."

I won't see him again, she thought with a feeling of desolation. Recklessly, she began to talk, "I was offered a position in the castle."

"I know, you didn't take it. I'm glad."

"I was going to, for I thought if you saw me perform some lowly task in your home, you would pass me by unnoticed, and that might bring me to my senses." Jean hesitated. "I couldn't bear the thought of that." She turned and ran swiftly down the hill. I have opened my heart, she thought. Maybe it was not wise.

Towards the edge of the field, she stopped and crept into the shadows when the sound of voices came from the other side. Two figures approached, Gypsy Willie and Eileen O'Hara.

Willie gave an angry exclamation. "Well, I'll be damned."

"What ails ye, m'darlin'?"

"Someone's taken the post office stones that I spent the whole bliddy afternoon hauling o'er here." He was silent for a moment, then said viciously: "I bet that Jean Chrystie was behind this. Come on, I'm goin' to take a look around the post office yard. You go to Chrystie's house and see if there's anything a-doing."

The two figures walked across the field. The tinker girl seemed to follow Willie unwillingly.

"Hurry up, will ye," he said impatiently.

"Ach," she muttered sullenly, "why d'ye want to be bothered with auld stones, m'darlin'?" And at that she began pulling at him.

## The Forgotten Duchess

He turned and laughing coarsely, tumbled her to the ground.

Jean was mortified. She couldn't get away without them seeing her and she couldn't bear to watch them either, behaving there like a pair of animals. She turned her face and tried to think of the profusion of wild flowers which grew in the hedge. But the coarseness of their talk penetrated her thought. I hope they roll into cow's clabber and get covered in it. Small thought that Willie had for his poor old mother lying ill.

Suddenly there was the sound of a dog barking on the hills. It stilled her agitation for a minute and in her mind's eye she saw the figure of a man and his dog walking towards the castle.

When the pair moved on, Jean sneaked towards the cottage garden to the woodshed for a knife to open her window. Thank goodness she had left by that way and bolted the front door. The knife was under her fingers when there was a patter of bare feet coming round to the back of the house; with a clatter it fell to the floor. Eileen O'Hara stooped to pick up a huge stone. "Where are ye, Jean Chrystie," the girl hissed. "Show yoursel' for Willie will be back in a minute and ye'll not escape." At that moment, the sound of Willie's boots came down the road towards the cottage.

"B'Jasus, she's here somewhere, m'darlin'," O'Hara called, going to meet him. "We'll drag her by the scruff o' the neck up to the factor's house and show him what a fine fella y'are, looking after lordie's property."

Jean felt cornered and frightened. She couldn't get into the cottage nor escape to the field. Then something came through the shed door and began to poke wildly on her chest; it was the long bamboo cane which Meg kept to rattle on the front window when she was on her own in the cottage and wanted to attract some passer-by to come in for a chat.

Tearing across the grass she clambered through her grandmother's window. When the pair came around to the back of the cottage the window was half-shut when Willie rushed towards it.

"Is that you, Willie Robb?" Meg scolded, "disturbing folk's rest to come courting my granddaughter when she's bin a-bed these past hours. Have a care, laddie, or I'll get the factor after ye."

Eileen O'Hara swore viciously and threw the stone to the ground as the pair moved away.

"Did ye get the job done?" Meg enquired.

"Aye, it was a good night's work."

"Ye'll try again, likely, and that'll set the Gordons thinking."

"We'll see," Jean replied, but her heart had gone out of the protest, for she realized now that the land and the position near the burn was much better.

The following morning someone brought a message that Gypsy Willie's mother needed more ointment.

"I'll swear she eats it, Granny."

"I wouldna put it past her, lass, hog's fat and leeks is tasty enough."

When she arrived at Robb's cottage a neighbour was looking after Sarah. Jean collected the empty ointment pot and as she was passing through the kitchen again, a snorting sound came from the loft. That lazy Willie, to think he was boasting about having risen from a farm-servant to farm-labourer and earning eight pounds instead of two pounds a year. If he doesn't get up and go to work he'll be earning nothing!

The neighbour nudged her. "Listen to yon. Willie's away to work and left that brazen baggage behind. Sarah doesn't know yet but the tinker girl is here to stay. She's been thrown out of the castle."

At least I'll get peace from Willie in future, Jean thought, and picking up her basket hurried off to make the next call which was to see Tessa McDonald's youngest child. Every time she thought of that house, her head began to itch.

Tessa came to the door with a spindle and whorl in her hand. She smiled slyly at Jean Chrystie's surprised expression and noticed how the girl's eyes went to the hearth which was swept clean, with a batch of oat cakes baking on the girdle and... Tessa chuckled to herself... a respectable visitor sitting in the corner.

The priest rose and greeted Jean. He was pleased to see such a respectable body calling at the McDonald house. Perhaps the girl would have a good influence on this wayward Glasgow woman. As Jean chatted to the priest she watched Tessa out of the corner of her eye moving about the kitchen, spinning away with a pious expression on her face. He must have wrought a Popish miracle, she thought. The illusion was soon shattered, for the minute the man went out of the house Tessa tossed the spindle and whorl up on the loft and began to laugh and dance around the kitchen.

"Thank God," she said, gaily "now I can relax for another week. Poor auld soul, I canna stand his blethering about mortal sin. Good thing he comes on the same day every week and I can have my wee act all ready."

"Good thing you don't belong to our kirk," Jean told her severely. "There'd be more than blethering from our minister!"

"Ach, sure," Tessa said slyly, "we papists are nearer the good Lord. Our holy man doesna need to go on about hell's fire and stool of repentance."

"Ye're an awful bisom, Tessa Mcdonald," Jean said laughing.

Her daughter Fiona came in with the baby. Jean took the child in her arms and touched the silky skin, then gently opened its mouth. "Why don't you come up to our cottage one evening, Tessa, with your spindle. It's great fun. Big Annie's husband brings his fiddle and her father tells old tales."

Tessa's face clouded. "Ah, I wouldna like, Jean. They look down on me. Thanks anyway, hen. You're the first person in this village to darken my door for a long time, and I canna mind when anyone asked me to enter their house."

"Ma," Fiona said eagerly, "can I go?"

"Yes," Jean replied quickly, "you can help me when it's time to give them a sup and bite."

The girl smiled at her happily and Jean suddenly realized that Fiona was growing up in a community where her family were not accepted. Her mother's way of life had made her an outcast and it was bound to affect this lovely young girl. She smoothed a little honey inside the baby's mouth, handed the child back to Fiona and said: "I'll be expecting you, then."

It had been decided among the women that it would be wise to move around the village as usual after the episode in the night. Jean didn't look forward to going to the post office. Her feeling of discomfort increased because the place had never been so empty. They had not kept their word.

"It's yourself," the postmistress said coolly.

"Hello, Elsie," she greeted her brightly. "Sarah Robb is ill again." The information rushed out of her mouth to ease an uncomfortable pause, though everyone passed on their news to Elsie.

"I'm not surprised with what she's got to put up with. There'll be more than her not well from what I hear about Willie's carrying-ons."

The door opened. Jean turned around, relieved, expecting to see one of the village women. It was Mr Marshall, the Duke's clerk. He gave her a quick glance then turned to the post-mistress.

Elsie said inquisitively as she attended to his order, "I hear the castle folk are not moving off today after all, Mr Marshall."

"That is so, Mistress Chalmers. Some important papers are on their way for the Duke and he can't leave 'till they arrive."

Jean's heart leapt. When he left, the post-mistress said:

"That man has done well for himself. Not many get the chance to rise from flunkey to be the Duke's personal assistant."

"The Duke must be a very reasonable man to encourage folk with ability, don't ye think," Jean said casually, wanting Elsie to go on talking about Alexander Gordon.

"Och, aye, but he and Mr Marshall have a bit o' music in common. The gentry take notice of common folk when the good Lord puts a gift in their hands."

"Is the Duke musical?"

"Indeed so, it was he who wrote 'There is Cauld Kail in Aberdeen'."

"Really?"

Elsie gave a wise nod. "That surprises ye! Mr Marshall is supposed to be a fine composer too. Young Rabbie Burns who's aye popular at the castle said Mr Marshall is the finest composer of strathspeys of this age. What d'you think of that? There must be great going-ons up there."

Jean hurried away from the post office feeling excited at the news about the delay in the Duke's departure, then tried to put him right out of her mind. The post-mistress had not complained about the stones re-appearing in her yard. She probably suspected who had done it and was too embarrassed to say anything, for in the beginning she had protested louder than anyone about the village being moved.

That evening, when a few neighbours called for a ceilidh with Meg, Jean rose from her spinning wheel, made them refreshments, then went to her room and dressed in her best gown, a deep green which went well with the gold-coloured shawl Meg had knitted for her.

"I'm away for an hour or two," she said, her heart pounding nervously at what she planned to do. Though she had tried, it had been impossible to put Alexander Gordon out of her mind. She remembered what he had said on the previous evening, that he had come to the hill hoping to see her. Perhaps he would come this evening?

"That's right m'love, enjoy yourself." Meg peered suspiciously. "That's no' your best gown, I see?"

"Aye, I want to show it to someone for the pattern," her granddaughter replied untruthfully.

"Ah, well, I thought maybe you were off with some laddie." Meg's friends began to laugh. Jean Chrystie with a lad. That would be the day! Who would be good enough for that lass? She was too stand-offish to encourage anyone, and her turning nineteen too.

Alexander saw her coming up the hill. How tall and graceful she looked this evening. The colour of her gown seemed to be reflected in her eyes. He should not be here but at the castle attending to the papers which had arrived. Somehow, he had felt compelled to come. It had been a tedious day of waiting. The Duchess was in a difficult mood because of the delay, and the children impatient. He moved into the shadow of the trees which were in Jean's path.

He looked so tall and stern standing there that her steps began to falter. A minute ago she had been on the point of going down the hill again because her conscience had begun to trouble her. It was difficult to forget the discipline of the kirk, particularly as she went twice to church every Sunday. The spiritual exercise satisfied something deep in her nature. But now, as she took the few steps towards Alexander Gordon, joy began to rise in her and everything else was forgotten.

"Did you know," he said, smiling, "that the male butterfly can smell the scent of the female when she is miles away?" He touched her face lightly. "I smelt your delicate rose perfume." A frown crossed his face."Why are you looking so serious?"

"I think," she replied with childish candour, "that I'm a bit frightened."

He rested his hands on her shoulders for a second and said quietly: "There is no reason to be frightened of me, Jean."

They walked on in silence through the tufted heather until a startled plover rose in flight just ahead of them. Instinctively, they paused and looked down on the glen which was filled with a soft, green light. Suddenly a shrill cry and a flashing movement drew their attention further up to where the bracken mingled with young birch trees. At first Jean thought it was the long-haired Highland hound after a deer, until Alexander said: "It's my Pomeranian bitch—an offspring of a wolf... Damn it, who's let it out at this time of day?"

Then before their startled eyes, the dog brought a deer down and tore out its throat. Alexander Gordon's angry exclamation was stifled when two fugitive figures emerged from the trees. They moved quickly, one took charge of the growling dog and the other, the deer's carcass, then they disappeared.

His face was grim. He caught her arm and drew her to the path on the left, away among the trees. "So, I wonder how many times that has occurred? The Pomeranian is a good-natured dog but sportive. They must have slipped it at a weak deer." He looked sternly at her. "Did you recognize them? Do they work on the estate?"

She shook her head, and clenched her trembling hands at the terrible scene. That thieving Willie Robb. Why was Ned Geddes, the butcher, getting involved in such dirty work? If I tell Big Annie she'll have the hide off her husband. Jean shrugged inwardly; no doubt there'll be a nice bit of venison tucked away in the butcher shop and I'll receive my portion.

She looked out of the corner of her eye to see if the Duke's anger was cooling. He caught her glance and returned it challengingly. Unexpectedly, the mutilated deer came before her eyes and to her dismay, bile rose in her throat. She rushed away among the trees and vomited. Ashamed of such weakness, Jean wiped her streaming eyes, then picked some hawthorn leaves and chewed them to clear the bad taste in her mouth.

He didn't say a word when she joined him, but simply took her arm considerately and guided her until they were on the path that led to the Quarry garden. Her first impression of the garden was that she had stepped into another world. There was a stretch of magnificent parkland laid out with paths, broken by many arbours, trellised with roses.

"Those carved stones you see," he explained, "came originally from Huntly Castle. The stone lion is a particular favourite of mine, he has such a benign expression, don't you think? His eyes follow one everywhere."

"It is like an enchanted place," she said slowly.

"It is my special place," he told her. "You see that little gazebo or summer-house on the high ground? I go there at times to think, work and escape from people."

"Does...the Duchess come here too?"

"She only comes by carriage when picnics are organised for the children and our guests."

The inside of the summer-house was simply furnished with a divan, table and two chairs and bookshelves containing a few books. A tiny fireplace was laid with twigs and cones.

"Sit down," he told her. "I'm going to give you something to settle your stomach."

Alarmed in case he intended to question her about the men, she said: "I'm fine. I must have got a fly in my throat."

He poured brandy into two glasses, handed her one and smiled. "Liar, but a beautiful loyal one."

Jean kept her eyes lowered, not knowing what to say. She was saved from any further mention of the killing in the glen when she took a sip of brandy and choked. "I think it needs a drop of water," she said, clutching her burning throat.

Alexander laughed. "I think that might be a sacrilege! We'll go and fetch some from the well behind the house."

"The Duke of Gordon going to fetch water from a well? Let me go."

"We'll go together," he said, taking her hand.

She knelt down and looked into the well while he dipped in a pitcher. Some hieroglyphics engraved on a stone caught her attention. "I wonder if this is a holy well?"

He raised her to her feet and said gravely: "It is holy now because you've gazed in it."

That's a right bit of nonsense, she thought. Nevertheless, his words moved and delighted Jean. When they returned indoors, he placed the pitcher on the table and took her in his arms. She felt alarm at first, followed immediately by an increasing joy. To her dismay, he dropped his arms again and turned away abruptly.

"I have no right to touch you," he said slowly. "And you're so young."

"You have every right, for I love you and will do so for the rest of my life."

He shook his head as though to deny her words, at the same time reaching out and drawing her towards him again.

"If only," she said reluctantly after a while, "I'd recognized you the first time we met. I'd have taken to my heels. The Duke of Gordon has always seemed like God. Then one day I met this polite gentleman, asking me questions, just like anyone."

He laughed. "Jean, you do me good."

"I don't know if you're going to me much good," she said wistfully.

"My dear ..."

"Your position, and the..."

"The Duchess?"

"Aye, she's beginning to be an awful weight on my conscience."

"You may find it difficult to understand, but sometimes when people marry young–as I did–they are appalled at how different they become from the person they choose to spend the rest of their life with. If love fades or matures, at least there should be companionship. But when two people are constantly finding fault with each other, then that relationship is very poor indeed."

She looked at him solemnly and thought of what people said about the grand folk. If you were poor you made the best of life as far as she could see. There was a sadness and regret in his words which somehow removed a barrier between them because it made him seem vulnerable—this man who appeared to have everything.

"I have no breeding nor knowledge of the world."

He looked at her steadily and said with a touch of bitterness, "What is breeding anyway? Some of the coarsest women I know are supposed to be well bred and they have not your grace nor wisdom."

Jean shook her head. "I have so little."

He went on as though she had not spoken. "I am told that you have an astonishing knowledge of herbs; no doubt you are equally skilled in other crafts."

"We village folk wouldn't have a shift on our backs if we didn't know how to make it."

He laughed. "Also, you are very kind if sometimes unwisely so!"

There was the sound of someone approaching. "Wait here, Jean. It may be Mr Marshall with a message for me."

He was only gone a few minutes when she heard voices shouting. He returned, looking angry.

"Jean, tell me who those men are?"

"Haven't they got away by now?" she asked, alarmed.

"The factor discovered what they were up to. Now a dozen men are trying to find them."

Jean thought of Ned Geddes, the butcher; a gentle little man and not very bright. The work he did for the Gordons was cutting up carcasses, which was their main source of income for few people in the village could afford to buy meat at his shop. The bairns, and Big Annie, on whose shoulders every burden fell.

"They're hunting them like animals, all those men and dogs."

"Apparently it's not the first time it has happened," he remarked with a coldness that shook her.

"I cannot tell you," she said stonily, unable to lie, or yet to betray her own kind. Willie Robb would be cunning enough to get away, but the butcher, with his slow thinking, might be cornered.

She made for the door. Alexander barred her way. "No, stay here, I want to talk to you."

Determined to go and find Ned Geddes, she went to push past him. He caught her arm. "Stay here!" he ordered.

Her alarm moved to anger. "Don't tell me what to do. You don't own me. The people in Fochabers have some rights too, you know. God didn't put the fish in the Spey or the deer on the hills for the sole pleasure of the Gordons, or for feeding that fat Hanoverian sitting on the throne. Oh aye, we all know that salmon and game are shipped to London to feed those usurpers. So I can't see any wrong if the people whose blood and sweat go into this land take a bit back now and then."

"If you could see the state of my dog–It will never strike another deer. At least we kill cleanly, not brutally." There was grief as well as anger on his face when he walked out of the summer-house, slamming the door behind him and turning the key in the lock.

Oh God, they've killed his dog. He's locked me in. Jean ran to the window of the summer-house and climbed through it. She jumped, and landed, not on hard ground, but on something soft. Looking down, she discovered that she was standing on Ned Geddes's back half-covered with bracken.

Fearfully, he turned his earth-covered face and looked at her. "Jean! You? They're after me, lass. I'm done for. Willie Robb clouted the Duke's dog when it turned on him and I fear it's dead."

"Ned, they'll be spreading out to trap you. They're down front, so you'll be clear for a moment. Keep moving on your belly past the wee well. If you can get into the woods you'll stand a chance, then make for the hills and stay there; there's blood on your clothes."

She let him get away, then followed, crawling past the well too into the woods where she tore off in the opposite direction. As soon as she reached the village she went to see Big Annie and told her what happened.

"He's a silly loon," Annie said, wringing her hands in despair. "He only went out for a bit of a dander and must've got caught up with that Willie."

I can't do any more, Jean thought dispiritedly, as she made her way home. The butcher would have to take a chance with fate. She remembered Annie's face during the few minutes they had been talking and how it had seemed to age. It was a hard, harsh life for all of them at times. And her own happiness... How short lived that had been. She would never forget the look of anger on Alexander Gordon's face, when only a few minutes before there had been love.

## Chapter 9

Alexander Gordon had spent a restless night. He rose early, dressed and went to the stables and saddled his horse. If only they had caught the cowardly devils responsible for last night's carnage. My God, how he would like to strike them down. He bit his lip to suppress the rising grief he felt at the brutal murder of his dog. The horse, aware of its master's anger, turned its head slightly, then broke into a fast trot and galloped away swiftly. They crossed the burn and went on to the Braes of Ordiquish. By the time they reached the top, he felt as though their speed had burned up some of his anger.

He recalled the fury on Jean Chrystie's face when she told him that the fish in the Spey and the deer on the hills were not there for the sole pleasure of the Gordons. Unwittingly, a smile touched the corner of his mouth. He had returned to the summer-house yesterday evening prepared to shake, slap the life out of her, until she revealed the identity of the men, but she had outwitted him. Though a warm south-westerly breeze blew strands of hair across his face, there were warning sounds from the deer on the hills of approaching autumn. Over in the corrie the loud roar of a stag indicated that it had broken into the hinds' ground and was proclaiming its presence for rutting activity.

A shout from the direction of Thief's Hill drew his attention. Coming down through the folds of the hill were a stream of pack horses, tied head to tail, loaded, probably, with clothes and wooden utensils to sell at Burnside market. He often wondered why these Highland craftsmen didn't make articles of artistic value. Surely all the ancient Celtic skills were not completely forgotten? He shrugged, the Highlanders were by nature of a practical turn of mind. He must discuss this point with Jean sometime. Jean... shades of regret crossed his face and in his heart there was an emptiness. He tugged sharply on the reins and the horse went down the brae again.

Dawn was the best time to pick house-leeks, when they were heavy with dew. Jean rose, put on a light-weight woollen gown then picked up the one which she had worn on the previous evening. She looked around for her shawl; it was nowhere to be seen. With mounting alarm, she realized that in her haste to leave the summer-house, it had been left behind. When the leeks were gathered, she would go up to the Quarry garden before the gardeners began their work.

With her feet planted firmly in the old apple tree that grew alongside the house, she stretched out and began to pull the rosettes of house-leek from under the web of silver-spun dew. By the time her basket was filled, an apricot glow was spreading across the purple horizon. She placed the basket in a dark corner of the shed and made her way across the village in the direction of Bogmore. The only sign of life was a heron, sweeping down across the valley, seeking its breakfast.

The garden was silent. She moved quickly towards the summer-house. Halfway there, the sound of a horse approaching came from one of the paths below. Alarmed in case it was the factor, she stood quite still, wondering what reason she could give for coming to this private and remote place so early in the morning. Before she could turn her head, Alexander Gordon called out her name.

He was beside her in a minute, and slipping off the animal's back; the horse moved away patiently. She lifted her eyes slowly.

"I didn't expect to see you here," he said quietly.
"I left my shawl behind."
"I'm not surprised, you made a hasty retreat."

"I had to," she answered defiantly.

His face hardened. "Yes, you did."

She looked directly at him. "Don't think me unfeeling about your dog. I was deeply distressed when I realized what happened. The man who did it... I was not shielding him. His companion, who foolishly accompanied him on an impulse, is a gentle soul whom I've never known to hurt man nor beast. Was he... did you catch them?"

"No," he said curtly, and added: "I am not a violent man, but if I ever find out who killed my dog, I'll horsewhip him."

Jean moved away. He was like a harsh stranger, towering over her. "I'll collect my shawl and bid you farewell."

"I was taking a last ride around part of my estate. We set out for Edinburgh today."

"Don't let me hold you back."

He walked on ahead and opened the door of the summer-house. "How cold it is in here." His hand came in contact with her hair when she bent over to pick up the shawl from a chair. "It's soaking wet," he said in surprise. "Where have you been?"

"Picking house-leeks from the roof of the out-house," she replied, looking bleakly through the window.

His eyes widened in bewilderment, then a smile moved across his face. "What an incredible thing to do at this hour."

"You wouldn't think so if you were ailing and expecting me to cure you," she told him with some sharpness.

Alexander put his hand to his forehead and suddenly began to laugh, then he stretched out the other one and drew her to his side.

"Jean, I have never seen you look so miserable. Come, let's put a light to the fire and dry you off." He reached for the tinder-box. As though anxious to cheer them, the twigs and cones sprang immediately to life.

"Kneel down," he said gently, and taking a silk handkerchief from his pocket began to rub her hair vigorously, pouring it through his hands and finally sweeping it back from her forehead. When he raised her up, their eyes met in a long searching look. Jean's heart raced furiously, followed by a bewildering feeling that made her draw away unsure, almost frightened by the response in herself.

"Some kind of power must be drawing us together," he said slowly. "The way we meet unexpectedly at odd hours." God, what must I do, he thought. This young, innocent girl is driving me mad. He reached out and crushed her against his body. She didn't draw away and, gradually, her shyness and feeling of alarm were diminished by the passion growing between them. His hand encircled her throat, her breasts, and tugged at the neck of her gown until the button snapped and his fingers were touching the smooth firm flesh. Alarmed by this unexpected intimacy and her increasing desire to encourage it, Jean drew back sharply, as shadows of guilt began to edge into her happiness.

"I must go," she said, breaking right away from his arms. Though her conscience was urging her to get out of the door and run away, the look of dejection in his eyes made her hesitate.

"I have no right to touch you," he said in a dull voice. She stared at him helplessly. "But I love you—more than I thought possible to love any woman. Make your way home, my love, and," he added in a flat voice, "try to forget what has happened between us."

As Jean stood there battling with the love and desire she felt for this man, he turned abruptly and stared into the fire. She noticed the clenched hands by his side and the look of despair on his face. She couldn't bear it; it affected her more than the voice of conscience, more than the voice of the kirk that threatened eternal pain and damnation for sins of the flesh.

With a quick movement she pulled across the curtain, then ran to the door and shot the bolt into place. He turned and watched with a puzzled expression. She came beside him, her hand slowly moving to the row of tiny buttons on the bodice of her gown. One by one she undid them until the gown slid off her body.

Nearly an hour later, the gown was still lying where she had dropped it, a warm pool in the firelight. She trailed a finger across his brow and said "I should have known better."

He raised himself on his elbow and looked down at her. "What do you mean, darling?"

"Imagine me not remembering that house-leek is a powerful love charm."

"House-leek? What do you mean?"

"Remember I told you that was why I got up early, to pick it for folk's warts and boils? I'd forgotten it has strong love-power, too." She sighed. "And now look where it has landed me!"

"Jean!" He laughed helplessly into the curve of her throat.

When they were about to part, she said reluctantly: "If you're away for a very long time, I may not see you again."

He frowned, alarmed. "What do you mean?"

She paused for a moment. "When my grandmother dies—she's very old and I must be prepared—I'll have to leave the village to seek employment elsewhere."

"Are you not fully employed here? The village needs you."

In a few words she explained how her aunt, after Meg's death, planned to retire and live in the cottage, or the house that would be built on the new site.

Consternation clouded his face. "I must know that you are safe and well in your new home when I'm away. Look, I'll have a word with the factor and make sure that the new house is in your name, and the rent to be paid from my private account."

"No! *Please*. What would Mr Ross think?"

"I don't care what he thinks, it's more important that you're independent and free from worry until I return again." The need to protect her was as strong as the need to protect his own children. "Jean," he said urgently, "I want you to listen carefully to what I have to say. If at any time you need assistance or advice in any way, will you ask Mr Marshall?"

"It won't be necessary. If you're determined to give me a roof o'er my head, I'll want nothing more from you."

When the Duke returned to the castle, he asked William Marshall to come to his study. After their conversation had ended, he sent for the factor.

"Sit down, James, I want you to arrange something for me. William Marshall already knows the situation."

When the Duke did not speak immediately (Alexander was trying to find the right words to say to this straight-faced man) the factor said: "What exactly is the nature of your request, Your Grace?"

Alexander pointed to the wall where there was a map of the site for the new village. "That house opposite where the new inn will be sited."

"Yes, it has been arranged with John Ord that his mother and niece will occupy it. He will be responsible for the rent, as he is at the moment."

"I want that altered."

"Altered? Where will the old lady and the lassie go? It would be a bad move to put them all under the same roof, for the inn-keeper's wife doesn't get on with her mother-in-law." As if he hadn't enough trouble in this village at the moment, the factor thought testily.

"I mean," the Duke said patiently, "that I want the tenancy of that house to be made out in Jean Chrystie's name."

"Excuse me, Your Grace, the old woman is called Meg Chrystie."

"I am aware of that. My concern is for her granddaughter. The house will be in the name of Jean Chrystie and the rent to be transferred from the estate accounts. I would like this transfer to be done with discretion, of course."

The factor's face turned a deep purple. He couldn't speak for a moment; indeed, he began to wonder if he had heard correctly.

Alexander was finding the discussion with his factor difficult and embarrassing. He understood the man's feelings, his moral feelings, as an elder of the kirk. But it had to be done if Jean was to be protected. He began to tidy the papers on his desk with a brisk movement. "If you would inform the inn-keeper of the situation and in due course, arrange the necessary details with Jean Chrystie."

"Your Grace," James Ross said stiffly, "I fear the inn-keeper's wife is going to be upset. She was planning to live apart from the business when...Meg Chrystie passed on. And if I may be so bold as to say, we would be collecting two rents. A lot of money is going to be drained from the estate for the major project of moving the village. The demands of the villagers are growing higher all the time." And, the factor, thought viciously, thanks to that wee besom Chrystie! "Even at this stage, Your Grace, would you not consider shelving the whole idea about moving the village?"

"No," the Duke said frowning, "economically, it will reward us eventually. I am sorry if all this is putting a burden on your shoulders. Mr Marshall will give you every assistance. Regarding Jean Chrystie, I have written my wishes down in a document," he added firmly. Then he gave a quick glance and a little smile.

James Ross rose to his feet. He was familiar with that expression, it meant that the Duke wished the discussion to come to an end.

As the factor walked down the corridor he felt confused and angry. What was the meaning of it? The Duke of Gordon had always been a man of honour, not running after women of the lower orders. Maybe there had been one or two wee slip-ups. This was different. He and the Duchess had their quarrels, he knew that, but they had a fine family. Then into his mind crept the insidious voice of Gypsy Willie, hinting at something.

Meg was alarmed at the expression on her granddaughter's face. Her eyes were brilliant and sparkling and there was an air about the lass as though an inner light was shining through her skin.

"Ye stirred yoursel' early this morning," she said abruptly. "I'm needin' m'oats."

"I won't be long, granny." Jean threw a few wood-backs on the fire and moved the iron pot over the flames.

"Who were you seeing last night?"

Startled, Jean swung round. "I'm not a bairn, granny. I don't have to account for every second I'm out of your sight."

"Ye've never told me a lie in yer life."

"I'm telling you nothing."

Meg accepted a drink. "Ye'll no' forget what I said about the kirk and your bedroom. Ye'll be particular to let the mannie lead ye up the aisle of Bellie kirk first, won't ye?"

Jean bit her lip as she bent to pick up the kettle again. There would be no kirk wedding for her now. She started.

The old woman was watching her granddaughter closely. "Is there somethin' amiss, lassie?"

"It's something I don't understand, granny."

"I fear ye've got a touch o' the Sight. I heard the way ye spoke to Milne that evening. But," Meg said sagely, "it doesna tak' the Sight to tell us about that laddie. He'll do well for himsel' a'right."

A few hours later, there was the sound of bagpipes coming from the direction of the castle. "Ah, me, the Gordons are off south again. That's the end of another summer," Meg said resignedly, as her granddaughter lowered her head over the stocking she was knitting. The dullness of the work did not trouble Jean this morning for her thoughts were far removed from the automatic action of her hands.

"Awa' ye go, love, and tak' a peep at the circus. It's a sight for sore eyes if ye can see the Duchess and the ladies."

Jean went and stood behind a crowd of villagers and listened to the farewell lament of the piper who led the procession. As usual, she had missed the first carriages. Though her heart felt heavy at the thought of Alexander's departure, she did not want to catch a glimpse of him dressed as he would be for such an occasion. She would remember him with his hair caught back casually in a ribbon, and gentle with love and laughter.

"I want a word wi' you, lass." Jean turned quickly at the sound of her uncle's voice.

"What is it?"

"I said wi' you, not half the village." He took her arm. "Come away."

They walked to a spot where there were few people about. "The factor has been around this morning. The wifie is in a wild state after listening to yon man."

"Yes?"

"The house across from the inn in the new village is going to be in your name. The factor said as you're such a useful person in the community it was considered only right. I 'minded him of the promises made to your aunt. He said it was out of his hands. The order came from the Gordons. What age d'they think ye are?" he said with a spurt of anger. "You're not old enough to be a feuar."

"I'm old enough when someone's ailing," Jean snapped with nervousness.

"Ah, well." John Ord frowned. "The factor's heart was no' in his words, I could tell that. When I asked who's to pay the rent, he mumbled something about you having a hand in getting the Cottage Industry started that the Duchess is so keen on." He looked at her sharply. "There's something no' right about the arrangement but I canna put me finger on it... not yet."

He turned and walked away abruptly. Jean was left with the dismal feeling that she was in danger of losing the warmth and kindness which Uncle John had showered on her since she was a bairn.

Sheena Ord skipped across the field, singing with delight. She couldn't believe her good fortune. She had been on early morning duty at the castle, helping with last minute stitching and packing, when the Duchess's companion hurried into the sewing room. There was an angry flush on Miss Tison's face. "Sit down," she ordered. Fearful that she was about to be dismissed, Sheena dropped her head in dismay. She loved working at the castle; it was a window to the outside world listening to the servants who travelled with the Gordons talking about Edinburgh and London. How she would have loved to visit those exciting places. As she waited for the dreaded words, Miss Tison said, "Lift your head, Sheena Ord, and pay attention to what I have to say or else I'll begin to doubt the wisdom of entrusting Lady Madeline into your care."

Sheena shot to her feet and stammered: "What do you mean, Mistress Tison?"

She was told that Lady Madeline had developed a fever and the Duchess had been advised to let the girl remain at the castle for a week or two. Sheena was to help look after her and in due course, accompany her ladyship in the carriage to Edinburgh.

"Prepare yourself to stay there for some time," the woman added abruptly.

On the way home, Sheena leapt over a shaft of unstacked corn, scattering stalks into the hedge, where they hung on a hawthorn bush like splinters of pale gold in the sunlight.

"Aye, aye, then," Morag Fraser called. "Are you coming to give's a hand wi' the stooking?"

"I canna, Morag, I have promised to take part in a waulking."

The Andersons' sons, wide-eyed, stood admiring her comely figure and fair face. Sheena knew that look; when Morag's back was turned they would try to give her a sly pinch. She couldn't contain her news a minute longer. When she had finished talking, Morag sniffed and said: "As long as it isn't your cousin going wi' the Gordons."

"What do you mean?"

"Folk are talking," Morag said in an ominous voice.

"What about?" Sheena asked warily, and felt alarmed when she recalled the remarks Gypsy Willie had been making at the inn. Jean, seen with the Duke of Gordon. God willing it wasn't true.

She walked away from the field, her head bent thoughtfully, thinking about Jean. Sheena always felt that she was years younger than her cousin. There was something in Jean's nature that set her apart from everyone else—a sort of aloofness, a stillness. Och, it was Granny Chrystie's fault for rearing her in such a possessive way.

When she arrived at the weaver's house, the web had been cut from the loom, ready for the waulking process. She and nine other girls, five sitting on each side, sat down and beat the damp cloth with their bare feet and hands until the loose fibre began to felt together. It was slow, tedious work. Sheena, in her clear, sweet voice, began to sing the waulking song. Each girl in turn took up a verse, then they all joined in the chorus.

The sound of gaiety attracted the two men coming up through the village on horseback. Robert Burns had called at Gordon Castle and had found that the family had already left for the south. They drank a tankard of ale at the inn while a young lad led their horses to the pond. Robert looked at the cottages and thought they were well tended with the care and love of poor men. He did not agree with Samuel Johnson that it was a place of ruined dwellings. Trust the blind eye of a Sassenach! They made their way around the cottages until they were in sight of the waulking. Sheena, suddenly aware that they were being watched, turned her head. Robert Burns removed his hat and bowed a greeting. She felt her heart bounce. After a second she smiled and called: "Don't come any closer, sir, or you'll be tossed in the web."

"Aye, I know the custom, lass, but I wouldn't mind if you did the tossing!"

His friend said: "Och, no' again, Burns. If you take a fancy to every bonny face on the way, we'll get nowhere."

Robert laughed and waved his hand to Sheena. "We'll meet again," he said cheekily.

Sheena found herself colouring at the feeling in his voice. It had made his words sound like a promise.

## Chapter 10

As the days drew in, it seemed to Jean that they were in for an early winter and the herbs in the physic plot could be lost. There was an urgent need to pick, sort and dry the precious plants which were so important during the long, cold months. Slipping out through the door one morning, she turned and saw the glaring, ugly words chalked across it: "Jean Chrystie, Duke of Gordon's whore." Her foot caught in the hem of her skirt and she fell over the resting-stone, banging her back against it. Terrified, Jean pulled a tuft of grass and began scrubbing at the door. That childish scrawl must be Willie Robb's work.

When the door was cleaned, she returned to her room, threw herself across the bed and wept bitterly. The throbbing in her back increased, then her whole body seemed to be churning. After a while she leaned out of the window and was violently sick. It's the wrath of God paying me back for my sins, she thought miserably. Rebelliously, she muttered, "You listen to me, God, I didn't go out seeking sin and it didn't seem like sin either." She clapped a hand over her mouth in horror. "Och, dinna take heed of my blethering, Lord."

"Are ye about yet, Jean?" came the plaintive voice from the kitchen.

"Aye, Granny." She pulled a comb through her hair and hurried to the old woman.

"Och, I had such a bad dream," Meg complained querulously. "I heard a noise and thought the Lord had sent the angel of death for me."

"Angel of death my foot, he'll come in person for the likes of you. Now stop greetin' and maybe I'll find a wee dram to sup wi' your oats."

"Ah, God spare ye, lassie. I'd like that fine. You're in great form this morning."

"Aye, the best."

When the oats were cooked, Jean poured out two bowlfuls, then skimmed cream from the wooden milk-dish with a scallop shell which had holes in it. She took a sip of whisky too, and after breakfast felt much better.

"Hurry yoursel' lass, for the village will be stirring early to see Alexander Milne on his way to seek his fortune in the New Land.

It had slipped out of Jean's mind. A few minutes later she left the cottage to join all the villagers as they marched down through the village behind the emigrant. When they reached the Spey the piper and the minister were standing waiting. Everyone was quiet while the minister shook Mr Milne's hand and spoke a few words. The pipes stirred again, and music rose in the air filling the valley with gay, rousing tunes. Milne looked towards the Bog o' Gight, where Gordon Castle stood and deliberately turned his back on it. Then he raised his hand in a final farewell to his family and friends.

When Alexander Milne was across the river, he walked away through the glen without a backward glance as the music of the pipes and the singing across the Spey grew fainter.

"It's awful sad," young Fiona McDonald said, as she walked by Jean's side on their way back to the village.

"Aye, he made a fine departure though, pride in every inch of his body," Jean replied, and thought of the loneliness that Milne would know before he rested his head in some quiet glen by the end of that day.

"Jean, ma says could ye do something about m' face."

They stopped, and Fiona lifted her face to be inspected. The girl certainly hadn't inherited Tessa's lovely complexion. The villagers thought her father was a foreign lackey who had worked at the castle. Well, Jean decided, he must have had a right sweet nature for there wasn't a scrap of Tessa's brashness in this girl.

"Come back with me and I'll make a mixture of oatmeal and rosemary."

"What'll that do?"

"The oatmeal will clean your pores and the rosemary will stimulate the circulation."

"Ye know," Fiona said shyly, "I like going to your house."

"You're always welcome."

"Your granny's teaching me to crochet. Och, I wish I could live there all the time."

"You will one day." The words which had fallen, unbidden, from Jean's lips, startled her. Fiona looked at her, puzzled. She put an arm around the girl's shoulder and said hurriedly: "I mean you can stay sometimes, if you like."

Bella Forbes was sitting on the resting-stone as they passed, a dumpy little figure with arms folded across her chest.

"Can I have a word wi' ye, lass?" she called.

"Run on in and have a chat with granny," Jean said to Fiona. "Is there something wrong, Bella?" She wondered nervously if Bella knew about the writing on the door.

"Well... maybe I shouldn't say this, but there's a bit of talk about ye. Gypsy Willie's telling folks that you've been seen wi' the Duke of Gordon."

"Did he?" Jean said quietly, her hands tightening on her skirt. "Well, I canna be seen wi' him now for he's no' here, is he? Don't mention that to my granny, will you?"

"Och, no," Bella said slowly, not taking her eyes off Jean's face. "That Willie is no' fit to live in this village. I hear he's wedding the tinker girl and by the looks of her, it's no' before time!"

That night Jean had a terrifying dream. The minute she woke she slipped out and opened the front door. The ugly, glaring words with more expletives were staring her in the face again. Three mornings in succession she rose early to inspect the front door, and each time she had to scrub it clean. She began to feel desperate, wondering when it was going to stop.

On the fourth evening, instead of covering the hot peat with ash, she built up the fire and filled the iron pot full of water.

When it was on the boil, she went down to her room and sat by the window in the dark. Exhausted by rising early every day, her eyes began to close. A chuckle of laughter outside the house roused her.

"She'll nae be able to get it off so easily this time," Gypsy Willie murmured.

The tinker girl sniggered. "Put that stuff on the wee stone, m'darlin'. Ye'll be for the long walk if the factor finds ye've taken it."

"Give's the brush."

Jean peeped out and saw something thick and glistening in a bucket. She rushed up to the kitchen, pulled out the crane and carefully lifted the pot off the hook.

"Are ye no' abed yet?" Meg called, twitching at the curtain.

"Hush, go to sleep, granny. I think there's a wild-cat outside my window. It'll have a go at the fowl if I don't get rid of it."

"Dinna go out or it'll have a go at you."

The two outside were crouching over the door with dripping sticks in their hands. Swiftly, Jean dipped her wooden wash basin into the pot, flung the window open and threw the hot water over them. Eileen O'Hara screamed and Willie swore. She quickly filled the basin again and while the pair staggered around clutching themselves she poured water into the substance in the bucket.

"In the morn', Willie Robb," she hissed, "I'm going to tell the factor who stole that stuff from the castle. Now clear off and don't come back here again, for next time I'll fling hot coals around the pair of you. And *don't* come to me for ointment for your burns either."

I've done a dreadful thing, she thought. I'm supposed to heal folk, not injure them. They would not come back tonight, but what would they do next time?

Later that morning, when Fiona arrived for further treatment, Jean suggested that the girl accompanied her across to the building site to take a look at the new houses. Every day now the villagers made trips to the site and stood around in little groups, laughing and pointing at the piles of wood and stones. They found it difficult to imagine that the grand building plan stuck up in the post office window would come to anything. Most people had accepted the compensation offered by the factor; there were still a few holding out.

As soon as Mr Marshall arrived on the site she told Fiona to wait while she had a word with him. William Marshall was taken aback by the girl's appearance. Her large green eyes had dark shadows under them and she looked very pale.

"You're well, I hope?" he greeted her.

"Yes." She suddenly found it difficult to get her words out.

He said gently: "I should tell you that his Grace has given me certain instructions regarding you, and I consider it to be my duty to assist you in any way."

She gave a tremulous smile. He frowned, remembering how this girl had stood up to the crowds by the old pillar.

"I would like to talk to you, Mr Marshall," she said carefully, "for I don't know who else to turn to." Then, hurriedly, she told him about Gypsy Willie, not even sparing herself by omitting the vile words written on the door.

What will become of her, he wondered. The people in Fochabers were God-fearing; if this story got around it could be very unpleasant for her. He had been feeling deeply alarmed since his conversation with the Duke, for he had never seen his Grace so anxious about anyone outside his family. The factor was another matter. James Ross was beside himself with rage about the situation. William Marshall sighed. They said the Duchess swept every obstacle from her path; by the look of it, she wasn't going to remove this one easily!

"I'll speak to the man," he assured her, "and don't hesitate to come to me again if I can assist you." They discussed the house which was being built for her, then Jean walked back to Fiona, feeling a sense of relief, and of shame.

Bella Forbes was helping Meg to spread a shawl across the bed so that she could work a scolloped edging around it. Jean was stirring a pot containing hanks of yarn which she was dyeing red with crotal; the rock lichen produced just the right shade. The sound of shouting made the three women raise their heads.

"Go and see what's a-doing," Meg told her.

Reluctantly, Jean left her work. She felt uneasy about mingling with the crowds outside because it was becoming apparent that people were talking about her. There had been no more writing on the door. It was a comfort to know that Mr Marshall had kept his word, more so, that Alexander had felt he wanted to protect her. She smiled to herself at that thought. Imagine anyone having to protect Jean Chrystie!

The shoemaker, who was the village piper, was swaying all over the road and not a sound came from the bagpipes. Behind him was a crowd of young men pushing a wheelbarrow in which Gypsy Willie was sprawled, his face blackened with soot. They were on their way to the village pond where he would be tipped in. I hope he can't swim, she thought, and looked at the pregnant tinker girl, who had brazenly tagged on to the group of men.

Back in the house, Meg said, "Well, well, so Willie Robb is gettin' married. It's time another woman came into that house to help Sarah."

Bella Forbes gave the shawl a vicious tug. "Aye, wed on Saturday. Some use that Irish tinker will be. Lays up half the day in the loft expecting Sarah to make her food. By the look of her, they'll have to push her in the barrow down to Bellie church."

"Ye tell me that, Bella?"

"And him just holding on to his job by the skin of his teeth, from all reports."

Some time later, Jean lifted out the yarn on the point of a stick to test for colour. Satisfied that it was ready, she rinsed it in cold water and hung it out to dry. While she was in the garden she remembered that Mrs Anderson down at the farm wanted a bunch of sage.

"Where's that going?" Morag Frazer poked at the sage suspiciously as though she expected it to snap at her fingers.

"It's for Mrs Anderson's indigestion."

"Indigestion, the cow's ass," Morag grunted, "it's nae for her belly, it's for her heed—thinks it'll stop her hair going grey. Her eyes roamed over Jean. "Are ye fit, lassie?"

"Aye."

"Ye've lost ye're bonnie colour. Why don' ye go to the wee well in the woods and take a sup, it's right good for bringing back the colour to a body's face."

As Jean walked through the woods to the well, she realized that Morag's words had made her aware of the lethargic feeling in her body. Still, she was always extra busy and tired at this time of year. She knelt down, cupped her hands and began drinking the fresh spring water, then rested on her heels and looked up at the leaves lacing overhead. Soon they would be carpeting the ground, for Meg was right, winter was trying to steal part of autumn. This morning there had been a thin sparkle of frost.

A stone struck her on the neck. It must be bairns playing somewhere in the woods, she thought, wetting her handkerchief and dabbing at the blood which was trickling down her back. As she scrambled to her feet another stone, sharp-edged, came at her arm, making her unbalance and slip on the muddy ground around the well. Then a rain of stones began to strike her. Jean covered her head with her arms and tried to crawl into the shelter of a bush. She hadn't gone far when she heard Willie Robb's voice and felt his hands tugging and beating her.

"Why don' ye call on Mr Marshall now, my fine lady? And where's your grand duke? Waiting for him to come and bed wi' ye? I wasn't good enough, was I?" He threw her roughly from him.

"Hold her, Willie m'darlin', till I crop her."

Terrified, Jean looked up and saw O'Hara waddling towards them with a huge pair of shearers. "Mother o' God, no one will want to look at her by the time I've finished. Weren't good enough for a kitchen maid, only lordie's bedroom suited ye."

Jean opened her mouth, but the scream that came from the woods was louder. "Mam," Fiona shouted, "Gypsy Willie and that woman are killing Jean Chrystie."

There was an answering yell from Tessa, who came running into sight clutching a huge stone. She'll split his skull, Jean thought when she saw Tessa lunging at Willie as he tried to make off through the trees. The Irish girl showed no fear, only anger at Willie's retreating back.

"Scoot off or my mam will clobber ye too when she finishes wi' him," Fiona said with a touch of compassion in her voice.

But the tinker girl couldn't run. She moved away heavily, shouting abuse at Willie Robb.

Jean was walking towards Tessa and Fiona when a sudden pain in her stomach made her double over.

"You're shivering, hen," Tessa said, taking her arm. "What ails ye? Did they knock ye about badly?"

"I've never had such a pain before... it's like a flaming sword going through me."

"Och," Tessa said worriedly, "we'll get ye home to bed. Are ye no' able to walk? Fiona, take the other arm."

"Oh mam, what ails her? They must 'ave clouted her wi' a boulder. Look at all the cuts."

Jean felt the comforting strength of Tessa's arms as they hobbled up through the woods. They were passing Lilac Cottage–not a cottage like the ones the villagers lived in, but a beautifully half-timbered house–when a woman in the garden called: "Has there been an accident, Tessa?"

"Aye, aye, Mistress Gubbay. A fine day," Tessa said, and urged Jean on.

"Has there been an accident?" the woman asked again, her eyes on Jean.

"Of sorts," Tessa said shortly. She didn't want the gentry folk knowing about their wee squabbles. She was good enough in her way and always paid Tessa well for her services as a washerwoman.

"Bring the girl over here," Claire Gubbay said firmly. "She appears to be badly injured."

Tessa was all for moving on when Jean's legs suddenly crumpled beneath her.

"Take her straight to the little bedroom," Mistress Gubbay said authoritatively, noticing Tessa's reluctance. She looked at Fiona. "Child, run to the kitchen and tell the servant to light the fire and put more blankets on the bed. And fill a tub with hot water."

When they were indoors, she said, "Tessa, help the girl to undress, I'll fetch the brandy. She appears to be in considerable pain."

The minute Jean smelt the brandy, weak tears poured down her face, and she remembered the Quarry garden. Claire Gubbay left the room when the maid carried in the tub.

"Come on hen, let's get them duds off ye," Tessa said cheerfully when the maid had shut the door behind her.

A few minutes later, the brandy and hot water eased away Jean's pain. Fiona put her head around the door. "Away to Jean's granny and tell her that one of our bairns is nae well and she'll be back later."

"Thank you Tessa... Oh God," Jean cried out, and bent her head.

"What is it?"

"Pain again," she whispered, and as she spoke blood gushed from her body.

Tessa McDonald looked startled out of her life, then in a flash she put her arms around Jean. "Kneel up, hen, grip the sides. I see now."

Sometime later, when she was wrapped in the bedclothes and the tub emptied, Tessa said, "Mistress Gubbay will come in a minute to see you." She sat on the edge of the bed. "Did ye no' ken ye were carrying? You were carrying a wean... a bairn."

Jean shook her head, hot colour flooding her face. "I'm often a month out. I thought I was anaemic. I've been taking a brew of nettle tops."

A baffled expression crossed Tessa's face. However did Jean Chrystie get hersel' in this trouble? Her thoughts were obvious. Jean lowered her eyes as Mistress Gubbay came into the room and said, "Thank you, Tessa. I think it would be a good idea if your young friend rested now. Come back in an hour or so and we'll see how she is."

She draw the curtains across the window. Utterly exhausted, Jean turned her face to the wall and shut her eyes.

She woke to find Mistress Gubbay by the bed pouring tea into a fragile cup with a delicately fluted rim. "How are you, my dear?" the woman asked, handing her the cup. "Drink this, you will feel much better afterwards."

"I'm feeling better now and I want to thank you, Mistress Gubbay, for your great kindness to me. I'll never forget it."

"Nonsense, you would have done it for anyone else. Tessa's in the kitchen. When you've had some refreshments, she will bring your clothes and help you to dress. My maid has cleaned your gown."

Later, when Jean was lying in her own bed back at the cottage, she tried to remember what the villagers had said about Mistress Gubbay: a mysterious lady they called her, not quite gentry, but grand enough for the Duchess of Gordon to call on her every time she returned to Fochabers.

Passages from the Bible kept running through her head. The

harshness of some of the words seemed as frightening as what she had experienced that day. Both were completely devoid of beauty and equally terrifying. She knew it would be hypocritical to deny what was in her heart for the sake of cleansing her soul, nevertheless she was greatly troubled after such a chastening experience.

Two days later Jean called at Lilac Cottage to return the shawl which had been lent to her. The maid led her into the drawing-room where Mistress Gubbay was pouring tea from a silver pot. She insisted on giving her some and waved aside a second attempt to thank her.

"I am glad I was at home, my dear. I must tell you that I have been hoping to meet you for some time."

"Me?" Jean said in surprise.

"I have seen you at the village fair surrounded by a magnificent collection of herbs, and heard your wise counselling to those who required to buy them. I am interested in this kind of knowledge and would be so grateful if you could guide me when I set about to grow some, that is, of course, if you have time to spare."

"Yes, I'd like to help you, if I can," Jean said, sitting uncomfortably on the edge of the chair, trying to imitate the way her hostess held a cup. There was a short silence. She tried to occupy her mind by taking in the magnificent room, the exquisite furnishings and the silk cushions that shimmered in the sunlight.

After a minute she glanced across the fireplace and discovered that Mistress Gubbay was studying her with a thoughtful expression.

"How would you like to work for me?" the woman said slowly.

"For you... you mean help with the housework?"

"No, not that type of work, my dear—well, not entirely. I have a housemaid and Tessa does all the washing and the heavier work. I mean as a kind of companion. I have an interest in a home for the sick in Edinburgh, you could accompany me there, your knowledge would be most valuable." Claire Gubbay folded her napkin and said in a brisker voice "I think you should get away from this village. I have no intention of asking you any personal questions, my dear, but someone has used you wrongly."

"No, no," Jean said protestingly, "it wasn't like that." She rose. "I must thank you for such a wonderful offer, Mistress Gubbay. I would indeed love to travel a bit." She smiled at the lovely, serene faced woman. "Especially with you, but you see—" She explained about her grandmother.

"Perhaps we can discuss it again one day. It would be an opportunity for you to see life outside Fochabers. As well as Edinburgh, I often travel to London where I have an apartment."

"An apartment in London?" Jean said in wonder.

Claire shrugged. "Well, it is more in the nature of some rooms in someone's residence. It's at Buckingham House in Piccadilly, the London home of the Duke and Duchess of Gordon."

Jean lifted her head quickly and the blood drained from her face. "The Gordons?" She turned quickly towards the door. Who was this Claire Gubbay anyway, she wondered, and why did the villagers not know anything about her?

## Chapter 11

The work stopped on the new village when the snow came. Every day Meg and Jean gazed out of the window at the garden which had become a white desert filled with vague shapes. The sun, reflected in the snow, scattered glittering points of light over everything, including the trees which had a hidden identity in their furry-white coats. The silent days of winter reminded Jean of a great broody white hen, not moving until the treasures underneath were ready to come to life. First there would be spears of crocus, then snowdrops defying their look of fragility. In the woods a mosaic pattern would appear when pale gold leaves, threaded with shiny strands of ivy, were revealed lying captive under the snow.

There was a restlessness among the villagers this winter. The older people dreaded the thought of moving from their homes and the younger ones were now impatient to go. At one of the gatherings in the Chrystie cottage, Big Annie said:

"If we dinna shift soon I'll be putting a knife in me man. I went out to the back hall last night and banged into a carcass hanging from a beam. Well, says I, Annie, if we're this tight for space and has to share it wi' a carcass, we may as well fill our bellies wi' meat." She looked around the kitchen, allowing a pause to build up a dramatic effect to her story.

"What happened?" everyone asked excitedly.

"I left the lamp on the table, picked up the carving knife... Ye'd have heard my loon's scream down in Bellie churchyard!"

There were shrieks of laughter. Meg called out: "The whole o' your man wouldna make a decent stew, Annie".

"Aye, right there, Meg," the butcher's wife replied calmly, her fingers flying over the knitting needles.

Jean smiled at Annie's story and remembered how she had threatened to take the chopper to any castle-man who attempted to shift her. She felt content these days. Gypsy Willie had left the village for good. After his attack on her in the woods, he had broken into the head gardener's house at the castle, and had stolen the man's life savings. Though the factor and every man on the Gordon estate searched for him, Willie and Eileen O'Hara got away. People thought they had taken to the roads with a band of gypsies who were travelling south. The other thing which had brought happiness to her was the increasing friendship with Claire Gubbay. Claire was different from anyone else she had ever known. Her charm and kindness enriched Jean's life and also, she was gradually learning about things in the outside world.

One day Jean invited Claire to visit the cottage. There was a pause before her invitation was accepted, which surprised Jean, then Claire smiled and said she would be delighted to come.

"Granny, do you mind keeping the curtains drawn back from your bed?" Jean asked before Claire arrived. "It'll seem unfriendly if you're shut in there. Folk who don't know you get startled out of their wits when you start gabbing."

"Mind? I do so. Your friend might be an awfu' girner. Well, I'll see, lassie."

When Claire came she stood in the centre of the kitchen looking about her. "My dear, it is enchanting. No wonder people resent leaving these lovely old cottages."

"Aye, right there, Mistress," Meg called. "But they're nae minding so much now since the Gordons decided to butter their palms, I'm tellin' ye. His lordship must've awfu' long pockets in his trews."

Jean rolled her eyes and nodded towards the curtains. She had warned Claire.

"Good afternoon, Mistress Chrystie. Your granddaughter talks frequently about you."

"Oh aye. Who may you be? I canna mind you a'tall."

"Perhaps not. I came to live here only a few years ago."

"Will ye draw back the curtains, lassie," Meg called. "I've a feeling I ken that voice."

A flash of alarm crossed Claire's face, but she crossed the kitchen and said calmly, "How nice to meet you."

"Aye, ye're welcome, Mistress. Have a sup and bite," Meg said with a piercing glance, and fell into an unusually long silence.

When they were walking back to Lilac Cottage, Claire remarked, "You know I am not entirely a stranger to your grandmother."

"I thought there was something."

"She was employed in Edinburgh by some friends of mine. I often visited the nursery where she worked, to see the children."

"It's a wonder she didn't talk to you about it."

"Of course, I didn't really know her."

"That wouldn't stop Granny."

"The people your grandmother worked for were related to Jane Gordon, the Duchess."

"Yes, she has mentioned that."

Claire was silent for a few minutes. "At that particular time of my life I was in a difficult position. I had a house in Edinburgh but I did not receive visitors nor was I welcomed into the social circle."

"Why not?" Jean asked in astonishment. "You're so cultured, so... Well, I was surprised when you encouraged our friendship."

"Don't under-estimate yourself, my dear. I did not have your beauty nor intelligence. I was quite a simple person who came from a very humble home. My father was a clergyman and we were a large family."

"What were you doing in Edinburgh? I've often wondered how you came to this part of the world. Few English people settle in Scotland."

"I had a position with the Gordon family. I worked with the children—not as a nursemaid, but helping to instruct them in their early years before a tutor took over. In truth, I think the position was made for me because the Duke liked my father. Then—"

Claire hesitated for a moment. "The Duke and I fell in love."

Startled, Jean stopped and whispered in alarm: "Alexander?"

The use of his name and the expression on her face made Claire say: "Ah, I see now. My dear, how could it be at my age? It was Alexander Gordon's father, Cosmo George Gordon, who died when he was quite a young man." Though her words were spoken without a trace of surprise, Claire was shattered. How did Alexander Gordon meet this girl?

"He must have been a great deal older than you," Jean said, turning away.

"The difference in our ages was similar to that between you and Alexander."

"You know?"

"You've just told me, haven't you?" They walked on in silence for a moment. "I am not going to pry, Jean, all I want to say–before it is too late–don't get involved. For if you do, my dear, you will have no life of your own. No husband, no children. You will spend weeks, months, waiting–always waiting. For a brief while there will be happiness which will be short-lived, then loneliness and frequently rejection from people. Life in those circumstances can be quite terrifying; and, as I said, intensely lonely."

"Were there no children of your union?"

An expression of bitterness clouded Claire's face. "Yes, one child. It was considered best that I should part with him, and I accepted that decision."

I would never have done that, Jean thought fiercely. I would have faced anything rather than give away a bairn of mine.

Claire said carefully, "When the Duke returns and discovers what has happened to you, he may well decide it would be wise to end your friendship."

"He must *never* know. I don't intend to be so...so close to him again." She flinched inwardly when she remembered the physical pain and the humiliation when she had miscarried. "I have my grandmother to care for."

"There's another thing," Claire said thoughtfully. "You would have Jane Gordon to deal with if the relationship between you and the Duke became serious. She would not tolerate such a situation. And I warn you, the Duchess does not let things stand in her way. Only I am so fond of you, I would hesitate before making remarks about a woman who has always shown me kindness."

One morning about a week later, Fiona rushed into the cottage on her way to school. "Och, Jean, I'm that full o' messages for ye I've gone and forgot to take my peat for the Master."

It was the custom in the village school for every pupil to take one peat to keep the classroom fire going throughout the day.

"Help yoursel' Fiona, from the stack by the side of the house, but he can't be short for a number of scholars went past early this morning."

"Aye, but our Jamie says they hid them o'er the hedge when they went sliding on the wee brae, and they all disappeared."

"They'll be burning in Sarah Robb's fire by now," Meg shouted. "Bella next door tells me that Sarah goes around folk's stacks at night filling her apron ever since Gypsy Willie scuttled away."

"Well she has to keep warm," her granddaughter said briskly.

"What messages are there, Fiona?"

"Ma says the wee bairn's got hiccups and keeps throwing up its food, and Mistress Gubbay wants ye to come to dinner tomorrow at four o'clock."

"Mistress Gubbay... to dinner?"

"Aye, she's got two friends from Edinburgh who've arrived in a fine carriage. Can I take a couple o' peat to soften the Master for I'm wild late?"

Why does she want me there, Jean wondered uncomfortably. She knows I'm not used to that kind of company.

Tessa McDonald was rocking the baby's cradle with her foot and her hands moved industriously on the spindle when Jean arrived. "Surely the priest isn't calling at this hour?" she asked, mixing dill seeds with hot water.

"He and Sam, the kenner, are comin' up from the Fisheries."

"Sam Duncan?"

"Ye're awfu' slow, hen, the priest is putting' the fear o' God into Sam 'cause he wants him to wed me." Her face softened. "He's the only man for me."

"Will he mind taking on all the bairns, though?"

Tessa tossed her head boldly. "Why should he when they're all his, apart from Fiona."

So much for village gossip. Tessa wasn't as wanton as they had made her out to be. As Jean poured the dill water from one vessel to another to cool it, she saw from the window, Sam and the priest coming up the hill. She handed it to Tessa to give to the child. "I'll be away now. Good luck, Tessa." Impulsively she bent down and kissed the Glasgow woman on the cheek. "I hope everything will be all right."

"I hope so," Tessa said wistfully. "I'd like fine to be wed like other folk." She caught at Jean's skirt. "Listen, Sam tells me an order has been sent from the castle to the ice-house at the Fisheries. Ye ken what that means, his Grace must be returning."

Jean dressed with great care for the dinner party at Claire's house. She felt nervous, wondering how she was going to manage in the presence of these ladies from Edinburgh. Though by now she was accustomed to the refinement of a tea-party—thanks to Claire—this dinner with its numerous accoutrements was sure to be an ordeal.

The visitors, a Mistress Ritchie and her daughter, were sitting in the drawing-room at a distance from each other to allow space for the silk gowns worn over pannier-hooped petticoats. The mother acknowledged the introduction with a brief glance and comment, "What glorious hair", then waved her fan and continued with the interrupted conversation. The woman's brusqueness surprised Jean though somehow Claire's smile seemed to make it appear less offensive. The daughter grunted with an ill-manner that she had not expected of the Quality. Jean felt a sudden urge to giggle because the girl reminded her of Bella next door when she sat in her wee house down the garden and forgot to shut the door.

"And as I was telling you, Claire," Mistress Ritchie went on, "the Duchess of Gordon's latest ruling passion is literature. I believe she wants to be the arbitress of literary taste and the patroness of genius. Tosh! She doesn't know a thing about it. Her early lack of culture rather disqualifies her if you ask me."

Jean listened intently to the gossip about Edinburgh society; it was widening her own world and allowing her to look into, at least a part of, Alexander's.

"But Elfrida," Claire said loyally, "the season doesn't get started until Jane Gordon arrives in town, and it is the same in London. She is considered to be the leader of fashion in both cities."

"Huh!" Elfrida sniffed. "Why shouldn't she be when she's married to the richest lord in the land."

"And," the daughter giggled, "the handsomest one too, not that she seems to be aware of it!"

Mistress Ritchie rolled her eyes. "The last time I was at her salon in Edinburgh she gave all her attention to that young ploughman poet, Robert Burns. I don't know why he is supposed to be a genius. Can't make head nor tail of the stuff he writes. All I can see about him is his wicked, roving eyes."

Claire laughed and turned to Jean, trying to draw her into the conversation. "I must confess Rabbie Burns makes me wish I were young again."

Elfrida Ritchie flashed her eyes in the daughter's direction. "I hope, miss, you'll have the sense to keep your wits and petticoats about you when you meet the Duchess's bard."

The girl flushed. "Oh Mamma..."

Her mamma needna be worried with that quine's long nose and buck teeth, Jean thought. The woman's next words riveted her attention.

"Jane Gordon was quite put out when she discovered that the ploughman was after one of her maids. At least he had the good sense to chase one of his own class. She sent the gal packing, back to where she came from."

Alarmed, Jean remembered Sheena's unexpected return from Edinburgh and her strange, quiet moods since. Throughout the meal, the gossip continued–malicious, and often laced with wit. Mistress Ritchie threw defamatory remarks about as nonchalantly as if she were discussing the state of the weather.

"I hear the Duke of Gordon is trying to raise another regiment since the American Colonies' Declaration of Independence," she announced, and added with a slight note of triumph, "There is some talk that the Highlanders are not willing to take up arms to help the Duke."

"The shadow of Culloden still hangs over this land," Claire said quietly.

"Money will talk. Mark my words! Some more of that delicious syllabub, Claire..."

The second helping of syllabub disappeared, and Jean waited, almost with impatience, to hear what the creature would say next. Now she could understand why Meg used to make dry remarks about the "Higher Orders" in Edinburgh.

"Mr Ritchie says I'll have to pull in my horns now that the tobacco trade has gone. What do you think of that, Claire?"

"You won't starve!" Claire replied with gentle humour.

Surely, Jean thought, this woman's husband wasn't one of the Tobacco Lords who made a fortune from tobacco imported from America? "Cocky Peacocks" the News-sheet had called them because they dressed in scarlet cloaks with laced hats and carried gold-headed canes. Then she realized that Claire's friend was referring to the fleet of ships owned by her merchant husband who, like many others, had done well from England's control of the colonies.

No sooner were they settled in the drawing-room when the maid came in looking flustered. "Madam, His Grace, the Duke of Gordon has called."

An expression of astonishment crossed Claire's face. She rose quickly to her feet. "Please show His Grace in," she said, and walked towards the door.

Jean was shocked, and in her panic glanced about to see if there was time to reach the door to the garden.

Claire was curtseying. "Your Grace, I am honoured by your visit."

The Ritchie women began bobbing up and down like over-loaded haystacks. Alexander took Claire's hand, bent over it and said, "The Duchess has asked me to call about some matter, but I see you have company..." He broke off as his gaze moved across the room to where Jean was standing. He looked incredulous for a second, then his lips moved in a smile and to Claire's alarm, joy lit his eyes.

She moved quickly in front of Mistress Ritchie and her daughter. "Your Grace, may I present to you my young friend, Jean Chrystie."

Alexander walked slowly across the room and quietly acknowledging that he already knew her, said: "How does your grandmother fare these days?"

"Very poorly, my lord," Jean murmured. "I must hasten home for I have been absent for some time." She turned to Claire. "It was most kind of you to invite me and I have enjoyed myself." After a brief farewell to the Ritchies, she went out to the hall, grabbed her cloak from the little ante-room, and fled from the house.

For a moment, Claire thought Alexander was going to follow her. Be wise, my lord, she prayed silently, for heavens sake be wise. There was a brief hesitation, then he turned to her friends and began to make conversation. He was taken aback by Jean's appearance. She had seemed older. The expression in her eyes had smote his heart; there had been a sadness and a look of maturity.

As Jean walked home, she began to wonder why Claire was so friendly with the Ritchies. A few days later she understood when Claire told her that the woman had shown friendship in Edinburgh when other doors had been closed against her. Also, she explained, Jean had been invited because she felt it would be a good opportunity for her to hear about life outside Fochabers. This had been phrased in such a way that it became obvious her friend was still hoping she would accept the position one day that had been offered when they first met.

Jean did not leave the house that evening, nor had she planned to. It was no longer possible to go out unless Fiona or one of the neighbours kept her grandmother company, for Meg was becoming very frail.

"Och, lassie," she complained the following morning, when her granddaughter was washing her. "I'm heart weary of lying here."

"I know, Granny, but spring is just around the corner. Wait 'till we move to the new village, it will only be a stone's throw from the burn."

"Aye, I'd like that fine. But dinna greet, love, I dinna think I'll be going somehow."

Jean lowered her head for she was afraid that Meg was right. "Lay back a minute, Granny, there's someone at the door."

A lackey from the castle handed her a basket. Lying on top of the linen cloth was a card which read: "From the Duke of Gordon to Mistress Meg Chrystie."

"Granny, the Duke has sent you some delicacies from the castle."

Meg gave her a shrewd glance. "Can I see?"

When the basket was uncovered, Meg said with pleasure: "Oh my, I'd like fine some of that honey mead with an oat cake."

After the old woman had eaten and fallen asleep, Jean sat down and tried to compose a letter to Alexander. She thanked him for the gift to her grandmother, then wrote a few more words expressing her own thanks for his kindness and friendship. Finally, she wished him success and happiness for the future. A quick glance at Meg and she was out of the door and hurrying up the road. Mr Marshall usually called about this time at the post office. He was taking the path to the castle when she caught up with him.

"Mr Marshall, can I ask you to do something for me?"

"If I can be of any assistance," he said carefully. He had been hoping with all his heart that the Duke's interest in this girl had waned. Yesterday when he had complied with his wishes and asked the housekeeper to arrange a basket, her sniff of displeasure had been unmistakable. There was no doubt about it, Willie Robb had made free with his tongue and there were few people who did not know about the Duke and this young lassie.

Jean hurried away quickly when she had handed him the letter. His reluctant manner made the colour rise to her cheeks for she could imagine what he was thinking.

Alexander Gordon was surprised to receive the letter and dismayed by its note of finality. With a bleakness in his heart, he turned to the desk and tried to concentrate on the plans to form a regiment. Heavens knows what this American War of Independence was going to do to the economy of the country.

"Spring has come at last," Jean said to Meg when she came indoors after tending the livestock. She had brought a few branches from a silver birch tree and put them in a jar beside the bed.

Meg looked at the delicate green leaves with pleasure. "Aye, Jeannie, the earth is stirring, and the power of it helping my old bones."

"Any day now you'll be wanting to get on with your knitting."

Though Meg nodded her head happily, Jean doubted her own words. She felt bone weary. Over the past weeks she had tended Meg night and day, often going without sleep to keep a fire burning throughout the night to make herb-healing drinks. Her eyes were strained from the long hours she had spent doing needlework, sitting by the Pier Man. The tall iron stand, with a candle stuck in it, made the old smoked beams glisten like glass. She liked the Pier Man for it made her think of olden days when poor men came begging for their supper and repaid the hospitality by holding a lit candle. The stand made that duty no longer necessary.

In the last few weeks she had become extravagant and had lit the cruize lamp as well. Her favourite light was from fir-candles, because the splinter of pine fir in the clip stuck into the stone wall filled the air with a resinous scent. During the silent hours, Jean often let her mind wander to the peat mosses where the pine log had lain, and tried to imagine what life had been like when it was part of a forest.

After they had eaten their dinner, Meg said: "I'd love a few snowdrops by my bed, Jean. Tak' a wee walk down by the hedge and I'll be fine until ye get back."

Pleased at her request, Jean took her knife and ran through the garden to the field, where she dug out a clump of earth threaded with snowdrop bulbs. She placed them in a little horn dish and put it beside Meg's bed.

"The hedge is a sight for sore eyes, Granny," she said cheerfully. "The green fronds are bursting through the old brown bracken."

Meg nodded her head happily, her eyes on the snowdrops. "Earth's treasures, tidy wi' their wee green pinnies. Mind me of you when ye were a bairn."

Happy with her grandmother's delight in the snowdrops, Jean began to make a batch of oat cakes. When they were baked, she called: "Granny, would you like an oat cake and a drop of honey mead?"

There was no reply. She went across to the bed and found Meg lying looking at the snowdrops with a faint smile on her face.

"Granny?" Jean said, then noticed the unnatural expression in her grandmother's eyes. "Oh my God," she cried, and turning, ran next door to Bella Forbes's cottage.

## Chapter 12

"Settle yoursel' lass, and go and fetch your uncle," Bella Forbes told her, putting a hand over Meg's eyes.

Jean tore through the village to the inn. John Ord's arm went around her shoulders. "Aye," he said quietly, "we were expecting it." He went and told his wife and shut the inn.

When they arrived back at the cottage, the laying-out woman had attended to Meg's body and the minister was standing by the bed. Jean took her place by his side. Her grandmother looked different now; the face small and remote, as though she had already travelled to another world.

Tessa McDonald entered the cottage, took one look and led Jean to the stool by the fireside. "I've just heard the news, hen. There, dinna tak' on so. She's awa' to sweet Jesus and his holy mother. She'll be as welcome as the flowers in spring. Kindhearted auld soul, wouldna say a bad word against anyone."

Bella Forbes nudged the laying-out woman. "She's going too far. Meg would've cut ye if she had a mind to."

"Aye, ye're right there. Them popish wans have some queer ways."

For the next few days, Jean was surrounded by people. They brought gifts of food and her uncle supplied plenty of drink. As each person entered the cottage, they lamented for a while over the body, then took a seat, ate and drank and were soon happily extolling Meg's virtues—finally shouting with laughter about some of the old woman's exploits.

"She'd doctor the cow's better than any loon," Big Annie said.

"Aye, and remember..." they went on.

Jean had nowhere to go to be on her own. Her bedroom was lined with benches brought in from neighbours' houses, which were continually occupied during the few days of the wake.

"I'm proud of ye, lass," her mother said, who had come up from Spey Bay with her husband. "It's the finest wake I've ever been to. Will ye no' come back wi' us? Your stepfather says there's a roof for ye."

Jean shook her head and thought briefly about how her mother had parted with her baby daughter when she had married this man. Over the past few days she had begun to think it would be better if she left the village altogether. There was no point in remaining alone in a community where girls married and raised families, and she certainly didn't want to go to Spey Bay where the sea howled like a pack of demons during the winter storms.

On the day of the funeral, the villagers formed into a procession and followed the coffin the few miles to Bellie churchyard. Afterwards, her uncle and several of the villagers invited Jean to come and stay with them for a while. She refused, wanting to be on her own, but as soon as she returned to the silent, untidy cottage, the loneliness struck her like a physical blow.

There was a tap on the door. Tessa pushed it open and came in, followed by Fiona. "We'll no' be in your way, Jean," she said briskly. "We thought we'd give you a hand getting the place straight again." Tessa gathered the chaff mattress from Meg's bed, carried it outside and spread it over the whin bushes.

As the three of them worked together, Jean reflected with surprise that Tessa and Fiona were the only people she could bear to have around her at that moment. Though Tessa was cheerful and free-and-easy by nature, she was also a very understanding person.

A few minutes after they left a lackey came from the castle carrying a basketful of spring flowers. He mumbled something about Mr Marshall asking him to deliver them. The freshness of their scent gave her the first spark of joy for days. But later, sitting by the fire, listening to the sibilant whisper of the flames, she felt the bleakness of the cottage close around her.

She needed to do something. Her body felt lethargic though and the thought of needlework, or any other task, seemed to be beyond her. Rising from the chair, she threw a shawl around her shoulders and went out to attend to the livestock. The crisp air made her feel better, and reluctant to return indoors again.

Walking down the field Jean thought about her grandmother's death which had left such an alarming emptiness. In among the trees where she used to collect moss for Meg's bed, she automatically stopped and noted that the ground was still dry and withered after the winter months. It would be a time yet before it was ready for picking. She turned abruptly, remembering that there would be no reason to bring her basket here again. Suddenly, the grief that had been frozen in her heart, seemed to dissolve and tears began to pour down her face. Sobbing bitterly, she flung herself on the ground.

Someone said her name, then she felt arms raising her up and holding her. In the blindness of grief she clung to him, half-afraid she was imagining it.

Alexander took out a handkerchief and wiped her face. "My poor Jean, I know how much you loved your grandmother."

"I didn't know you were at the castle, someone said you had gone away again. The flowers... I thought Mr Marshall had sent them."

"I wish I could have picked them myself. The gardener grows them under glass."

"They smell just the same whether you picked them or not," Jean said blowing her nose.

He smiled. "That's better. I was coming to see you when I saw you walking across the field."

She freed herself from his arm. Now was the moment to tell him what was in her mind.

He put out his hand and touched her face. "What is the matter?" he asked gently.

"I'm thinking of leaving the village," she said hurriedly. "Now that my grandmother is dead there's nothing to keep me here. Claire Gubbay has offered me a position, but I don't think it would be a wise choice to make. I would rather go right away and seek employment."

He was silent for a moment. "You are needed in the village, Jean. The nearest physician lives nearly thirty miles from here. I've heard how skilful you are in applying your herbal knowledge." He hesitated, then said bluntly, "I don't want you to leave. I want you to be here when I return."

"You have no right to ask that of me."

He lowered his head and said simply. "Perhaps not, but I love you. I want you to be part of my life, always."

She tried to shut out his words, and said quickly in half-anger: "'Tis not right for anyone to have everything they want. You want two wives and that's against the law of God."

"I have to have a duchess but I also need someone who loves me. If love had remained in my marriage — " He shook his head as though trying to stop the words. "Jean, I know the church will not bless our union, but before God, I swear that I will love and cherish you for the rest of your life."

She walked away from him. "Don't speak so, it is wrong." She stumbled, suddenly aware that some wisdom in her mind seemed to be counselling her.

Alexander looked alarmed, took her arm and said anxiously: "Jean, my love, you're ill. I have no right to keep you standing here in the chilly air. Let me take you home."

Submissively, she allowed him to lead her across the field. As they went along, she began to wonder if her legs would carry her the short distance to the cottage. The village seemed unusually dark and silent, no light nor friendly voices coming from the inn. The people were still mourning the death of her grandmother.

When they entered the cottage, he shut the door behind him. Jean pulled the curtains across the window and poked life into the fire.

"Let me do that," Alexander said, taking the poker from her. "Sit down and rest." He crouched over the fireplace, adding kindling until the flames were leaping up the chimney. Then he walked around examining and looking at everything with interest. Picking up a stone jar from the dresser he filled it from the kettle and took it down to her room. When he returned, he poured whisky from the flask into a mug and added hot water. "Drink this, my love, then you must go to bed. You are ill from grief and shock. You shouldn't be alone tonight. Was there no one who could have kept you company?"

She took a sip of hot whisky and told him that Tessa had offered to let Fiona spend the night with her, and she mentioned the kindness of the villagers. When she turned to look at him, he was squatting on the earth floor, arms around his knees, gazing into the fire.

He looked up and smiled. "I've always heard that there's a great comradeship and neighbourliness in this village. Jean, when you move to your new house, could this girl, Fiona, come and stay with you? I don't like the idea of you living there on your own."

When she didn't reply, he said lightly jumping to his feet, "Well, we'll discuss it another time. I think you should go to bed now." He took her hand and kissed her on the forehead. "Goodnight, darling. God bless you."

Feeling completely exhausted, Jean went to her bedroom where she found her nightgown wrapped tightly around the stone jar. She was soon fast asleep.

When she awoke at daybreak, a feeling of desolation swept over her. How she had been dreading this morning after the funeral. A sound in the room made her turn quickly. Alexander was stretched out on the chair beside the bed, fast asleep. She touched his hand and found that it was icy cold. He opened his eyes.

"You didn't go home?"

"And leave you to sleep in a house with an unbolted door?"

"Alexander, you're frozen."

"It's a cauld wee hoose," he murmured.

Incredibly, Jean felt laughter catching in her throat and a feeling of happiness came that was stronger than the twinge of guilt. She drew aside the plaid on the bed. "Shift yourself, my lord, and feel the warmth of my bed, then you must go home before the workers stir."

She saw his hesitation, then the quick response when he noticed the pleading in her eyes. Tenderly, he took her in his arms and for a while tried to restrain his feelings, until their love became too demanding and they were lost in each other.

Some time later, he said, stroking the hair off her brow, "I thought you were going to send me away for good."

"I had intended to," she replied solemnly, and thought, I have kept faith with my heart, it is no longer possible for me to battle with my conscience. "Alexander, I hear footsteps on the road. I'm anxious about you leaving the cottage unnoticed. Would it be beneath you to climb out of my window and go around by the field?"

Laughter lines formed around his eyes. "It would not be beneath me, but it certainly might be beyond me! What if I stick and the village carpenter has to come and free me?"

"I'll push you!"

"Right, I'll suffer that indignity so that you needn't get up and bolt the door after I leave."

"I'm getting up anyway."

He tucked the plaid around her. "No, you're not. Settle down and go to sleep. You look frail, my darling. I want you to have enough energy to walk up to the Quarry garden this afternoon. I'll be working in the summer-house. Will you come?"

"Yes," Jean said eagerly.

He climbed through the window and was gone. She snuggled into the clothes and fell fast asleep again.

During breakfast, she noticed the horn dish containing the bunch of dead snowdrops; it had been pushed into the corner of the window-ledge beside Meg's bed. It was a wonder no one had thrown them out. Perhaps they had considered it unlucky to take such an action before the funeral for they all had heard how Meg had died while she was gazing at them.

Jean was not looking forward to this morning because it was the custom for neighbours to call again. She didn't feel like seeing anyone. Her eyes fell on the withered flowers and suddenly knew what she would do; take them to Bellie churchyard and plant them on Meg's grave. It would get her right away from the village for a few hours.

As she was passing Tessa's cottage, she remembered to call in and warn Fiona that she would not be at home this morning. Fiona, who had promised to come and see her, might hang around with endless patience.

Tessa, looking flushed and happy, said: "The banns will be read this Sunday."

# The Forgotten Duchess

"I'm happy for you, Tessa."

"Aye, I know you are. I hope you'll get your happiness too." Jean dropped her eyes. As though she could read her thoughts, Tessa said, "Your affairs are safe wi' me, hen. You were always a good friend. Naebody but yoursel' came to gie me a hand in days gone by. I'll not forget it. And dinna go grieving about your grannie. She's at rest. Everyone says how worn out ye are, nursing her. Just look at ye, not a pick on your bones." Tessa frowned. "What's that in your hand? You're no' goin' to the graveyard so soon?"

"Yes, I want to put these snowdrops on her grave."

"But they're as dead as..."

"I know," Jean said quickly. "The bulbs have life though. They'll bloom again next spring. It's... just something I want to do."

There was the sound of a cart and horse drawing up outside the house. "That's my man, he'll tak' you down."

Before Jean could protest, Sam Duncan came in.

"Sam," Tessa said, "Tak' wee Jean to Bellie churchyard."

The kenner looked alarmed. "Aye, so, I'm going that way," he said reluctantly. Then quickly–"Come wi' me for the drive, Tessa, and bring the bairns." He felt uncomfortable with Jean Chrystie–a tall, pale quine in a black cloak. She'd scare the daylights oot of the horse.

"Och, I'd like that fine," Tessa said delighted. "Wait till I fetch me bonnet." She returned wearing a bright silk hat.

Fiona fell into fits of laughter. "Mam, it's no' fit for the graveyard, it's meant for kirk."

Her mother tossed her head. "I'm starting a new fashion," she said unabashed, shooing the children out of the cottage.

Jean sat uncomfortably between Tessa and Sam Duncan while the children rolled around in the straw at the back of the cart.

"My, isn't it fine up here, grand view of the countryside," Tessa said happily. "The drive will soon put colour in your cheeks, Jean."

"Ma," one of the children called as they went down the Bellie road, "there's horses coming."

Sam pulled in and tweaked his cap as Alexander and a groom passed. He smiled at the children and went to nod to the grown-ups when he saw Jean sitting up beside the driver of the crude cart. She gave a slight inclination of her head and gazed straight in front of her, while her heart leapt wildly at the look in his eyes. Tessa's elbow went into her side. "My, did you see yon, hen," she whispered, behind the kenner's back. "I'd say he was fair daft about you." Tessa thought: 'Tis true what folk say, the Duke has never been seen around the place so much before. Sam thinks it's because he's sold the forest of Glenmore where the Duke used to hunt. Tessa thought otherwise! She gave Jean an anxious glance. Och, I hope that wean will no' be in trouble again.

They were dropped off at the churchyard where the children began to play hide and seek among the graves. The first thing that caught Jean's eye was the imposing arrangement of flowers on her grandmother's grave. "With respect from the Duke and Duchess of Gordon." she read.

Tessa rolled her eyes and went down on her knees to pray for Meg's soul. She scrambled up after a minute. "Listen to them weans, they'll waken the dead."

Jean planted the bulbs on the freshly dug soil and turned away quickly. How glad she was of Tessa's robust presence in this lonely place. Later, she would bring pebbles from Spey Bay and brighten up the grave. Tessa chased the children out of the graveyard and Jean walked slowly after them, taking the path over by the trees. After a moment she became aware that someone was keeping pace with her a few yards away where the growth was thick and dark.

"Who's there?" she called out, feeling alarmed. There was no movement now, but she could hear breathing. One of the children, perhaps, playing a game? A foot, too heavy for a child's, broke a branch under its weight. She turned and hurried through the graves and out to the road where the children were climbing into the cart.

The sun was shining brightly when Jean reached the Quarry garden that afternoon. She was surprised to find Alexander working at a table covered with instruments. He rose, took her wool cloak, and said: "You looked very prim and proper sitting up in that cart chariot!"

"You, my lord, should not have greeted me so warmly. That

was Tessa and her family. She said when you passed: 'Did you see yon. I'd say he's fair daft about ye.'"

Alexander threw his head back and laughed. "She's right, you know. I am fair daft about you. Come, let me show you my work."

"What are all those pieces?"

"I am making a clock."

"A clock?"

"That surprises you, doesn't it?"

"I'm glad," she said simply. "It's good for folk to work with their hands."

"Mr Marshall is supplying the brain-power. He's a kind of genius, you know."

"Aye, so folk say."

"He, too, is making a clock which I believe will be here long after we are all dead and gone. It is an incredible piece of work which he intends to give to me for Gordon Castle. I shall lay down in my Will that it must never be taken away from there."

"What is so special about this clock?"

The Duke began to speak enthusiastically about the design.

"It seems an awful lot of bother when all folk want to know is the time o' day. I tell it near enough, by the sun."

When Jean turned she knocked against a book on the shelf. Picking it up she noticed that the leather cover was peeling.

"What a pity," he said, taking it from her. "It's a German classic which I studied at Eton."

"Let me mend it for you," she offered eagerly.

"Could you? What a resourceful girl you are."

"I'll keep it by me until you return. It'll be a sort of... talisman."

Alexander raised his eyebrows and smiled. "How could a book be issued with magical powers?"

"I have used the wrong word, It'll be a power between us because you have handled it."

He frowned slightly, scarcely understanding what she was trying to say. Then he said lightly: "In that case I, too, must have my amulet."

"Shall I make a sachet of special herbs for you?"

He laughed. "No, I demand something more intimate." He put

down the instrument in his hand and took a strand of her hair. "Would it be a sacrilege to cut off a piece?"

Recklessly, Jean took the scissors, cut and plaited a strand of hair. He put his hand in his pocket, took out a small lace-edged handkerchief and placed the hair in the folds. "Remember, I fished its owner out of the river one day?"

Her eyes filled with tears and she put her arms around him, feeling a strange maternal love for this man. He rested his chin on her head. "You know, my darling, I'll never let you go, so don't ever suggest such a thing again. Promise?"

She didn't reply.

"Come on," he said quietly, "let me take you for a walk, you have spent long enough indoors these past few months. We'll come back here later and dine."

"Shall I make you a herbal stew? There's savoury mugwort and nettles growing behind the house and I see some oatmeal in the cupboard."

He laughed. "You're determined to give me herbs in one way or another, aren't you? I cook oats for breakfast when I come here early to work. That is one dish I can cook to perfection... well, apart from a few lumps."

"Oh, I was forgetting, thank you for the flowers on the grave."

He took her hand as they walked down through the garden. "You will be one of the first to move to the new village, you know. It will help you to get over your grandmother's death. So keep busy in the meantime, preparing to move."

"I suppose I should make a start in clearing the out-houses."

"There's no need for you to do that type of work, I'll see that a servant is sent from the castle."

She pulled her hand away. "No, Alexander, you mustn't do that. What will people think?"

"I don't want you to do heavy, unnecessary work," he said firmly.

"I have always worked hard."

"It's no longer necessary. I am responsible for you now."

She stood still. "You are *not* responsible for me. I have accepted a roof over my head, I want nothing else. You can keep your house if you think it gives you the right to tell me what to do."

"That's being childish," he said quietly, with a touch of anger in his voice.

"I'm not being childish. I don't want to be like Claire Gubbay sitting alone in a grand house for the rest of my life–idle, bored. I would work hard even if I had a dozen bairns to care for."

He looked at her in alarm. "Children? Jean, I hope you don't wish for children. It would be too difficult for you. I couldn't bear you to have that kind of problem."

She turned her head away, her mouth curving into bitter lines. Yes, she thought, it is all right for me to accept your love but I must not bear your children.

"Darling, what have I said to upset you?"

*What had he said?.*

He put out his arm and drew her close. Jean's mind struggled to be independent but as usual her heart betrayed her. They walked on in silence until they were near the place where the golden eagle had its eyrie. A noise overhead made them look upwards. An eagle was flying right above them. It went into a breath-taking dive with a rushing, thundering noise, then it regained its height and sailed across the hill towards the Spey. They smiled at each other and continued through the glen until they saw smoke rising just ahead of them.

"Alexander, do you think there's a clachan over there? I've never been as far as this before."

"I don't know, let's go and take a look."

They scrambled through the bushes and crossed a lea-rig which brought them out behind an old cottage.

"There's enough smoke coming out of that roof for a dozen cottages." He frowned. "It must be my property."

The row of hens sitting on the half-door flew off in all directions as they approached. "May I enter?" He called in a loud voice.

An old woman limped towards the door. Her face was a mesh of wrinkles, with bright alert eyes. She stopped and looked at Alexander, took a step backwards and bowed her head. "My lord Duke, is it not?"

"It is. Who may you be?" he asked kindly.

"Och, an auld body who hasna the sense to tak' hesel' off to Bellie graveyard." She chuckled at her own words.

He stroked his chin. "Well, since you are alive and well, tell me

*The Forgotten Duchess*

who you are."

"Auld Eva, wife of Angus MacPherson, resting in Bellie this past twenty years.'

"I'm sorry. You are quite alone then?"

"Nae... Herself likely saw ye comin' and has taken to the hills."

"Herself?"

"Aye, my daughter, a lassie of seventy years," she chuckled.

"I'm ninety." The old woman looked shrewdly at him. "My, you grew to be a bonny lad, and did ye ken I worked at the castle when I was a lassie?"

"Did you really?"

"I mind the day news came that your father, Cosmo George, was dead in foreign parts. Ye were only about nine years old. Just a bairn with the great hoose of Gordon on your wee shoulders."

Jean glanced at Alexander; his eyes went swiftly around the interior of the cottage, stopping at the fire in the centre of the room with a hole above to let the smoke escape. He put his hand in his pocket and laid some money on the table. The old woman, with amazing agility, moved and grabbed it.

"God speed ye back from foreign parts m'lord. Did ye ken that Bonnie Prince Charlie lay up here when the soldiers were searching for him?"

He shook his head.

"I saved him. Kenned when the red-coats were coming, bad luck to them." Her expression became crafty. "Many's a body seeks shelter about here. I can tell ye things if ye've a mind to ask." Her eyes went to Jean. "My, but that's a rare beauty."

Jean turned away.

They took the road to the left, past the cattle-shed. Alexander put his hand on Jean's shoulder. "I must get the factor to call here. What an appalling place this is. I remember her now, Eva the Witch, she was called."

"Aye, I've heard of her," Jean said, recalling the day, years ago, when Eva came to their cottage and asked Meg for some kind of herb or potion. Her grandmother had been upset and had said in an angry whisper: "I may be a white witch but ye're as black as sin."

## The Forgotten Duchess

Some trees attracted the Duke's attention and he went off to examine them. Jean walked on until she came to a three-cornered field surrounded by stone walls. She went through a gap and saw a row of fir trees, entwined in mistletoe and woodbine. Beyond them was a group of tiny, round cells and in the centre of the ground a broad stone lay horizontally on four smaller ones.

"Where the druid priests offered their sacrifice," a voice muttered.

Jean swung round. Old Eva was standing close to the fir trees. "This is sacred ground, lassie. No doubt, one such as yoursel' will feel its power. Here the druid hermits lived and prayed." She looked up into Jean's face and said softly: "Come to the Green Cairn on mid-summer's eve. I could tell the future which is as plain as the eyes in your head." The woman frowned and turned away, muttering: "Maybe ye could tell it yoursel' if ye'd give the power within ye a hearing."

Out of the corner of her eye, Jean caught a movement behind one of the druid cells. Perhaps it was Eva's elderly daughter who had not wanted to meet them? When she was on the road again, she glanced back at the cottage; to her alarm she saw Eva entering the house followed by a younger woman. The incident in Bellie churchyard came to her mind.

Jean ran until she reached Alexander, who was sitting on a hedge examining a leaf lying in the palm of his hand. "Is she chasing you?" he asked, smiling.

"No, but I think some druids are," she said, touching his arm and quickly forgetting her moment of alarm.

He laughed. "Shall I go and charge them?"

When they returned to the summer-house in the Quarry garden, his servant was waiting for them. A saucepan of soup was heating on the fire and a platter of meats and other food was laid out on the table. The man had a cheeky, warm expression and spoke with an odd accent. Alexander told her he was an Englishman, a Londoner.

The man served the food and left. After they had eaten and were sitting by the fire, he said: "Jean, I want you to accept a package."

She looked at him in surprise. "A package?"

"It contains some gold."

She frowned.

He took her hand. "Listen, I have important work to do when I leave Fochabers. I want to think about you, but not to worry about you. Please, for my sake, accept this gift." Looking disturbed, he continued, "I am aware that our... friendship may have altered the pattern of your life, indeed I am constantly terrified that a day may come when you'll want to marry a man of your own age. I know it is selfish, yet I cannot bear the thought of it."

She raised her head sharply. "What have I to offer any man now? My heart and body belong to you, but my independence, Alexander, that is different, it is a quality that you cannot control or take from me."

"Why is it," he said with a trace of bitterness, " that the women I fall in love with have this extraordinary feeling of independence? My wife–she was only eighteen years old when we married–immediately wanted to change the running of my estates. Though we have several homes, she now wants to run a farm of her own over at Kinkara. How well she has established her independence."

"All right, I will take the money and if I need it I will use it. You're forgetting that God gave me a pair of hands and that's all I need to buy my oats." And, she thought, if the Duchess of Gordon used her hands a bit too, she might find a greater contentment in life. Imagine having a Frenchman in her employment to fiddle with her hair. It wasn't natural.

They sat by the fire talking contentedly. She felt that their friendship was gradually developing in depth. The hours out on the hills walking had brought a companionship which she had not experienced before. He rose and unlocked a small cupboard and took out a package; from it he withdrew a box lined in black velvet which contained a bracelet and necklace set with emeralds surrounded by diamonds.

"They belonged to my grandmother," he told her. "She had long, slender hands like you. Hold out your arm and I'll put on the bracelet."

The magnificence of the stones stunned her. The dear, daft man, what a gift to give a village girl.

"When we dine together again you must wear them."

To please him she said: "I'll make myself a gold silk gown to show off their beauty."

He smiled. "Do that." Although he realized that the gift was quite impractical he knew it had great value. If anything should happen to him, at least she would be well provided for.

Large spots of rain began to beat against the window. "We're in for a storm."

"It'll be a bad one," Jean said looking out at the dark clouds folding over the landscape.

After a while he glanced at her and frowned. "Is something the matter?"

She hesitated for a second before replying. "I think I should get back to the village."

"If that's what you want," he snapped, feeling frustrated and disappointed.

"You don't understand. I *don't* want to go, I want to stay here with you 'till morn. I just have this feeling I'm needed there."

"Has old Eva had an effect on you?"

"No! Alexander, I'm sorry. I just can't explain it. Look, I'll go now and come back again."

"Certainly not," he said quietly, rising to his feet. "You'll catch a cold if you run around in this damp air." He longed to take her in his arms and lay her on the couch and shut out the night, but her look of preoccupation had put a barrier between them. He picked up her cloak.

She wrapped it around her and went to the door. As soon as it was opened, a howling wind and rain beat against them. On their way to the village, the fragile spring bushes were bent with a savage relentlessness, as though the wind was testing their strength. Near the cottages, where it was more sheltered, a woman struggled towards them, carrying something white in her arms.

"Alexander, we'd better part now." Before he could turn away, Bella Forbes ran towards them. "Och, am I glad to see you, lass. You've been needed this past hour."

"What has happened?" Jean asked, her voice sharp with alarm.

"Gypsy Willie's mother has shot hersel'." Bella's eyes went to the tall figure standing behind Jean. "Your Grace," she said in awe, as though he were a holy vision.

"What do you mean, she's shot herself?" Jean demanded.

"The poor cratur was taking a gun out of the loft and it went off. Her leg's badly injured. I'm just goin' now to put her bed in order. There's not a clout in the cupboard to make her decent for the minister," Bella declared, as though the injured woman was being prepared for a nuptial.

"If the woman is badly injured one of my servants had better go for the surgeon at Kingussie," Alexander said anxiously.

"Many a one gets a shot wound and there's no surgeon," Bella muttered belligerently, then cowered when he glared at her.

"I'll see how she is first and send word to the castle if it's necessary. I must get home at once and fetch some things." Jean turned and hurried down the road.

The bleakness of the cottage without a glimmer in the hearth struck her forcibly. However, her mind was soon occupied checking over the items she would need to put in her basket. A dose of valerian to settle Sarah Robb's nerves and make her sleep. Antiseptic ointment, bandages and scissors.

"I've been sorely needing ye, lassie," Sarah said when Jean went into the room, stepping over the grey, blood-sodden clothes that Bella and the shoemaker's wife had stripped off the bed.

She examined the leg which had been wrapped in an old cloth. "The bullet grazed it, it's not embedded in the flesh. I've seen worse gun wounds. How did it happen anyway? And what were you doing with a loaded gun in the house?"

"Och, it's one Willie had. He must have forgotten about it when he went off."

Jean cleaned and dressed the wound and gave Sarah a potion to drink. "I'll stay here tonight, just in case."

"No need for that," the shoemaker's wife said hastily. "She's my neighbour and I'll bide by her, same as she's done by me in the past."

"All right then. Bella, are you coming down the road now?"

"I'll make my own way and in my own good time," Bella said in a surly voice.

Startled by her manner, Jean said quietly: "Very well. I'll see you in the morning, Sarah."

As she went through the silent village she felt depressed and tired. All the time in the sick room, the two women had chatted away to each other, deliberately ignoring her. And now she would have to face a freezing cold cottage and icy bed.

The glow of the fire shone through the curtains. She opened the door and ran in, calling the Duke's name. The cottage was empty. On the table there was a note. "Sorry I cannot wait, my love. I'm off to Inverness early in the morning on military matters. Ugh, but it's a cauld wee hoose!" Jean found herself laughing and without flinching, looked at the empty box-bed and said: "Och, Granny, you would have liked him."

She was slipping down between the sheets when her foot touched something; it was the package and jewellery which Alexander had carried and she had completely forgotten about. Alarmed, she stretched under the bed and prised up a stone. In the cavity she placed them and pressed the stone down firmly. Never again would she run out of the house and leave the door unbolted.

## Chapter 13

The following morning Jean called out a greeting to her neighbour as she was passing. Bella Forbes turned her back and ignored her. Determined not to be snubbed, Jean walked across and said: "I'm on my way now to see Sarah Robb. Do you know how she fares this morning?"

With blazing eyes Bella turned on her. "It was all true, wasn't it? Every word Gypsy Willie said was true, you wee strumpet. Meg Chrystie must be turning in her grave." And with that Bella rushed into the house and slammed the door shut.

Jean went on up the road, her face scarlet. She felt like turning back home, for Bella's voice had rung out and people had come to their doors, some even settling themselves on their resting-stones, waiting to be entertained.

Fiona came running after her. "You'll be coming to the wedding? Mam and the kenner are making... Are ye well, Jean? You look funny."

"Yes, of course, Fiona," she answered quietly.

The girl kept giving her little glances. It wasn't like Jean Chrystie to walk up the road with her head down. And some folk were looking the other way too, as if they didn't want to greet her.

When Fiona turned into the school-house, Jean felt like running across to the field and going up by the hedge. Determinedly, she stuck to the road.

"What sort of night did you have?" she asked Sarah Robb.

"Well enough. It'd been better if the clacking tongues had kept still."

"They both stayed with you then?"

"Aye."

While she was attending to the injured leg, which seemed improved, Sarah said: "You're a good lassie, and who's to blame ye if ye want fine clothes and the likes. Bin working hard since ye were a bairn. Old Meg seen to that! 'Tweren't fair the way ye didn't have a chance to play like other bairns."

Jean's cheeks began to burn with shame. So that's what they thought, she was after fine clothes and money.

For the next few days she didn't leave the cottage, apart from going up by the field to visit Sarah. What, she wondered, would happen on Friday night when the village women came to the cottage to do their sewing and spinning?

She spent Friday afternoon baking and churning mounds of butter. There were piles of oat and honey cakes, also ale and wine. She sat down and waited. It's my life, she told herself, they have no right to interfere. But her hands were gripping the needles and not producing a stitch. Finally Big Annie, who was always late, came in with her husband, then Fiona arrived.

"Mam says she'll come too when she's wed."

"She'll be welcome, Fiona."

"She'll be fit!" Annie said tartly.

"Why did you come this evening?" Jean asked Annie, glancing at her formidable face.

"Is it true or no'," she snapped. "That's what I want to know, or is it just a cruel bit of village gossip. I want to hear the truth from your own lips."

"Is what true?"

"That ye're carryin' on wi' the Duke." Annie nodded at the box-bed as though she suspected he was hiding under it.

"The Duke has been kind to me," Jean said carefully.

"Ye must be out of your mind."

"Out of her clothes, more likely," the butcher chuckled.

There was a muffled laugh from Fiona.

Furious, Jean's voice burst angrily on Annie's husband. "How dare you use such ill-chosen words. Get out of my house."

"Och, stop blethering, lassie, and give's a bite to eat," Annie said wearily. She pointed the knitting needle at her husband. "Ye'd be as well up in your own corner."

The butcher shuffled down the floor and out through the door. Annie rolled up the stocking she was knitting. "What's to become of ye, Jean? Is it true he's building you a fine house?"

Jean thought of her visit to the building site and the alarm she felt at the size of the house. Mr Marshall, who had been aware of her embarrassment, had explained that the extra rooms would enable her to make a positive start in organizing the Cottage Industry. As he had spoken, the look in his eyes had been kindly but sad. She had returned home that day without a glimmer of enthusiasm. They both knew that the Duke had made a mistake by providing her with such a pretentious place.

When Annie went home, Jean filled her basket with the cakes and accompanied Fiona down the road. The darkness would protect her from glowering expressions, and the painful realization that the people whom she had always helped were shunning her.

"I'm right glad to see the pair of ye," Tessa said in a muffled voice as she tried to struggle out of a white silk gown. "Mistress Gubbay gave me this, I was going to wear it to be wed."

For the first time in days, Jean dissolved into laughter and Fiona fell into helpless giggles. "Oh ma, you look like the Christmas pudding poking itsel' out of the cloth."

"God's heart, I'll be like a black pudding if ye dinna git me out of here. My blood's stopping."

Jean wiped her eyes. "I'll have to cut you out, Tessa."

"There's nae room for scissors," Fiona told her.

The seams of the exquisite material were snipped carefully. "Don't worry, Tessa, I'll help you to find something to wear."

"Way down to the room," Tessa said to Fiona, "and see to the bairns."

"I'm wild worried," she whispered.

"What's wrong? I thought you were happy about..."

"It's no' that, I'm jumping o'er the moon about getting wed. It's Fiona. When Sam moves in...you see, she sleeps wi' me."

"Oh, I understand. Well, let her come to me. The...Duke has suggested that when I move to my new house she should stay with me. To tell you the truth, I could do with her cheerful company."

Feeling happy about the arrangement, Jean made her way home. It was a pity, she thought, that Claire Gubbay had gone to Edinburgh; her company would have been a great help over the past few weeks. She badly needed to talk to someone. There was Sheena. Perhaps if she slipped through the back door of the inn she might avoid meeting customers.

A sudden footstep behind her on the isolated part of the road from Tessa's cottage made Jean start with alarm and take to her heels. She ran swiftly until she saw the cheerful light of the inn. Without thinking, she ran through the main entrance.

A complete silence fell on the customers. "Come away to the snug," her uncle said gruffly. "Sheena isn't here, she's gone to visit her cousin at Buckie."

"Uncle John, do you think I could sleep in her bed tonight?"

He looked at her, frowning, and saw the tremble in the hand that held the shawl to her throat.

"No, you can't."

John looked at his wife who had entered the room. "Go and look after the customers, I'm taking Jean home," he said shortly.

Out in the road, he took her arm. "Now what is this all about?" he asked briskly. "Ma's ghost hasn't been bothering ye?"

She had to smile in spite of herself. "Why should my poor granny haunt me?"

"I wouldn't put it past her if she had a mind to," he said drily. "I've been wanting a word wi' ye. Tell me why there are all these awful rumours."

When they were inside the house she said, looking straight at him: "They're not rumours, uncle."

He rolled his eyes towards the beams and shook his head. "Ah, lord, lassie."

Before her courage went she began to tell him how she and the Duke of Gordon had met and the way they felt about each other. She waited for his disgust and anger. To her surprise he shook his head sadly and said: "I'd give my right arm to live my life again and know the true love of a good woman. With your granny's help, I sold mesel'."

Shocked by his words, she said: "You've got Sheena."

"Aye." He passed a hand across his face and tried to smile. "I've got my lovely lassie, and here I am moaning about a lost love."

"Who was she, Uncle?"

He hesitated. "She married William Marshall. My, but she did well for herself. A fine man, his fiddling would make the dead dance out of Bellie churchyard." He frowned. "I shouldn't be talking to you like this. I should be telling you to behave yourself and get away from Fochabers. If only your grandmother had yelled at ye about the wrath of God."

"What could poor Granny do? She didn't know where I was going."

He looked at her for a minute. "That was no' the impression she gave me, when I come to think of it. She knew there was something going on and she was right pleased, if you ask me. Och, if I'd only taken more heed of what she was saying at the time." He shook his head. "I'm right feared for you, Jean. The folk in Fochabers will no' like this situation."

"I'm not asking for their opinion, no doubt they'll give it anyway."

He shook his head sorrowfully. "Aye, brave words."

In bed, she reflected on the way her life had changed: the quiet happiness and content had gone. She was either full of joy or feeling vaguely threatened by something or someone. Tonight, she had not only bolted the door and windows, but had checked twice that her home was safe. Fear was a sensation she had rarely experienced before. Indeed, she was beginning to wonder if the unaccountable incidents which had occurred were becoming exaggerated in her mind.

There was something else that troubled her; in the lonely cottage she often found herself making silent comments directed to her grandmother. But the memory of Meg as a frail old woman lying in the box-bed was gradually fading, and now she remembered her as the tall, dominating woman who had reared her.

The piper led the long stream of guests down through the village after Tessa and Sam Duncan were married in the Catholic church.

Everyone was pleased to see the Glasgow woman wed at last, and to the kenner—"a good catch," they said.

"Bonny, she looks," someone commented. "As well set out as the Duchess."

Tessa had every reason to be as well set out as a duchess for she was wearing Jane Gordon's gown, the one Sheena had given Jean some months back. It had required a lot of alterations and the three of them had worked hard to get it ready in time. The day was fine and a table had been placed outside the cottage laden with drinks which were dispensed by the blacksmith. After the feasting, the floor was cleared for dancing.

Jean, who had spent the previous day baking, was feeling rather tired, but as soon as the music started, her feet began to itch to dance. The generous amount of drink had lessened people's reserve towards her, some were still avoiding her though. Alarmed, she realised that a few men were eyeing her with bold testing glances.

Fiona was sitting in a corner looking enviously at the other young girls who seemed to have no problem in finding partners. She went across to her and said: "Come on, Fiona, you and I will dance the next one together." They took the floor and joined a group forming for a reel.

"It's no' right for lassies to be dancing together," the blacksmith's daughter said disdainfully. "You'll spoil the set."

Fiona ran from the floor, embarrassed. Furious, Jean turned on Nellie the Blacksmith. "We'll not spoil it as much as your big, flat feet." She turned and walked out through the door and sat on the resting-stone, feeling quite miserable. She was no longer treated as one of them, just like an outsider whom they did not particularly care for. The party would go on for hours but it held no enjoyment for her.

The sound of music and laughter followed Jean down the road. It was good to be out in the fresh air on this lovely evening with the smell of damp sweet earth around her. Silhouetted against the sky on the distant hill was a row of trees, reminding her of the Japanese picture she had seen hanging in the summer-house at the Quarry garden.

She was approaching the cottage door with the key in her hand when she heard a shuffling of feet over by the rose tree. The figure of a man was pressed against the wall. Perhaps it was a tramp hanging around the door waiting to beg for food, as they sometimes did. Then she became aware that he was dressed in the clothes of a gentleman. To her horror, she saw that the cane in his hand was held like a weapon. In that terrifying moment before a scream could escape her lips, the man quite suddenly staggered backwards and disappeared around the corner of the house.

A slight noise from the other end of the cottage made Jean swing round, standing there was the tall, bent figure of her grandmother. "Granny," she gasped, and slid to the ground.

She felt her shoulders being lifted and cradled by someone, then a vaguely familiar voice said: "Cor, you didn' 'alf give me a fright, miss." She opened her eyes and saw Alexander's servant, Dobson. She struggled up. "Did you see that man? Did you see my granny?"

"I saw a bloke clearing off around the side of the building. I didn't see any woman." He glanced over her shoulder. "Maybe she's gone into the house."

"She's dead. She died some weeks ago."

"Christ!" He looked at Jean, his eyes wide with fright. After a second, he said briskly: "I'll see you safely indoors."

"Has the Duke returned?" she asked, suddenly realising that this man always accompanied Alexander.

"He's at the castle. He asked me to call and let you know. I came earlier and they told me at the inn there was a wedding."

They entered the cottage together. Dobson began moving about as though he were inspecting an enemy camp. "Okay, miss," he said smartly, "all safe. I'll go now and inspect the outside premises then return to the castle and let his Grace know you're at home."

After he left, she shot the bolt in the door and quickly changed her soiled gown. One thing began to stand out in her mind: the intruder had been as alarmed as herself when he saw Meg standing by the cottage. Why should a stranger be frightened by the unexpected appearance of an old woman who had died weeks ago? Unless it was someone who knew that she was dead.

At the sound of footsteps she looked through the window and flew to the door.

"What a wonderful welcome," Alexander said, putting his arm

around her. He frowned. "Dobson told me you were troubled by someone hanging around the cottage." The Duke began to look worried. "He might have been in the Quarry garden when I was showing you the jewellery."

"I didn't think of that, Alexander. The package is safely hidden."

"I'm concerned about your safety."

"Surely that Gypsy Willie wouldn't have the nerve to show his face in Fochabers again?" she said thoughtfully.

He looked at her quickly. "That's the man who stole my head-gardener's savings. He must be found at once. I'll have him whipped and deported."

Alarmed, Jean said: "I didn't see his face. He was dressed like a gentleman."

"That was no gentleman, my dear. He probably stole the clothes. He was waiting for you to open the door and would have burst in after you. You mustn't go out after dark until he's found, promise me?"

"All right," she said quietly. To change the subject, she enquired how he was getting on with the recruiting.

"At the rate I'm going," he said with a shrug, "the need for my regiment will have passed."

"There's many a man who will not lift a finger to fight for England again," she told him bluntly.

He frowned. "Is that the opinion in the village?"

"Many left here to fight at Culloden and never returned," she answered. "But as far as the opinion in the village is concerned, I no longer know what they think."

"What do you mean?"

She could have bitten her tongue for she had had no intention of complaining to him about people's attitudes. "I'm so busy preparing to move into that disgraceful house you've given me."

"You do like it, don't you?" She could hear the anxious note in his voice.

"Aye, indeed, it looks very fine. But have you no sense? The size is no' right for a simple village girl."

"There's nothing simple about you, my Jeannie. I would staff it with servants if you'd let me."

"I'd take to the hills!"

He looked anxiously at her. "You're sure there's nothing troubling you?"

Jean was thinking about all the rooms in the new house and her few possessions. There was money enough to furnish them but she hadn't the faintest idea how to go about it. "At this moment I'm perfectly happy."

"That doesn't answer my question." He smiled. "Perhaps it's the same with me, when I'm with you everything else is forgotten." He drew her towards him, and gently kissed her brow and eyes; when their lips met, the passion between them broke with a demanding urgency. He picked her up roughly and kicked the bedroom door open as though it presented an obstacle to the fulfilment of their love.

The following morning Jean filled her basket with herbs and a jar of ointment, also a few vegetables. Sarah Robb lived on tatties and didn't bother to grow kale. A pot was simmering on the side of Sarah's hearth: curious, Jean lifted the lid and saw roughly cut joints of rabbit. She sprinkled a few herbs around the meat and was straightening her back when her eye caught sight of something bundled behind a bag of oats in the corner. Casually, she went across the room, almost certain of being watched. Pretending to look outside, she glanced down and saw a pair of leather boots wrapped in a coat.

"Is that yoursel', Jean?" Sarah called.

"Aye." She strolled down to the room. "That's a fine stew you've got on the hearth. Who shot the rabbit?"

"Bella Forbes' husband."

"Think again, Sarah, he doesn't use fire-arms since he had that accident to his right arm." Her hands moved quickly and efficiently on the injured leg, applying ointment and fresh bandages. "Tell Willie that the Duke of Gordon has ordered men to search for him."

Sarah's hand gripped her wrist. "Tell him. He's up in the loft, sleeping."

"Where's his wife? Or did he ever marry her?"

"Left him, the devil take her."

"He left her, more likely."

"Och, dinna dawdle, lassie, tell him or his mother'll die of a broken heart if they catch him." Tears began to stream down Sarah's face. It was the first time Jean had seen her cry.

The same Willie wouldn't care if you did, you poor soul, Jean thought and hurried out of the room. "Willie—"

"Buck off, you nosey quine."

"They're coming for you."

"Who?" he asked surlily, but there was fear in his voice.

"The factor and his men. You have cheek to come back to the village. You'd better get to old Eva's and lie low, where you were skulking the other day. If you don't clear off you'll be flogged and deported." Well, Jean sighed, I had to keep my word to that poor old woman. Truly, I would be happy if he were caught. Nevertheless, she shuddered at the thought of his punishment.

There was a flurry of movement in the loft. Before Willie could jump down, Jean picked up her basket and hurried out of the house. Over by the glebe the factor and several men were advancing in the direction of Robb's cottage. She ran towards them. "Willie's gone, he cleared off in the night."

The factor looked at her disapprovingly and turned to his men. "He'll be heading south. Get after him. You're about very early, Jean Chrystie," he said suspiciously.

"It is my way when folk are ill. If I had your business to attend to, I'd have been here at dawn," she said brusquely, and brushed past him.

At midday she was beating chickweed into hog's grease in the pestle and mortar when there was a swift, impatient knock at the door.

"May I enter?"

Startled, she looked at Alexander. "I thought you'd be on your way by now." How rash of him to come here at this time of day. The entire village would be on their resting-stones. His expression made her take a step backwards, and the welcoming expression died on her face. "What's the matter?"

"I ordered my factor to organise a search for that man. Because of your stupid action and misguided sympathy, my men have wasted hours on a fruitless search. He was seen slipping away from his home when they were already heading south. The factor is furious and so am I."

Her gaze fell before the anger in his eyes. "I couldn't let them take him. I promised his mother; she's lying in bed, ill."

"You're a silly girl," he retorted.

Furious, she looked at him. "That seems to be the opinion of the villagers too, and not because of any action I have taken over Willie Robb."

He flinched slightly and his gaze dropped. "Jean," he said quietly, "do you realise that Dobson has been keeping watch on this cottage all through the night?"

"He must've been frozen," she said stiffly, and felt guilty at the thought of the man's discomfort.

"Mr Marshall told me that Robb abused you in some way. For that reason alone he must be found."

What would he say, she wondered, if he knew that Willie Robb and the tinker girl had beaten his child from her body?

She put ointment in a jar and made her way to Anderson's farm. Morag Frazer wasn't in the kitchen, nor was Mistress Anderson around. She left the jar on the table and walked down to the Spey. Perhaps Morag was washing clothes in the river. She went in the direction of the Boat o' Brig. There wasn't a soul in sight, only a tiny boat which she did not remember having seen before.

An unfamiliar bird sound attracted her attention. Quietly she moved through the trees, trying to catch a glimpse of it. A heavy rustling noise in the branches overhead made her look up. She froze in alarm when Gypsy Willie swung down in front of her. A shaft of sunlight caught the glint of a knife in his hand.

"A bit o' luck," he said softly. "If it isn't the Duke's whore." He caught her wrist. "Let me see how willing ye are."

Jean took a step backwards. "Please, Willie, I gave you the chance of getting away."

"Aye, to please Ma, telling me to go to old Eva's where I'd be cornered."

"I didn't tell them you—" Her words were shattered when he caught the neck of her gown and ripped it from her shoulder. Paralysed with fear, she saw the knife coming towards the strap of her chemise.

"Don't make a sound or I'll mar your beauty, then I'll be off. A good friend has put his boat at my disposal. Thought the signal was a wee birdie, didn't ye? I'll be across the Spey in no time."

Before his hand could clamp across her mouth, Jean twisted her head swiftly and let out a scream. Almost immediately there was a shout and the sound of a horse. Furious, Willie slammed his fist into her head and as she stumbled against a tree, he made to bound towards the river.

"Drop that knife," Alexander Gordon called out as his horse reared up threateningly, blocking Willie's path.

He tried to cut through the trees. In a second the Duke was off the animal's back and facing him. Without looking at her, he said: "Leave us, Jean."

There was a cunning expression on Willie's face. She wasn't going to run and leave Alexander to die on the point of that devil's knife. Opening her mouth, she shouted as loud as she could. Oh God, where were Dobson and the others?

The crust of bark under her fingers suddenly came away in her hand. In a flash it was flying through the air into Willie's face blinding him. The Duke, who had been moving towards him slowly, gripped his wrist and twisted it until the knife fell on the ground. His height and strength was too much for Willie Robb. She shut her eyes. Sweet heaven, Alexander was going to kill him with his bare hands.

Dobson, panic-stricken, came thrashing through the trees. "Your Grace—" He put a whistle to his mouth and blew frantically. When there was an answering shout, the Duke said: "Dobson, take Mistress Chrystie home."

Jean, clutching her torn gown, replied: "There's no need," turned and ran. She hurried along the river to a large boulder where she sat and pinned the tear on her gown with a brooch. Across the Spey, by the little saw-mill, she noticed a lot of activity which meant they were preparing for a log-run. At that moment, voices came down the river and she saw the Spey floaters moving along the banks, holding long flexible poles with sharp hooks at the end of them to guide the lumber. Some of the team were jumping from rock to rock, while others stood on lightly constructed rafts. There was a rhythm and beauty in their movement which took her mind off that frightening incident. The skill of these men had been handed down from one generation to another and Jean knew that all the holes, shoals, rocks and shiftings in the river were as well known to them as the backs of their hands.

Raised voices, came from the woods. She jumped up quickly, ran to the bothy and sank down on the heather strewn floor. Here, the Spey floaters rested after a hard day's work, every man wrapped in his plaid, a gill of whisky in his belly and feet toasting at the fire in the centre of the bothy. After a while her eyes moved to the corner where there was a small cask with a horn cup hanging around the neck. With a feeling of guilt, she rose and poured a drop into the cup. As she sipped it her eyes moved to the circle of clear, blue sky showing through the smoke-hole in the roof. It seemed like a far-off place up there, reminding her of the country where Gypsy Willie would end his days when he was deported for the crimes he had committed. She felt no pity now, only a deep feeling of relief that he would no longer be around to threaten her.

## Chapter 14

At one time, Jean had been dreading the thought of leaving the friendly cluster of cottages in the old village. Now, when the day came to move to her new home, she felt relieved. Tessa and Sam helped to pile all her things on their cart, then drove away while Jean remained to take a last look about her old home. "Rest in peace, Granny," she said softly, before closing the door for the last time.

The new inn–the Gordon Arms–was directly opposite Jean's house. Although her aunt and uncle had moved in only a few days before, the inn was already open for business. It would seem strange living in a street with a neat row of houses opposite. She was fortunate to have a corner position on the old road which ran down to the burn.

When she put the key in the lock, Sam Duncan said: "You should have a man of your own, Jean Chrystie, to carry you across the threshold."

Tessa's elbow shot into the kenner's side. "Shut your gob," she whispered.

The three of them entered the house cautiously as though they had no right to be there, then stopped in amazement at the sight that met their eyes. There were rugs on the wooden floor in the hall and in the sitting- room, which was also completely furnished. A letter on the mantelpiece from Mr Marshall explained briefly that His Grace had requested him to furnish the house. "If Mistress Chrystie did not find the furnishing to her taste, she was at liberty to change it. The house and the entire contents belonged to her, according to the orders laid down by the Duke of Gordon."

The three of them stood in silence for a moment.

"Jean, where are you going to put your bits and pieces?" Tessa asked. "They'll nae fit in here."

"Let's go and find the kitchen," she said uneasily.

It was a large kitchen with built-in cupboards stocked with china and kitchen utensils; apart from that, it was completely empty. The three of them sighed with relief. Tessa pointed.

"There's a back door and a wee room, that could be your still-room. Bring the things in through that door, Sam, and spare the fine rugs in the hall. Jean, you sort your bits and pieces and I'll lay a fire in the hearth. God spare us, a kitchen without a fire is like a body without a soul."

Fiona, who had arrived too, tugged at Jean's skirt. "Come away upstairs, it's like heaven."

There were three bedrooms on the first floor, and on the next, one small bedroom with a door leading into an enormous attic. Each room had richly coloured bedcovers and lengths of material ready to be made into curtains.

"What a grand view. Look, Jean, you can see away down the Spey."

"This will be your room, Fiona; bring your things over and no one else will sleep here."

Fiona's eyes filled with tears. "Och, do you no' think it's too grand for me?"

Jean put an arm around the girl's shoulders and said in a whisper, "To tell you the truth, I think it's all too grand for me too, but we mustn't let on to the house! We'll try and get used to it together." Laughing, they ran downstairs.

When Tessa and her family left, Jean walked right around the place again and down through the garden. She had given all her livestock to Tessa and Sam, for she was going to concentrate on building up a herb garden, and grow flowers to fill the large earthenware jars that had been placed in every room.

After a few weeks, her new home seemed like a large,

expensive toy. Every day she dusted the elegant rooms and shut the doors again. Apart from the kitchen and garden, the place felt like part of a dream world: unreal, slightly alien. This house needs people, she decided; their talk and laughter to warm the atmosphere. In her mind she began to gather together a group of those who still smiled and greeted her, if not too warmly, at least in a way which did not make her feel a complete outsider.

One day she called on the few who were already installed in the new village, then crossed to the old village. The reply was similar everywhere she went. "We'll see... They weren't sure..." They'll come, she decided; their curiosity will get the better of them. Deliberately, she left Big Annie to the last.

"Away down to the room, lass, and talk to me da, I'll be wi' ye in a minute," Annie said, who was busy in the shop.

When Jean entered the room, the old man gripped his stick and stumbled to his feet. "I'll no' be in the same place wi' the likes of you, Jean Chrystie. Ye're a disgrace to the village. Take yoursel' out of this house or I'll lay me stick across your back, you wee besom."

"Mind your own business, you lazy old loon," she snapped. "You've been sitting in Annie's corner since the day she was wed, a right plaster."

"Aye, aye, what's going on?" Annie, with a chopper in her hand and a blood-stained apron around her waist, stood in the doorway.

"I came to invite you to my house, Annie, but I'm not begging folk. No doubt you'll all come fast enough when you're ailing. And as for him," Jean pointed scornfully at Annie's father, "next time he gets a boil on his backside he can sit on it for all I care!"

Be damned to the lot of them, she thought, as she hurried home. I can live without them.

"How're ye getting on, lassie?" her uncle John called from the door of the inn.

She crossed over and said, "Would you and Auntie like to come and see the house?"

Her aunt, who was standing in the hall hanging up a picture, said, "I'm no' going to a house of sin."

"I was only asking you out of manners. Indeed, if you did come

I'd run and hang a rowan bush outside my door to stave off bad luck."

"Now, now, lassies, stop girnin' at one another. I'll be over as soon as I can, lass."

Sheena slipped past her mother and took Jean's arm. "I'll come now. Do you want help with making the curtains?"

"No thanks, Sheena. I think I'm going to have plenty of time to do them myself."

As though her cousin couldn't contain her thoughts a minute longer, she said excitedly as they crossed the street, "There's going to be a grand party when the Duchess comes back to celebrate the new village. All kinds of people are coming... Robert Burns and," Sheena went on hurriedly, as though his name had slipped out, "Mr Marshall is writing a new Strathspey for the occasion. I believe he and... Mr Burns are working on it together."

Jean glanced at her cousin's excited expression and said casually, "I hear the ploughman poet is a great favourite of the Duchess."

"Aye, but nothing in it, mind. He's too young."

Sheena took a step backwards, alarm crossing her face, when she entered the sitting-room. "Oh Jean, it's wicked, all these things must've come from the castle."

"No, they didn't. Mr Marshall ordered them from Aberdeen."

Her cousin turned away with a look of dismay. "All this, and you so young."

"You're not the first to comment on my age," Jean said angrily. "I didn't hear folk being bothered about that when I had to attend to their aches and pains. Another thing, Sheena, I'll have you know. I'd love Alexander Gordon if he had a pack on his back and a creel hanging by his side!"

When all the preparations for the house-warming party were completed, Jean and Fiona took a seat at each corner of the fireplace and waited. Fiona was gnawing anxiously at her fingernails when there was a thumping on the back door. To Jean's surprise it was Big Annie with a lump of pork in her hand; her house-warming gift.

"You're early," she said with pleasure.

"I'll no' be staying," Annie said uncomfortably, "things to see to, ye ken."

Each room was viewed in stony silence. When they reached Fiona's Annie said mournfully: "Poor bairn, out o' the girdle into the fire."

"Annie!" Jean winced at the blunt words. Then with a spark of anger: "Tessa's wed now."

"And no' afore time!"

When they were downstairs again, Annie said: "Och, lassie, folk are nae going to take kindly to this arrangement. Best not to let anyone past the kitchen."

"All right," Jean said quietly, wondering why she had been so foolish as not to realise that people would be shocked at the sight of the things which Alexander had provided for her comfort.

Tessa, accompanied by her husband, arrived, dressed in all their wedding finery.

"It's a pity you didn't bring the bairns for no one else seems to be coming," Jean said with bitterness.

"The bairns are no' far away, hen. Wee Jamie has them in the cart in the lane." Tessa hesitated. "I brought them for I ken what folk are like, and know what it is to be shunned. Let them all stew in their own sour virtue."

Sam made free with the whisky bottle and took a glass over to the corner where he sat glumly, looking as though he'd rather be somewhere else. He'd get a right jarring the morrow when he went to work, that was for sure. There was a lot of talk about Willie Robb, and though he had been a right blaggard, blame was beginning to fall on Jean Chrystie.

The children came tearing into the house as though they had been tied to a tree and left without food for days. Fiona made them sit on the floor and each was handed a plate piled with food. Tessa pushed a drink into Jean's hand. Before the potency of the whisky took effect, she had a gloomy vision of herself and Claire Gubbay visiting each other in their well furnished homes. She would sadly miss the friendliness and gaiety of village life, and the work she loved, the healing of the sick. She was sure they'd die now before they'd let her put a hand on them!

Tessa clapped her hands for silence. The kenner, flushed after several big drams, started to play the mouth-organ and the children began to dance. When the second youngest wandered off to "git the wee fl'ers" from the rugs in the sitting-room, Jean followed and watched his efforts to pick the rose-patterns out of the carpet. Laughing, she picked him up in her arms and cuddled him. The warm softness of his body filled her with a terrible longing. Then with dismay, she remembered Alexander's words that day.

Late one afternoon, several weeks later, Jean was sitting by the fire sewing and Fiona was at the table trying to do her school work. "I'm a terrible scholar," the girl complained dolefully.

"You're a terrible old misery the minute you open a book."

Fiona could giggle about anything except her school work. "Ma says I needn't kill myself at my books, that I'd be best just to take heed what you do."

"I'm not having anyone around me who keeps their brains in their boots. When the Master is pleased with your work I'm going to set you the task of copying out lists of herbs and the potions I make." She was really amazed and very pleased at the aptitude Fiona was showing when she helped her in the still-room.

"I might get things wrong and poison someone," Fiona said gloomily.

Jean went over and put a hand on her shoulder. "Don't think so badly of yourself love, you're still catching up because you missed so many days from school when you were younger."

A figure passed the window. "It's Dobson," Jean said excitedly, rushing to the door.

"Evening, miss. His Grace hopes you are well and wished to know if it will be convenient to call?"

"Yes, of course."

The man bowed and his eyes went past her to Fiona.

"Isn't he right handsome?" Fiona said, then coloured as she hurriedly gathered her slate and things together.

"Scoot out o' the way," mam had warned her, "and dinna fret if the Duke forgets to go home."

Sadly, Fiona realized that Jean's fairytale romance had another side to it.

"I hope you'll forgive me for coming by the back entrance,"

Alexander said smiling. "But the back door is not overlooked."

She held out her hands and led him to the armchair by the hearth. "You are very welcome." It seemed a long time since she had seen him. She thought briefly on their last meeting, then pushed it right out of her mind again. She would not mention Willie Robb's name unless he brought it up.

He raised his eyebrows. "Are you not going to invite me to your sitting-room?"

"Oh," she said, embarrassed, "there's no fire in there."

He walked across the kitchen and down the hall. She followed slowly, feeling confused and a bit ashamed. He didn't seem to realize that she lived in the kitchen all the time. "The house is beautiful, Alexander, and this is a lovely room, but it's a bit lonely.'

"Of course it is, because you have rejected it. There is no sign of anyone living here. Is your young companion in the house?" He went across to the wall and pulled a round, brass knob which Jean had thought was there for decoration. A bell tinkled somewhere upstairs; at that moment a shriek was heard, followed by Fiona fleeing down the stairs.

Jean ran out to the hall. Fiona, white-face whispered: "Oh Jean, my wee room is haunted. There's a bittie o' a box up on the wall and it began to ring with nae a hand to stir it."

Alexander came out to the kitchen as Jean was trying to explain the bell system. He smiled kindly at Fiona, who in an agony of shyness bobbed up and down.

"So this is Fiona? Do you think you could light a fire in the sitting-room while Jean shows me her garden?"

"Yes, my lord... Your Grace..." Fiona was terrified. The Duke of Gordon. He was like the King. She rushed around, gathering kindling and peat. She was right clumsy when it came to lighting fires. Please God, she prayed, if it doesn't light, make me drop down dead. Holy Virgin, stick ye're hand out and work a miracle.

After a while, light footsteps came across the room. "How are you getting on, Fiona?"

"Och, my hand won't stop shaking."

"Let's cheat." Jean went out to the kitchen, picked up the tongs, and put red coals in the bucket.

Fiona shut her eyes. "Holy Virgin, don't let the arse fall out."

Alexander inspected the neat rows that formed Jean's herb garden. He noted how she had moved bushes from the old cottage. He must arrange for some roses to be delivered from the castle. She had told him that roses were her favourite flowers. When he returned indoors, the fire was blazing and the low table laid with refreshments. Jean was busy preparing tea. During the past weeks she had been practising the genteel art of brewing from the scented grains that were in the compartments of the inlaid rosewood box which she had found on the sideboard.

When Fiona placed a few dishes on the table and left the room hurriedly, he said "That's a little character. I can imagine her bubbling over with laughter in the kitchen."

"I don't know what I'd do without her." As she spoke he caught the momentary bleakness in her eyes, but when she handed him the cup, her smile was radiant.

Afterwards she took Alexander through the house. He was delighted with the way she had arranged everything. The still-room really impressed him. Jean felt that his presence had made the house become alive in some way and she knew that it would not feel quite so lonely again.

The wide, sumptuous bed had caused her many sleepless nights. Now she stretched, enjoying the space and comfort which let Alexander sleep so deeply. The moonlight streaming through the window caught the glitter of the satin, quilted robe lying across the chair, and the slippers to match. He had also brought a pair of silver-backed brushes, a hand mirror, and a length of material to make a gown.

When he opened his eyes, she said: "When do I wear the robe and slippers?"

"In the evening when you are not receiving callers."

"Callers?" She gave a dry laugh. "Not a soul has been past my door in days."

He put his arm around her. "Tell me... I would rather know."

She told him how the sewing evenings had suddenly ended, and about her efforts to invite people to see her new home. "I'm not complaining, Alexander, but there are those who pass me by, when I venture out, who should remember the times they came to seek my help."

He withdrew his arm and sat up in the bed. "How dare they treat you so."

"I suppose it is only natural."

"Would you consider going to live in Elgin?"

"Live in Elgin?" she said horrified. "I think I would die living in a town."

"Then you must stay here. When Claire returns you will have her friendship."

But, she thought sadly, I want the friendship of my own people.

When Alexander was dressed, he said: "I will call in the morning before I leave for Edinburgh."

"Call in broad daylight? You wouldn't do that?"

"I will," he said crisply, tucking the silk quilt around her shoulders.

She was awoken by a timid knock. "Come in."

Fiona's sharp little nose edged slowly round the doorway. "I've got the oats on. Shall I bring your breakfast? Oh, my, what fine clothes."

"No breakfast. Ladies have morning tea, I believe."

"Dinna ask me to make that stuff. Ma says it tastes like—" Fiona swallowed the word and put her hands on her hips the way her mother did. "Och, ye look right bonny this morning."

Jean stretched out her hand. "Give me the looking-glass till I see, then make your piece, collect your peat and away to school."

When she went downstairs she was pleased to see that Fiona had left the place tidy. The grate was cleared in the sitting-room, the china washed and returned to the cupboard. The oats were a bit lumpy, but with rich cream added, they tasted good. Alexander had suggested previously that she should pay Fiona a small wage. Fiona had rejected the offer at first, but when it was pointed out that it would give her a chance to buy material to make clothes, the girl became delighted with the idea. "Ma will skin me for taking money, for you're right good to us."

Jean was in the still-room when the carriage drew up at the front door. She threw off her pinny and went to answer the knocking. Dobson bowed. "His Grace has asked me to accompany you to the carriage."

"The carriage? I don't understand."

Dobson stood aside and pointed. She drew back and whispered: "No!"

"Blimey," the man muttered in alarm.

"There's been some mistake," she said quickly, and turned away from the door, not before she saw the crowd of faces at the windows of the inn. She sat down in the sitting-room, her hands clenched. Alexander was going too far.

The front door slammed shut, and he was standing before her. "Why did you refuse to accompany my servant to the carriage? It is my intention to drive you through Fochabers and point out the work which has been done and that which will be done in future."

Without looking at him, she said: "I can see it myself and can wait to see the rest." She lifted her head. The Duke was magnificently dressed in a blue frock coat with a high stand-fall collar but his eyes were without warmth.

"I am asking you to accompany me on a tour of the village."

"You can't be serious."

"Certainly I am. Go and fetch your bonnet."

"I'm going nowhere," she retorted. "The people have a bad enough opinion of me. What do you think they'll say if I drive around brazenly in your carriage?"

"They will see that I respect you. You have been slighted by them, now I wish them to respect you, too."

Angry colour flamed in her face. "Who do you think you are—God? You won't change *their* way of thinking."

"Don't blaspheme," he snapped.

"Don't order me what to do."

He took a deep breath and said slowly: "If you don't walk willingly out of that door, Jean Chrystie, I will order my servant to carry you out. I am not leaving this house without you. Fetch your bonnet."

Jean went across to the cupboard, took out the bergère straw which she had been trimming, and banged in on her head.

"Most becoming," he said coolly.

She didn't see the laughter forming around his eyes. Her hand went up, and the hat was spinning across the room, knocking over a vessel.

He picked up the vessel and the hat, which he placed on her head. "It will do," he said briskly, and taking her arm, led her out of the house.

She held her head high but her eyes were lowered. She could have died of shame.

Her uncle, across in the inn, passed a hand across his face and muttered: "God in heaven, what next?"

His wife Kitty poked him in the ribs. "Ye see that? The brazen wee besom."

"Stop yer havering, woman," he said weakly, his legs nearly going from under him.

The customers left the window and slowly walked back to their glasses of ale. No one spoke. Every head moved disapprovingly from side to side as though a strong wind was blowing through the inn. Then, in gloomy condemnation, they looked at John Ord.

John lowered his head to hide a sudden wave of mirth that had taken him. They looked like a flock of Elders about to condemn some poor body to the Stool of Repentance. Aye, you parsimonious auld loons, there wasn't one of ye who didn't try, at one time or other, to pinch the lass when she passed through the inn. Ha! ye won't try it again. The Duke of Gordon has seen to that.

When Jean was settled in the carriage, the strange sensation in her head came for the last time; nearly thirty years later she was to remember that moment, and understand the meaning of it all. They went up the street, through the square, then proceeded on to the end of the village, near to the part where she had seen, in her mind's eye, the vision of Mr Milne's school. They turned there and went down again.

This time they went slowly around the square. The new post office had a large window which was adorned with wide-eyed faces. "I'm entertaining the village," she said crossly. "Look at them gawping at me."

She felt his hand cover hers; his touch was gentle, not matching the severe, haughty expression on his face. Oh aye, Jean thought, now there's no more doubt in their minds. Another thought suddenly struck her; there would be no more sly hinting either.

He was letting the people know the position she held in his life, and telling them to respect her for he was the ducal lord who owned the village, the land and every penny they earned.

To Jean's surprise, the postmistress came right out past her door and made a low curtsey, then, smiling warmly, she nodded to Jean. Cautious Elsie! She was pleased though. The postmistress was well looked up to in the village. Outside her house again, he took her hand, kissed it and said: "God bless you, my darling. Now I must proceed to Edinburgh."

She didn't want him to go; she wanted him to come inside for a few minutes, take her in his arms and reassure her. He saw the pleading look in her eyes; for a second their glance held, bringing to life the feeling between them which made every separation painful.

Jean turned, walked slowly into the house and lay down on the couch. She felt as though she had climbed to the top of the Cairngorms and down again.

## Chapter 15

Two soldiers from the Duke of Gordon's new regiment, the Northern Fencibles, were in Umphray's store in the High Street of Fochabers when Jean and Elsie Chalmers entered. They were purchasing red and white hose and black shoes with silver buckles. The main items of uniform were sold over in Huntly but the village store had increased their stock to meet some of the regiment's requirements. Jean turned her head to avoid the glare of the men's scarlet jackets; her attention was held when the storekeeper said, "I hear the British army have lost four thousand men in Saratoga. Will you be going out there to replace them? Or is the Cock of the North taking you elsewhere?"

The soldiers gave him a quick look, then the older one shook his head, the plumed feathers dancing on his high-diced bonnet. "We'll not be going to the colonies, our work will be protecting the North-east coast from the havoc caused to shipping by American and French privateers."

"A traveller was telling me that a buck called Paul Jones entered the Forth and was threatening Edinburgh."

"'Tis true," the soldier said, "he's one of the leading privateers."

When the men left the shop, Elsie said to the storekeeper: "They say the Duke is disappointed at the poor turn-out of volunteers from his estates and that some who have joined strongly object to crossing the border to England."

"Let England mind her own coast," he replied, "and the Scots can take care of ours. Mind, you'd think three guineas for enrolling would be an enticement. Ah well, maybe the thought of eight hundred lashes for a punishment is no enticement either."

Without thinking, Jean said quickly, "The Duke of Gordon has a great aversion to that type of punishment."

Her words were met by silence.

On their way down the street, Elsie turned to Jean and said sympathetically: "I hear the minister called to see you yesterday."

"Yes," Jean reflected briefly on the harrowing few minutes he had been in the house. The minister had lashed her with scornful words. He said that he would not believe what people had told him about her until he saw that disgraceful spectacle with his own two eyes. Then he preached about the wrath of God until she had said despairingly: "How do you know what God thinks? How do you know how he judges me?"

To that he had replied sadly: "Jean, I am only his messenger," and walked out of the house.

For the first time in her life she had given herself a dose of valerian and gone to bed.

Elsie broke into her thoughts. "I've been wanting to have a word with you, lass. Come over and take a look at the poor lot of work the women have left with me to sell to the Aberdeen dealer. They're sorely missing the work-evenings in your cottage."

"It's up to them, Elsie."

"And to think you were going to teach some that Shetland knitting. They'd have made a fortune."

The pile of knitted hose in the post office store room was of a very poor quality. "Since Holland has stopped buying from the Aberdeen market, the Deans o' Guild have set a very high standard and they'll pass nothing with loops or hanging threads," she told the postmistress.

Elsie rolled her eyes. "That Big Annie gave me a pair of stockings with different size feet."

Jean began to laugh.

"Aye, but 'tis well for us to remember that King George passed an act about penalties for bad work."

She was about to leave the post office when Elsie handed her a letter. While the postmistress looked on curiously, Jean opened it excitedly. It was the first letter she had ever received and it was from Claire Gubbay. Claire wrote... She had heard the sad news about Jean's grandmother's death. She, herself, had been ill and the doctor had advised her to go abroad in the autumn. She wondered if Jean would like to travel with her as a companion?

Elsie said without hesitation when she told her about Claire's suggestion: "I think you'd do well to get away from this village, lassie, for a while. There are few doors opened to you. And think of the long winter."

Excitement grew in Fochabers as the time drew near for the festivities to celebrate the new village. Some people had refused to move from the old site, others were still waiting for their new homes to be built. The factor was furious with those who would not sign the agreement. He had put a notice in the post office window warning them that the Duke had threatened to take legal action.

One morning when Jean was working on the physic plot, she heard the sound of bagpipes coming from the direction of the castle. Though her heart leapt, she knew that Alexander would be surrounded by his family and guests this time. He had told her that he always went to the Quarry garden on the day of his return.

When she climbed to the top of the hill, she looked down on the new village and thought how clean and neat it looked. The streets crossed each other at right angles and the great road to London went right through the square. London. In the autumn she and Claire would go there before they set out on their travels. A herd of red deer passed some distance from her, and over by the rocks a few goats were browsing. At one time Meg had kept a couple of goats there too, because they ate only the finest rock herbs which gave their milk great medicinal restoratives.

She crossed a little stream into the birch wood. It was taking a roundabout way to approach the garden but she wanted to pick some camomile which grew on the other side. Just as she was coming out of the woods, a peregrine falcon streaked across the sky, then swooped downwards. She ran up a hillock, then crept quickly out of sight when she saw Alexander some distance off with the falcon on his glove. The bird went up again, wheeling and circling around lazily as though enjoying the breeze which made the clouds go scudding by.

Alexander never took his eyes off the falcon. Suddenly, it seemed to become motionless, then it went plunging down towards a bleached stump of pine. She drew back in alarm when a wild cat sprang into the air to attack it. The bird swept around then came plummeting down again. The cat gave a hissing sound and its bushy tail went up ready for fight. As the falcon wheeled and swooped once more, the cat sprang even higher to meet it. The expression on Alexander's face never changed. Jean could imagine him silently commanding the bird to keep away from its fierce quarry. When the falcon finally descended on the glove, she slipped back into the woods and made her way home.

That evening he called. Jean chatted away as though her life in the village had resumed its former pattern. After a while he said: "Unfortunately I cannot stay long; with the castle full of visitors I am constantly in demand. There is a late supper and Robert Burns, who is one of our guests, is working on a new strathspey with Mr Marshall." He laughed. "I promised to attend their rehearsal before the Duchess makes them perform in our little theatre."

"The Gordons are so gay," her cousin had told her once. "When the Duchess is in residence, the place becomes alive."

As soon as the door closed behind him, she felt depressed. Now, no one seemed to need her–not even Alexander. How quickly he had hurried away.

The post office was crowded the following morning. Big Annie was bartering meat for groceries, and Tessa, dressed in a peacock coloured gown, was leaning against the counter. Tessa enjoyed her weekly outing to the new village. Life had never been so good: a fine husband and the bairns well fed and clothed. 'Twas a pity there was another one on the way... A blessing, the priest said. God look to his wit! As if she hadna enough wee "blessings" in the house. She glanced through the window as a carriage drew up. Her eyes widened when a handsome young man jumped down. Then she saw the Duchess's woman, the wee Edinburgh body, assisting the Duchess of Gordon to alight. Sweet God, they were coming in, and there was Jean Chrystie over by the counter as large as life.

The postmistress flew around the counter to welcome her important customers. "And how do you like your new dwelling, Mistress Chalmers?" the Duchess asked, her eyes sweeping over the group of women. "I hope there'll be no more dallying with any of you," she said pointedly, "and that all your agreements have been signed. We want the land over there cleared as soon as possible, it is causing the Duke a lot of inconvenience."

"God curse me boots," Morag Frazer said in a loud undertone. "Didye hear yon? *We're* causing the inconvenience." Morag gave the Duchess one of her wild glaring stares and strode out through the door.

"What did she say?"

The companion hurried to her side. Really, she thought, Jane Gordon has no refinement expressing herself to these common people. She has no right to mix with them in this manner.

The Duchess shook off her hand and turned on her heel. "Rabbie," she called, "have you finished your business with the postmaster?"

The bard came sauntering through the shop, smiling broadly at the women. "Not quite, Your Grace, with your permission I will walk back to the castle later."

"Very well."

Phew! Tessa took a deep breath; the way the Duchess's eyes had lit on Jean, as though the wee cratur was a wraith.

Jean looked steadily at the string of dried fish hanging from the ceiling; the smell was competing disagreeably with the Duchess's musky perfume. So this was the ploughman poet. What chance did her cousin stand against the allure of that man. His dark eyes seemed to be burning with intelligence and sexuality. No wonder women fell in love and into the hay, at a glance. To add to his charms, he had a most attractive voice.

"It's an honour to meet you, Mr Burns," Elsie Chalmers was saying importantly.

"The honour is mine, Mistress Chalmers."

On her way home, Jean thought of the handsome Duchess and wondered why the Duke bothered with herself. Then she recalled how he had hurried away on the previous day. Perhaps it had been loneliness that had made him seek her company, she thought bleakly, opening the door of her silent home.

"I wondered if I dare go and search for you—"

Joy leapt into her eyes and she ran swiftly towards him. "Alexander."

"What's the matter, darling? You seem so tense."

"I saw the Duchess in the post office and wondered why you bothered with me."

"Because," he said simply, "I love you."

Jean raised her arms and touched his face. The quickly spoken words removed all her doubts. He thought of the scene his wife had created that morning before he left the castle. To lose her temper with the factor sometimes, was understandable, but with William Marshall, it was unforgivable. William had devoted his entire life from the age of twelve to the Gordons, writing and dedicating his music to the family when there was cause for celebration. His work on the estate was incomparable. He was a kind friend and an honourable servant. And all because that damn Frenchman, the Groom of the Chambers, had spoken out of turn.

"You're frowning, Alexander."

"Am I?"

"I saw Robert Burns over in the post office too."

"And what do you think of the bard?"

She pretended to swoon. "I'd have taken to the roads if he'd asked me," she said impishly.

His arm tightened around her. "Don't you dare."

As Jean prepared some food, he picked up her pestle and mortar. "Are you busy these days?"

"No one seems to be ailing in the village any more," she said airily. "Will the Duchess miss you?"

"As long as she has several men to dance attendance on her, I will not be missed." He glanced at his watch. "I must be home in time for dinner at four o'clock though. That will give us a few hours together."

She lifted her eyes and looked at him, and wondered if their love would always feel so perfect.

It was a fair day. The gypsies, in flamboyant clothes, had returned from the south. They brought their caravans to the edge of the village green and decorated them with pine, juniper, and rowan branches. Then they laid out their goods and kept the spectators entertained with good- humoured raillery. Jean and Fiona worked together at a stall where they displayed different kinds of herbs, pots of ointment and skin lotions.

Fiona picked up a bunch of marigolds. "You don't often use these."

"No, because it is a bother to grow. Did you know that marigolds were supposed to be the Virgin Mary's favourite flower? The priest told me when he was passing the garden one day."

"Ye dinna say? Och, I know nothing. What are they supposed to do?"

"It is good for skin complaints that are slow to heal. I use it mostly for nervous ailments."

"Nervous...our wee Jamie's in a right state because mam has to take him to the tooth-man."

Jean put down a bunch of sorrel. "Fiona, you'd better go and give her a hand, it's nearly her time."

Fiona's face fell. "Och, Jean, I canna bide that mannie with his gob full o' black teeth, and all the time pretending to split his sides wi' laughter to drown the sound of bairns crying."

"All right, you stay here and I'll go."

Jean was not sorry to leave the stall because she had noticed people walking past slowly, glancing at her as if she were part of the spectacle. The tooth-drawer was at the other side of the green. As she approached, he held up a huge molar in his pincers. "I had it out in the twinkling of an eye," he boasted.

"Aye, from some auld cow," Morag Frazer shouted.

"I'll have all yours out, wifey, if ye dinna keep ye're gob shut."He looked about him and called: "Come on, laddie, next one."

A little boy came forward, then took a flying leap into the crowd and disappeared. The next customer was a tiny girl who started to scream. At that the bagpipes began to stir, and the piper, who was paid a shilling for the job, marched smartly up and down, drowning the cries of the terrified child. She was pushed on the stool, and in a flash the man was holding up a tiny, pearl tooth.

"You didn't take the right one out, you silly loon," the mother shouted at him. "I told ye it was the one next to it."

"Can't keep changing your mind about these matters," he said, turning his back on the irate mother.

He should be banned, Jean was thinking, when Tessa pushed her eldest son on to the stool. Jamie's eyes were standing in his head with terror. She ran forward and caught Tessa's arm for she looked about to drop.

"Go over to the stall, Tessa, and have a rest. Fiona will give you something to drink."

"Aye, lass, I'll be right pleased to get off m' feet. Ye'll see to wee Jamie, then?"

The tooth-man, anxious to gather customers, and also to keep his audience entertained, held up another giant molar for inspection. Suddenly a woman's laughter peeled out, making everyone turn their heads. It was the Duchess of Gordon. She, and a group from the castle, had joined the crowd surrounding the man. For their amusement, he began to produce all shapes and sizes while Jamie sat quaking on the stool, waiting. Furious, Jean tugged at the man's arm.

"Will you stop that nonsense and look to this bairn."

The man bowed in the Duchess's direction and said: "I beg your pardon, Your Grace. I have been ordered to attend to other matters."

A silence fell over the crowd. The people stared at Jean, then at the Duchess. The pincers began to waver over Jamie's mouth. Jean shot forward and pushed them aside. "First of all, wash the last person's blood off them and then find out which tooth is hurting the lad."

The man swung around angrily and snapped his fingers in her face. "Give me your money first afore I start, wouldn't put it past ye to run away, you brazen hussy."

Jean looked at Jamie and he stared back helplessly. "Och, Jean, Ma's got it in the pocket of her pinny and I'm aching somethin' awfu'."

She looked around the silent and mostly hostile crowd. Where was Morag Frazer? She must have gone. Was there not a soul to help her? Then she noticed someone moving in her direction. Robert Burns was by her side holding out a fistful of coins to the tooth-drawer.

"Take what you want and make a good job of it," he said smiling. "I think you are a better comic than a dentist!"

"Thanks, Your Honour," the man grunted, putting down the pincers to extract his fee.

Jean picked them up quickly and plunged them into the pail of clean water. As she lifted her head to thank the bard, she noticed, to her dismay, that Alexander had appeared at his wife's side. This was the first time she had seen him at a fair. Even the Duchess's presence was unusual. Now she remembered Claire Gubbay telling her that the Duchess's friendship with people like Robert Burns was influencing her, and that it was fashionable to mix with common folk.

"Maiden in distress," Burns said, joining the Gordons and explaining to the Duke what had happened.

"Surely she should have been able to get assistance from someone in the crowd," Jane Gordon remarked, looking puzzled. "I was under the impression that girl led the village by the nose. Remember, Alex, how she wrote that rebellious letter about the moving of the village?"

He was silent for a moment. "It was not rebellious. She merely represented the wishes of the people and asked us to re-consider our plan," he said evenly. "I think I'll mingle with the people." He turned to his daughter. "Are you coming, darling?"

"Yes papa." The girl moved eagerly to his side.

The Duchess shot her hand out. "Oh, no, miss, I have other plans for you."

As the Duke walked away, Jane Gordon, with narrowed eyes, turned to Robert Burns and said, putting a hand on his arm, "You, Rabbie, are one of the most intelligent men I have ever known, can you tell me why my husband always flies to that girl's defence–that Jean Chrystie? It has happened a few times."

"Your Grace," he replied smiling, "we men are always protective where attractive lassies are concerned. Now I think I'll try my luck at the shooting booth over there."

Jean returned to the stall and found Fiona enjoying the responsibility of running it. "Ma's away home. She says if ye can spare the time will ye look in and see her on your way back."

Unsettled by Alexander's presence, Jean took her purse and

went off to look at the other stalls and booths. He was busy talking and laughing with some of the tenant farmers. Determined to keep out of his way, she went in the opposite direction and immediately noticed Robert Burns. Remembering that she owed him some money, she was just about to move towards him when he began pushing his way through the crowd. Then she saw her cousin. The bard approached Sheena eagerly and drew her out of sight.

"You've come," Sheena said, her heart soaring to the heavens as the pressure of his hand tightened on her waist and he led her through the trees. This was the moment Sheena had been waiting for since she left Edinburgh. Her hasty and unexpected departure from the city had surprised everyone, and had upset Lady Madeline, of whom she had become very fond.

A few days after Sheena had arrived in Edinburgh, she had been on duty in the drawing-room where the Duchess entertained all the people of note. Moving about the room unobtrusively, offering refreshments to the guests, she had lifted her eyes and noticed Robert Burns gazing at her. The plate slipped from her hand, spilling biscuits all over the floor. He had moved swiftly to her side and while helping to pick them up, whispered a few words, arranging for them to meet.

After that day, stolen meetings had occurred frequently. Sometimes he had slipped out of the drawing-room to meet her in the pantry or he had come to the sewing-room where she spent most of the time. Occasionally they had walked together when she had time off. Then one day the shattering news came that Sheena had to return home. In a way, her feelings had been mixed, because she realized that she and the bard were becoming too close.

The last time he had come to the sewing-room, he had locked the door. Their feelings had nearly got the better of them. Sheena was not able to resist his love-making because his dark eyes and smile nearly made her heart stop. When he had led her to the old couch in the sewing-room that day, she had barely known what she was doing. If only she had stayed on her two feet, with the hard edge of the table digging into her back.

There, on the couch, with a pile of mending beneath them, he had coaxed her with gentle kisses; gradually they had become fierce and demanding. She had blushed when his hands went to remove her gown. The action had suddenly chilled her. No man was going to make that free with Sheena Ord until she was wed.

Robert's voice had grown loud with pleading. A maid passing the door had heard them and had gone to see the housekeeper. Sheena had been packed off home on the next carriage returning to the castle for supplies.

Now, as Robert Burns led her into the green shade of the woods, Sheena hoped with all her heart he would speak the words that she long to hear.

Tessa was in bed when Jean called. "Will ye run for Bella Forbes, hen? All the bairns are still at the fair and Sam's nae home yet." Her face contracted with pain. To Jean's relief, Sam came in at that moment. When he hurried off to fetch Bella, she made Tessa a potion of raspberry leaf tea. She thought of the jasmine flowers in her still-room which would have helped to relax the womb and ease the birth. There was no time now. She tied a clean towel around her waist and prepared Tessa for the birth. Bella Forbes came through the door just as the child gave its first cry.

With a frosty expression, Bella took over. When the baby was washed, she handed it to Tessa, who was beaming with happiness. "Och, the wee hen, God love it, as ugly as its da."

Sam burst into the room as though a bull was chasing him.

"Och, dinna fash yoursel' man, go and pour the midwife a dram."

"Are ye right, Tessa?" he asked anxiously.

"Aye, right as rain and nae the worse than I was at the birthing of your other four."

Sam coloured and smiled sheepishly.

The old priest acted wisely getting these two wed, Jean thought. Pity Sam wasn't man enough to get the idea first. She shrugged. Men always make the decisions in these matters, one way or the other. That's the way it has always been, at least for women of our station. Not the Duchess of Gordon; they say she's a law unto herself.

"He's a greedy wee loon," Tessa said, "will ye gie him a pat on the back and break the wind."

As Jean held the child against her shoulder, she felt as though her heart-strings were being tugged: the scent and the feeling of the baby moved her deeply. "He's lovely. I could take him away with me!"

"No doubt I'd hae nae trouble in replacing him," Tessa said promptly.

Bella Forbes sniffed disapprovingly and Fiona giggled uncomfortably.

The empty spaces and broken-down cottages in the old village were a depressing sight. One thing caught Jean's attention as she walked away from Tessa's house, a high stone wall was being built to enclose the castle and the ground for the new parkland. People were coming from the fair. To avoid them she turned and walked towards Bogmore.

The sound of music and laughter made her move in the direction of the Quarry garden. Unable to resist the temptation she knelt down and peeped through the trees to see what was going on. There was a pile of hampers outside the summer-house and two lackeys spreading rugs on the grounds. Mr Marshall was playing a violin and Robert Burns, blind-folded, was trying to catch the Gordon children. The Duchess was sitting on a low chair with a group of men surrounding her. Fascinated, Jean watched as though it were a tableau being performed for her entertainment.

"I don't think it is very becoming for you, Mistress Chrystie, to be intruding on the privacy of the Gordon family."

The factor stood a few yards from her where he had emerged from the trees. Impatiently, he straightened his waistcoat and brushed moss from his breeches.

Jean sprang to her feet, colour rushing to her face. "I was out walking and heard the music," she said lamely.

"I must ask you to leave. When the Duchess and her family are in residence, it is my duty to see that their privacy is not disturbed."

Her temper began to rise at the contemptuous expression on the man's face. "Perhaps you're not aware that the Duke has given me permission to come here."

"I am aware of *that* arrangement," he said, dropping his words with icy deliberation. "But even you must see that your presence here is in bad taste."

Realizing that there was some truth in what he said, she turned abruptly and walked away unheedingly, until the pungent smell of burning juniper began to guide her footsteps. It was coming from the direction of Whiteash Woods, near Gallows Hill, where she and Alexander had walked that day.

Old Eva's cottage seemed to be growing out of the earth like the trees around it. Jean peered through a hole in the broken stone-work of the byre and saw smoke pouring from one of the animal's stalls. A pot was boiling on a fire of juniper wood; it contained a liquid thick with sprigs of juniper. They're practising the old religion, she thought with alarm, remembering that the brew was used for sprinkling on a sick cow, while the smoke purified the air around it.

As she hurried away, she began to realise that the feeling of apprehension came from the strange power that was within herself; in this place, she was more aware of it. She felt the touch of fear, for there was a disturbing rumour in the village; some people were whispering that Jean Chrystie had other powers as well as the gift of healing and that she had ensnared the Duke of Gordon.

When she was passing Sarah Robb's cottage, there was the sound of a young child. Jean leaned over the half-door and looked in. "It's yoursel', lassie," Sarah said. "I'm right glad to see ye. Come away in."

The old woman was nursing a lovely dark-haired bairn while she ground meal on the quern by her side. They both seemed well and happy, and the house had never looked so clean.

"You're surprised to see the wee thing–'tis Willie's. A wee laddie."

Jean expected her to burst into tears at the mention of her son, but apparently the child had already taken his place. Neither Sarah nor anyone else in the village knew about her part in the incident by the Spey which had finally led to Willie's capture and punishment. She admired the child, then opened her purse and pressed a piece of money into the tiny fist. Sarah put it into a little box which had been hidden in a hole by the hearth. "Thanks, lassie, that'll help. No matter what folk say, you're nae bad."

Suddenly, Jean was reminded of Tessa's reaction when she had given her new-born child the gift of money. Tessa had put it in a linen pouch hidden under the mattress. "I'm saving for the future," she had said. "I'm no takin' any more chances, life seems too good at the moment for auld Tessa." Her words had made Jean feel strangely uneasy.

## Chapter 16

Alexander was coming for supper. A young chicken was braising in wine and herbs and a syllabub was ready for serving. A bowl of soft, pink roses were arranged on the table which was covered with a lace tablecloth.

When the Duke arrived he was immediately struck by her elegance. "Where have I seen that gown before?" he enquired.

"You haven't. You gave me a gift of the material. I could wear the jewels," she said hesitantly.

"I will fetch them from your safe, or is Fiona about to serve supper?"

"Fiona isn't here. She's spending a few weeks at home with her mother who has had another bairn."

When the meal was over and they were sitting by the fire, he said: "I will remember this picture of you when I'm away, you by the firelight with the emeralds glowing on your neck."

Jean laughed. "I won't be sitting here all the time."

"Well, in the evenings."

"I meant to tell you, Alexander, Claire Gubbay has asked me to travel with her in the autumn. She has been advised to go abroad for the winter."

"Going away with Claire Gubbay?" he said in alarm. "You might not come back. Claire has a place in London and house in Edinburgh."

"Well," she said teasingly, "I'll see you in either of those places."

He raised his eyes and looked straight at her. "I'd rather you didn't go."

"Why not? It'll make a change from sitting here waiting for your return, and wondering when the villagers are going to accept me again, if they ever do."

He frowned. "I thought they had. Look Jean, one day we'll travel anywhere you wish."

"Och, dinna be daft," she said broadly. "It was bad enough going around the village in your carriage."

"If Claire is beginning to find the Highland winters too cold, she may want to settle elsewhere and keep you with her. You might feel sorry for her and accept a permanent position."

His words quietened Jean, for Claire had hinted at that.

"And she'll be mixing with society."

"I hope so. I want to meet people for I'm heart weary of the folk in this village."

"What," he said with bitterness, "if you meet someone else."

She turned on him angrily. "I believe we've had this conversation before. Will you please unfasten this necklace, it feels heavy. Perhaps you'd better take it back in case I do meet someone and don't return. I can't very well tell my suitor that everything I own belongs to the Duke of Gordon."

He looked at her, the colour leaving his face. She held out her arm. "And this. It feels like a chain."

"Why are you behaving in this way?" he demanded. "It is not like you."

"Because," she shouted, "I thought our bond was as sacred as if the church had witnessed it. Because I have put myself outside the kirk and I sorely miss it. I think you'd better return to the castle and reflect on how selfishly you're behaving." She stared into the fire, battling with the tears that threatened to spill from her eyes.

He was silent for a long time, then he said quietly: "In that case I must say goodbye to you now." He rose and walked towards the door. "God bless you, Jean, whatever you decide to do. Of course I have no right to make such a claim on you."

She swung round swiftly. "What do you mean, goodbye?"

"A messenger came this afternoon. I must leave in the morning with my regiment. Unfortunately I'll miss the village celebrations."

Alarmed, and forgetting their quarrel, she held out her hand. "To think I nearly sent you away in anger."

"It was my fault," he said quietly, sitting down again. "I was jealous, anxious, in case I lose you. Forgive me."

Jean put another log on the fire and sat on the rug by his chair. When she felt the touch on her hair, she took his hand and held it to her face. There were no more words, just a quietness as though the minutes passing had to be treasured in silence.

After a while, the pressure on her hand increased. With a swiftness that took her by surprise, he slipped down on the rug beside her. With the fire glowing around them, they lay close together, forgetting everything, their angry words and his imminent departure.

"Alexander, I wish I could go with you."

"No. I respect you too much to make you a camp follower. I'll think about you every day and long for you."

You won't, Jean thought sadly, you are a soldier and will fight with all your heart and strength for England. A sombre expression crossed his face. Jean leaned on her elbow and looked down on him.

"You know," she said teasingly, "it is not becoming for the Duke of Gordon to be lying by the hearth like a poor beggar-man."

When Alexander left the cottage, Jean went up to her room to lock the emeralds away safely. She was startled to find that he had placed a large amount of money in the safe. Troubled by his generosity, she went to bed, forgetting the important task that must always be done.

A few hours later she awoke suddenly and remembered. Jumping out of bed, she ran downstairs to the still-room and reached to the top shelf where she kept a pot of herbs. It was not there. She lit a fir-candle and searched frantically; after a while she realized that the special herbs which protected her from conceiving a child had disappeared.

It was too late to go and see Fiona, for only she could have touched them. To improve the girl's knowledge, Jean had explained about the contents of each jar in the cupboard. Fiona had accepted the explanation about the unmarked jar with a shrug of indifference. Although the girl had a rough knowledge about the facts of life, Jean was aware that it was combined with an innocence. But why had she taken it away?

Tessa was feeding the baby when she arrived the following morning. Sam had already left for the salmon fisheries. "What ails you at this hour?" Tessa asked.

When she told her, Tessa coloured guiltily. "The Lord love ye, it's been thrown out—not the jar, but the wee bitties inside it."

"What do you mean?"

"Fiona thought the jar had been pushed to the top of the shelf in your cupboard 'cause you had no use for it. She brought it to me and told me what it was for. Och, I thought you'd have a nice fresh supply. Anyway, when I fell asleep, wee Jamie came in and took a fancy to the jar. He emptied the stuff in the midden."

Jean ran out of the house; all she could see on the midden was a pile of tattie peelings, covered with flies. She turned away, bitterly disappointed. Some of the herbs in the jar she had been able to identify, others were still unknown to her. Meg had taken her knowledge to the grave, for bearing children was not considered to be an illness, or something to be avoided.

A week later, the village celebrations began. Jean took no part in them for she felt like an outcast. Though she had often sought solitude—indeed, with her busy life in the village, it had frequently been difficult to find—she now felt, for the first time in her life, very lonely. She even dreaded going to the post office to buy necessary provisions, because when she entered a silence fell on the customers. Elsie did her best.

From her darkened bedroom window she watched the feasting and fun away over on the village green, and the light from the bonfire burning brightly in the village square. Fiona was spending the night at Big Annie's so Jean locked up early and went to bed.

The illness that followed the celebrations alarmed everyone. People blamed the seamen who had come up from Buckie, but it was pointed out that others had travelled to Fochabers from as far as Aberdeen. The news seemed to have drifted across the

## The Forgotten Duchess

Highlands in the wind, reaching every clachan and glen. Though the source was no mystery, really, for it was carried by the men of the roads: the pedlars, hawkers and tinkers, who were often talented craftsmen. They could all make a better deal at cottages or at fairs by passing on an interesting bit of gossip. However, word of the feastings for the new village had reached far and wide. Many families had walked for miles through the glens. With the scent of the gorse and heather in their noses, and fine food and wine at the end of the journey, it was a rare treat.

There were other attractions too: while the gillies and stewards drank their fill of whisky, the Spey and the hills above Fochabers were left unattended.

"They'll fill their bellies for weeks on the pickings," Morag Frazer said gleefully. "And good luck to them, the Gordons have too many worldly goods."

This was a comment Jean could agree with, though she felt guilty when she thought of her share of those "worldly goods", hidden away in the safe. If only, she thought, there was a way in which I could use the money to help the villagers. As events turned out, the sickness came, and that wish was to be granted.

A couple of nights after the celebrations, Fiona ran into her bedroom, calling, "Jean, wake up, there's a wild knocking at the door. We'd better not open it for they say there's some sassenachs about the village."

Jean jumped out of bed and opened the window. At that moment a head appeared. It was Big Annie standing on the ladder.

"I've bin knocking to wake the dead," she complained.

They ran downstairs and opened the door. Annie hitched the ladder on her shoulder and put it back where she found it, then began to look sheepish.

"It's the auld man, lass, he's taken bad. He says you gave him somethin' afore to take the pains away."

"Where's he got the pain?"

"In his throat and he's wild hot."

"I'll find some poison for that auld rascal. Away over, Annie, and I'll follow you in a minute."

"You've a heart of gold, lassie. There's nae one else I'd turn to in trouble."

Jean gathered the things she required, put them in her basket, and set off up the village street. Dawn had cracked the shell of the sky and a rose coloured light was rising across the hills. "Many's a dawn I'll be seeing from now on," she said aloud, as though someone had put the words in her mouth. A terrible foreboding fell on her. The houses in the square looked as though they were huddling together to ward off an unwelcome intruder in their midst. Dear God, she prayed, not the plague, the pox.

"Annie," she whispered, bending over the old man, "his temperature is raging. I'm afraid he's very ill." She gave him a distillation of bramble leaves to gargle and to soothe his mouth which was furred with the fever, then applied all the skills she possessed to bring down the heat in his body.

One hour later he died. While the laying-out woman was attending to the body, Jean sat in a corner going over the symptoms of his illness. Alexander had given her a book called *Buchan's Domestic Medicine*. She thought of the illness caused where cattle and their masters lodged under the same roof. That was in the old village, Annie had plenty of space in this house.

Neighbours began to stream in, then Fiona came, her eyes wide with alarm. "Our wee Jamie's just been. Ma's husband has takin' bad."

Annie and Jean's eyes met. Previously, Jean had told her that if anyone else became ill, she was going to be really worried.

Annie said quietly: "If there's anything I can do, just call on me."

"There's one thing you can do right away, Annie. Send all these people home. If there's an infection in the village, numbers can be dangerous."

"You do it, lassie. I canna very well."

When Jean explained, everyone moved to the door quickly, fear on their faces.

Seeing Tessa in tears alarmed Jean far more than the sick man by her side. She took one look at him, lifted the child from Tessa's arms and said, "Fiona, wrap the bairn well, tuck him into his cradle with all his clothes. Tessa, I think you'd better go to my house, you and all the bairns. Jamie will get the cart ready."

Tessa shook her head. "I'll no' leave my man."

"It's only for a few days, he'll be well looked after. Fiona will take care of you and the wee ones."

"I'm nae going," Tessa repeated stubbornly.

"I don't know what ails him," Jean said sharply, wringing out a cloth and wiping Sam's brow. "Big Annie's father has...been very ill. Think of the bairns."

Tessa's eyes went across the room to where her children were lined up against the wall, watching her with frightened expressions. She moved slowly out of the bed. Jean helped her to dress and climb on to the cart, then she said to Fiona: "Get the bairns to pick me as many rushes as they can find and leave them outside the door."

She returned to Sam and gave him a sup of herbal brew which Meg used to call "The Life-Saver".

"What ails me, lass?" he asked in a hoarse whisper. "I haven't bin feeling right for days."

"Don't worry, Sam, you'll soon be fine. I'm just going to change the bed. I'll try not to disturb you."

She found that the few sheets in the cupboard were ridged with mending. She sorted them out, changed the bed and soaked the soiled ones in lye. There was a rattle at the door.

"It's me, Jean," Bella Forbes called out, and she entered the house with her arms full of rushes.

The two women looked at each other for the first time since Bella had accused her about the Duke. "We'll spread them on the bedroom floor, Bella, for it's in a very bad state."

"Aye, right, lass, as soon as we walk on them they'll release their scent and freshen up the air."

"It was kind of you to come."

"I'm going to help ye all I can, for as far as I can make out, Jean, you'll be needed in more houses than one. The post-mistress is poorly."

"Oh, no! Look, Bella, I'm going home to collect a pile of linen. I'll drop in on the way and see her. Wash your hands in that solution in the basin and make a gargle with the herbs in the jar; it'll give you some protection."

"Aye, away ye go."

Oh God, Jean prayed as she ran across the field, help me, don't let this sickness spread.

The postmistress was sleeping and didn't seem to be too ill. Jean didn't disturb her and went on home. Fiona had everything well organised. Tessa was asleep in one of the bedrooms so she was spared having to tell her how Sam fared. She collected a pile of linen and filled her basket from the still-room.

"Jamie, will you take that pile of sheets over to your cottage and leave them outside the door on the resting-stone?"

"I'll push them through, Jean," he said, his eyes wide with a fear he did not understand. "Fiona says there's wild sassenachs around."

Dear heart, she thought, smiling at his little toothless face, if sassenachs were the only thing we had to worry about. Before evening fell there had been calls of help from several houses. The older people were, the more severe the attack seemed to be. Sam was gradually getting worse. He caught Jean's hand and whispered: "Get the priest."

"What does a big man like you want prayers for?" she said cheerfully. But it wasn't prayers alone, she was to discover when the papist minister called: it was something more solemn. The priest put a white cloth on the table beside the bed and placed on it two small candlesticks, also holy water and oils with which he anointed the sick man. All the time he prayed in Latin, a beautiful, melodious sound of words that wrenched at her heart.

She went out to the kitchen and made a dish of tea. She and the priest sat drinking it by the fire and talked in low voices. Jean was glad of his company. He told her that he was a "heather priest", that he had been trained and ordained over in the Braes of Scalan where a Bishop Gordon had founded a seminary in a stone, turfed hut. "I was lucky to get away with my life after '45 when Cumberland's troops were in the glen looking for Bonnie Prince Charlie," he said grimly. "The blackguards burnt the seminary to the ground, but praise be to God, it is thriving again." He looked at her. "Now, child, go and stretch out on that settle over there and try and get some sleep. I'll spend an hour saying my Office."

Jean, weary in every bone, took a look at Sam, wiped his brow then went and rested on the bed. Soon, she had fallen into a deep, dreamless sleep.

Two sounds filled her ears when she awoke: the birdsong outside the window and the voice of the priest. In a strange way, she had the impression that the song of the birds was a background for the chanting of the *De Profundis*. She went into the room. The priest's head was bent. Sam's hands were joined on his chest with rosary beads wound around his fingers; on his face was the still look of death.

Jean fell on her knees beside the priest and wept bitterly into her hands. Poor, dear, Tessa, who'd had so little in her life, now had to face this. She felt a hand on her shoulder. "I'll go over to your home now, child, and break the news to Tessa."

Bella Forbes, who had met the priest on the way, came hurrying in. "I'll go and fetch the laying-out woman, lass. Oh, by the way, the minister's goin' to bury Big Annie's father today."

"So soon?" Jean said wearily. "I suppose it's wise."

"Aye, but poor Annie, she can't even have a decent wake to help her over her sad loss."

When Bella left, Jean went into the dead man's room, covered his face and stood for a second sniffing the air around her. There was nothing malignant here, only the smell of death and the crushed rushes. She shut the door quietly then poured hot water into a basin and thoroughly cleansed herself.

The laying-out woman rushed in ahead of Bella Forbes, as though she couldn't wait to perform her macabre and necessary task. She was a sparrow of a woman who went around the village as though apologising for her existence, but when she entered the homes of the dead, her head was held high.

"Jean..." Bella Forbes hurried in again.

"Not someone else?"

"A message has come from the Duchess for you to go to the castle straight away."

"The Duchess...me?"

"Aye, I think maybe one of the bairns has takin' bad."

She swallowed with fear. Dear heaven, one of Alexander's children. Don't let it be serious.

Jean met the housekeeper in the castle kitchen. "Go through the hall to the room on your left, the Duchess will see you there."

"How's the bairn?"

The woman frowned. "There's no bairn ill here." She moved out of the way when two lackeys came through the kitchen carrying a huge trunk.

## The Forgotten Duchess

"Why was I sent for then?"

"It's the Duchess's woman."

"Has she got fever?"

"Not that I noticed."

"Has that Chrystie girl come yet?" Jane Gordon called.

Picking up her basket, Jean said: "Tell the Duchess I've got a village full of sick people." She went quickly towards the door.

"Jean Chrystie."

She stopped, turned and faced Jane Gordon.

"I would like to see better manners from my villagers," she announced imperiously.

Anger stirred in Jean's body. "The only reason I came, Your Grace, was because I was given the impression that one of your bairns was ill."

"It's my woman. I want you to come and stay here and attend her. I don't want her condition to get worse."

Jean's hand tightened on the basket. "Has your physician seen her?"

"We've had word he's ill."

That information filled her with dismay. She had intended to see Mr Marshall about fetching the physician to the village. She looked straight at the Duchess and said: "There is no question of my staying here to look after one person. There's illness in the village and two people have already died."

Jane Gordon lifted her eyes in alarm and raised a lace-edged handkerchief to her nostrils. "As bad as that? Two people dead. What is the cause?" she asked quickly.

"I wish I knew," Jean told her wearily.

"Well, now you're here, come along and see Mistress Tison."

They went through a corridor which led to the great staircase where there was a stone bust of Caesar with eyes that seemed to follow her disapprovingly. On the first floor were the dining-room and drawing-room. She remembered Sheena telling her that the Bed-chamber of State was here too. What a place! The door of the room opposite was open. She glanced in and her heart turned over. There he was, Alexander, looking down at her from a portrait on the wall.

The Duchess gave a short, quick knock on a door and opened it. "I've brought the Chrystie girl to see you," she announced.

It was immediately apparent that the wee Edinburgh body was

put out. She gave such a jump in the bed that Jean was reminded of a salmon leaping in the water. "Well, you've got plenty of spring in your bones anyway, Mistress Tison," she said drily, placing a hand on the woman's brow. "As cool as a cucumber," she reported, aware that the woman was shrinking under her touch.

Sweet heaven, Mistress Tison thought, Jane Gordon's brought the Duke's harlot into the castle. Someone ought to tell her. Everyone knows–everyone but my bold Duchess!

The look on the woman's face was so distasteful that Jean said: "Well you haven't got fever anyway, likely something disagreed with you. A physic for your bowels might get you on your feet in no time."

The Duchess gave a snort of laughter, then said impatiently:
"Are you going to be fit or not to travel with me, Tissy? I'm not hanging around Fochabers a minute longer than is necessary." Without turning her head she gave a wave of dismissal.

Jean hurried out of the room as fast as she could, wondering if her manners were any worse than those of the Duchess of Gordon.

"You know, Tissy," the Duchess said in a thoughtful voice, "that girlie is really far too superior for one of her station. Don't you agree?"

During the following weeks, the sickness lingered in the village. Several elderly people died, and others were seriously ill. Jean worked day and night, but without the help of Bella Forbes, Tessa and Fiona, she knew what she would not have managed. After Sam's death, Tessa had been ill too, though it was a slight attack. For days she had lain in bed with a grim expression, deprived of her husband, and of her baby, who had to be weaned. Jean had felt desperately worried, for Tessa had looked alarmingly withdrawn. Then one morning the situation changed dramatically. She was startled out of her sleep by a yell, and flew to the sick room to find Tessa tottering around the bed, shouting, "Give me my clothes. I'm doing nae good for mesel' or anyone else lying in this bloody bed."

The children, delighted to see their mother getting back to normal, hugged and kissed and hung around her. Their love and attention gradually eased the harshness of her sorrow. Within a short time, Tessa had other children to care for as well as her own. A young child died in a house where the parents had been affected. After that, in similar cases, Jean brought the children to her own home.

For the first time, she began to realise what a joy money could be. She bought large quantities of meat to make pots of broth for her own household, and finer cuts to make beef-tea for those whose appetites had been diminished by the fever. One thing which she was desperately short of, and which money could not buy, was bed-linen. No pedlar or hawker had ventured near the village since the sickness began. When it rained people were not able to get their sheets dried, and in the poorer homes, one change of linen was all they had.

"What are we going to do, Tessa?" Jean asked one morning, worriedly, looking at her empty cupboard. "No one will come near the village for it's rumoured we've got the plague–so the minister told Bella."

"Aye," Tessa said, with a far-off look in her eyes, "but they havena got the plague in Lhanbryd and it's near the time of their fair."

"Much good the fair at Lhanbryd will do us!" Jean said impatiently as she chopped mint.

"Plenty of good if we saddle the horse and cart, put a wee bittie of money in our pockets and keep our gobs shut."

Jean ran and hugged her. "What would I do without you, Tessa?"

On the fair day, Tessa and her two eldest children set out for the next village. She was going to buy supplies for her new home as well, which was nearly completed. The family would not be returning to the old one for it had been pulled down. After Sam's death, Jean went to see Mr Marshall who had been very sympathetic when she explained how Tessa was dreading going back to the house where she had been so happy for such a short time. As Sam had already signed the agreement to move they were able to get priority.

When the cart returned that evening, everyone rushed to their doors in astonishment. Tessa, looking like Queen Boadicea, was dressed in a black satin gown with her red hair flowing down her back. "A wee body sold it to me," she explained, throwing the reins to Jamie. "She said it was a sack dress."

"A Watteau gown, Ma," Fiona interrupted, giggling. "It belonged to her mistress."

"Ah well, it's very old," she added, dancing around the floor with the massive folds of material falling around her body. "My, I feel grand."

"You look grand, Tessa," Jean remarked, anxiously examining the bolt of white material they had bought for making sheets. "Any news from the outside world?" she asked idly.

"Not a word," Tessa said promptly.

Something in her manner made Jean look up quickly. When Tessa turned her eyes away from her gaze, she looked at Fiona, who like her mother, seemed to be avoiding her glance. "There's nothing wrong anywhere, is there?"

"Dinna fash yoursel' about the outside world, hen, you've got enough right here in the village."

As Tessa helped to store the provisions, she thought of what she'd heard at Lhanbryd. Some said the Duke of Gordon's ship had perished, that he and his regiment were at the bottom of the ocean. Others said that France and Spain had decided to go to the aid of the colonies and the Duke's ship had been attacked by the French fleet. Och, maybe it was a lot of auld blether.

Jean was becoming increasingly tired. Though she hated to admit it to herself, the continually crowded house was, at times, very trying. One morning she was in the wash-house with her head over a bucket, when Tessa came in.

"God look to ye, I think ye're breedin', hen. Fiona and me have bin worried about ye this past few weeks."

"Aye, I'm afraid so." She wiped her mouth and took the mug of water Tessa offered. "The Duke won't be pleased."

"Well, you can stop—" Tessa clapped a hand across her mouth. Heavenly Mother, she nearly let it out.

At that moment there was a knock on the door and Tessa, relieved to get away from Jean's enquiring look, rushed to open it.

Big Annie walked into the kitchen. "Where's Jean?"

"She'll be with ye in a whiley."

Jean splashed water on her face and went up to the kitchen.

"I'm right sorry to be the bringer of bad news, lass, but Ned went down to Spey Bay with the meat cart and your mother wants ye down. Her man has taking bad...ye dinna look well, lass," Annie said frowning.

"I'm all right, Annie. Thanks for coming with the message."

"Thanks for nothing, but I'll tell ye one thing, Jean Chrystie, the folk in this village will never forget your kindness to them in these bad times." With that announcement, Annie stalked out of the house.

"Aye," Tessa said drily, "you're a'right now, the village has forgiven your sins. I had to be wed and widowed, and ye've had to half-kill yoursel'."

Jean said quickly: "Tessa, I couldn't bear to go on being treated the way it was before. I hope they won't change their minds for I'm not going to change my ways."

God help her, Tessa prayed, if the rumour was true, the Duke wouldn't be tempting the poor wean to sin her soul again. "Wee Jamie will take you to Spey Bay in the cart and come back to fetch ye."

"I'll be glad of a breath of sea air."

Jamie, flushed with importance, stood up behind the horse while Jean settled herself on the pile of old sacks. Just as they were moving off, Mr Marshall came hurrying across the field. "Whoa boy..." Jamie pulled on the reins and the horse jerked backwards sending Jean sprawling across the floor of the cart.

"Are you a'right, Jean?" Jamie asked anxiously over his shoulder. "I thought the auld bugger had us in the ditch."

Laughing, she scrambled to her feet and climbed down. Mr Marshall bit his lip anxiously as he looked at her smiling face, then her noticed her pallor. The girl wasn't well and no wonder, the way she was looking after everyone in their hour of need. And now he had to impart had news.

William Marshall drew her aside and, as gently as he could, told her about the confused reports concerning the Duke. "No definite word has come to the castle yet, my dear, so we mustn't disturb ourselves until we hear the details."

Stricken with horror, she gazed at him. "When do you think you'll hear?"

"I promise you, as soon as word comes through–good or bad–I'll come and see you immediately."

*The Forgotten Duchess*

She nodded her head and walked slowly away.

Jamie jumped down from the cart. "Och, ye're nae well, Jean. Come away home to ma."

"No, Jamie. I've got to go and see my stepfather."

When they reached Spey Bay, she found that he had a bad cold which had brought on a slight temperature. "Stay the night, Jean, in case he gets worse," her mother suggested.

"I can't because there are too many people sick in the village."

While she drank some tea, her mother went on in a monotonous voice about things which seemed to have no importance at all. Perhaps, she thought, I've got used to Tessa who throws a bit of life into every sentence. Her heart was heavy and at that moment she did not want to talk to anyone. It was with relief that she left her mother's house and walked towards the sea.

"It's yourself, Jean Chrystie."

She lifted her head and saw Mistress King Milne approaching her–so called because one of her ancestors had carried King Charles the Second ashore on his back when he landed from Holland in 1650. It's a wonder she spoke to me, Jean thought, for she's a right snooty body, for ever talking about how well King Charles had been received by the Knight of Innes at Garmach House, as though it had happened yesterday. The woman looked out of the side of her eyes and said slyly, "I hear there's bad news about the Duke of Gordon, and the Duchess kicking her heels down in Edinburgh."

"I don't know a thing about the Gordons, Mistress King Milne. Good day to you."

"That's not what we hear around here!"

Jean ran down to the shore, ignoring the woman's taunts. Alone by the sea, she thought of Alexander and tried to get her mind to reach out to him. There was nothing. Where was the power now that she had so often rejected? With her back against the high bank of stones, she recalled the first time they had met. Tears began to pour down her face and she was weeping as though her heart would break.

Unnoticed, the sea began to race towards the shore. Water trickled around her feet as if reminding her that it was claiming its territory. When the wet hem of her skirt touched her ankles, she looked at the grey pewter waves hurtling on the shore and retreating again with their bounty, like clawing monsters with foaming jaws. She went to scramble up the high bank of stones, but the waves rose higher and came after her, knocking her down; then the bank of stones began to move and she felt herself being carried towards the boiling foam.

A minute ago her desire for life had been low; now, suddenly, she thought of the child in her womb. She tried to dig her hands into the stones and found they were like a moving wall beneath her.

The weight that fell across her body winded her, then hands were clutching at her hair, her back. The roughness of a rope dragged across her face, and fell heavily on her shoulders to her waist.

"Dinna slacken, Mistress Milne," Jean heard Tessa yell above the roar of the sea. She was pushed and pulled upwards until she was lying on the rough sea-grass. Opening her eyes she found Tessa and Mistress King Milne sprawled beside her, exhausted after their strenuous efforts to haul her to safety. Fiona and Jamie were standing at each side of the horse's head where they had been urging it forward to take the pull of the rope.

"Her mother's no distance," the woman panted, after a while.

"No, I want to go home," Jean gasped.

"Right, then." Tessa scrambled to her feet and they helped her to the cart.

She looked gratefully at the two women who had saved her life.

"I directed them to you," Mistress King Milne said importantly. "Saw you going there. The devil's playground. Got my old uncle that way–happens in a flash."

"Thank you," Jean said, and shut her eyes.

"I'll call and see how she fares when the plague passes."

As the cart rattle up the road, Tessa said indignantly: "Sweet Christ, did ye hear yon? The plague, she says. We'll keep a few germs for ye, Mistress King Milne!"

Jean felt laughter well up inside her. "Oh Tessa, I'll be grateful to that woman until my dying day." She put out her hand. "And you...Tessa! you're wearing your new widow's robe. It's ruined."

"I dressed up to come and meet you. Och, bedam to it, Sam's poor ghost would run in fright if he met me."

That was the first time Tessa had mentioned her husband since he died. "I'll make you a beautiful new gown when all this has passed," Jean said gently.

As the cart gathered speed and tore up the rough Bellie road, Jean felt as though the life was being jolted out of her. And part of it was. When they approached the village, the searing pain she had experienced before, gripped her body. "Tessa," she said wearily, "I think I must be one of those women who can't carry well—"

Tessa's hand fell on her shoulder. "Ah, well, wi' the North sea beating at ye, it's no wonder."

## Chapter 17

Some days later, lying in her comfortable bedroom, Jean realised that her body had been yearning for this long rest. She had sent word to Claire Gubbay weeks ago, declining the offer to travel, for she was unable to say when the sickness would cease, or if she herself would escape it. Now that the sickness was dying out, she was in no condition to contemplate a long journey, nor did she want to. Mr Marshall had called days ago, and unable to see her, had written a brief note in the kitchen which Fiona had brought to her room. 'The Duke is safe. He had been injured, but not badly. They were awaiting further news.'

Tessa was delighted with their new home, situated over behind the inn. Though she was always full of life, a forlorn look often crept into her eyes. Jean felt as though they were her own family, and their happiness and welfare important to her. Fortunately Tessa had developed a skill and liking for needlework; also, she had been offered a job at the inn.

The last autumn fair was, in a way, a joyous occasion for the village. The sickness was behind them and they were no longer treated as lepers. Even the factor was moved to allow some kind of celebration and had given permission for a bonfire to be lit in the village square. Gossip from the castle said that the Duchess was returning with important guests. Some thought it was the Prime Minister, others swore it was the King.

## The Forgotten Duchess

"The King?" the postmaster said. "Nae — That Hanoverian bastard is too daft to travel."

Elsie told Jean that her husband, whose father had been killed at Culloden, smiled for business when English guests from the castle came into the post office, but he'd as soon stick a dirk in their backs. Jean wondered if that Robert Burns was coming. Uncle John was anxious for her cousin to get wed as he needed another man to help run the business which was now flourishing. He complained that Sheena didn't seem able to set her heart on any lad. Jean knew where Sheena's heart was—with the bard. And a right waste that was!

As she had neither the time nor energy, Tessa and Fiona had taken over her stall at the fair. Tessa had made dozens of lavender sachets and herbal pillows for the "quality who couldna sleep". Jean turned a blind eye to some of the herbs her friend used. Old Mother Wet the Bed was stuffed in with those of a more delicate nature.

"If they had to work like common folk they'd nae have the complaint," Tessa said airily.

Jamie had copied the gypsies and made heather-besoms. He was also developing a skill for shaping simple wooden utensils. On the day of the fair a silence fell over the crowd when the Duchess and her guests came to the green. Everyone was looking for the Hanoverian; apparently he had not ventured so far north.

"Just the thing you need, Tissy." The Duchess held up a sleeping pillow.

"Aye, Your Grace," Tessa said, "I've made them specially for auld maids—I mean maidens."

Jane Gordon threw back her head and laughed, then tapped Tessa's arm and said with unexpected kindness: "I hear you've been widowed. If this is your work, you'll have no problem in earning your oats." She opened her purse and placed a generous amount of money in Tessa's hand.

As the fair drew to a close, the bagpipes began to play gay airs, many composed by Mr Marshall. The sound of a carriage made all heads turn. It stopped by the green and the Duke alighted.

"Alex," the Duchess said, "I didn't know you intended to travel north." There was little pleasure in her voice.

"I decided," he said easily, taking the walking-stick which

Dobson offered, "that to get really fit I needed a breath of Fochabers air."

Jean, who had been helping to pack the things which had not been sold, turned her head and saw him. "Alexander..." His name flew from her lips, and her face filled with happiness.

He turned, looked at her and smiled. Alarmed by her impulsive action, she lowered her head and moved away. There was complete silence for a minute, then the piper began to play again. As Mr Marshall crossed to the Duke's side, he thought, now the Duchess knows. God help us!

Mistress Tison took a quick look at Jane Gordon's angry face and helped her into the carriage. It serves you right, madam, she thought, you've flaunted your charms too freely, too often, behaving as though you were wed to some daft Highland loon. Perhaps if you'd bothered more about your Duke and less about that crowd hanging around the Hanoverians.

"Get in," the Duchess snapped. "How long has that been going on? I suppose I am the last to know."

Though Mistress Tison enjoyed the privileges attached to her position, there were times when she hated her work. Occasionally she felt that the Duchess did not really like her, but there was a childhood bond. Their mothers had been friends when they all lived in Hyndsford's Close in Edinburgh. Jane Gordon had been brought up in comparative poverty, and when she met the Duke of Gordon she became determined to catch him—with her mother behind her with a strong net!

"How long, I asked, has *that* been going on?" the Duchess asked icily, then added quickly, "Are there any bastards?"

"I don't know... to both questions."

"Find out! I didn't work and slave to make Gordon Castle one of the finest places in the land to discover that after all my husband has been cuckolding me behind my back with some village strumpet."

"They fair showed their feelings," Mistress Tison said without thinking.

"They showed too much, Tissy, before my very eyes. I'll soon bring an end to it."

Alexander Gordon went for a short walk by the Spey with

William Marshall. His leg and side were still painful. He knew in his heart, that a few weeks of Highland air would do him more good than a hundred physicians. The two men discussed the village, and the Duke heard more details about the illness which had lingered so long. There had been alarming rumours in Edinburgh. With a slight reluctance, Mr Marshall told him how Jean had ministered to the sick. "Without her aid half the village might not have pulled through," he said with honesty.

Alexander lowered his head, aware of how much this man disapproved of his relationship with Jean. "William, the nearest doctor is a long way off," he said thoughtfully. "We must set about getting a physician in the village. See to it, when you have time. He can have free fishing and shooting, but I want no whisky man."

"Very well, your Grace. I will attend to that."

The minute he arrived back at the castle, the Duchess pranced into his dressing-room. "No wonder you've been so fond of staying up here in your misty glens during the past year or so."

He looked at her sharply. "What are you talking about?"

"You've had your amusement all laid on when my back was turned."

Alexander picked up a paper-knife, studied it for a second then looked at her briefly, and said: "It is a pity you turned your back so often, that you have not cared to spend longer by my side, on my estates. No sooner are you at Gordon Castle than you want to set off again elsewhere. This situation between us has been going on for years. Don't pretend to be the hurt, loving wife. You have abused your position many times."

Jane Gordon walked swiftly across the room, about to fire a mouthful of angry words. He rose slowly and looked directly at her.

"I have not enjoyed being tittered about by the Duchess of Devonshire, or your other cronies. I have found it extremely painful to hear that you have cast doubt on the parentage of some of our children."

The Duchess took a step backwards, alarmed at the quiet anger on her husband's face. She shrugged her shoulders and said: "A jest — "

"How dare you make such a jest."

"How dare you take up with that Chrystie girl. She's half your age."

"I am aware of her youth. I am also aware of her maturity and refinement."

"Huh! An ignorant village girl."

"No, Jane, she is not an ignorant girl. Your knowledge is of politics; hers is more profound and valuable. Many people in this village would have died if she had not the knowledge and skill to heal them over the past few weeks."

Jane Gordon tightened her lips. "When you go off again with your regiment, I'll have her out of this village, if it's the last thing I do."

"What do you mean?" he snapped.

"I'll tell the factor to give her notice to quit our property."

"You can save yourself the trouble, the house in the High Street belongs to Jean Chrystie. I have made all the necessary arrangements. And, since we are being frank, in case of my death, she will receive an income for the rest of her life. You cannot touch her."

The Duchess stamped her foot. "You... bastard. No wonder the coffers are so low supporting all these... Claire Gubbay and now this wee strumpet."

"Will you leave my dressing-room please. When you are in control of your temper we will discuss this again."

"*Never*! Her name will never pass my lips again. You do what you like, and I'll see that I do exactly the same!"

He raised his eyebrows. "I was under the impression that such a situation existed. So far, I have not made any objections to Buckingham House being used as a feeding place for every political upstart, hanger-on and admirer. Take care, or I may have to ask our lawyers to draw up another settlement regarding our financial arrangements."

Jane Gordon pretended to remove a thread from her skirt to hide her expression of fear and anger. By heavens, he would do it too. She had better play her cards right.

The door opened and their eldest son stood there. "Momma, Papa," he said disapprovingly, "your voices are being heard all over the place."

The Duchess put her hand on his shoulder. "Come on, George, your papa is well neither in mind nor body."

Seething with anger she went to her room. "Tissy," she yelled.

"Yes, Your Grace?"

"Get the maids to pack my bags. I'm leaving for Edinburgh in the morning."

"But the Duke... the guests. He is not in a fit state to look after them."

"He'll be fit enough to visit Chrystie, I have no doubt."

Mistress Tison had heard the angry voices coming from the Duke's rooms. She had never seen such a defeated expression on the Duchess's face. For the first time in her life, she felt sorry for Jane Gordon.

"Sit down, Jane, I must talk to you as a friend. You are a wise woman... don't do anything rash."

The two women sat for a long time talking, then the Duchess said with her customary frankness: "For once, I think you're right, Tissy. I have too much to lose to give way to my feelings. I'd be daft not to heed your words. But when you think of him doing such a thing, setting her up and airing her in his carriage. It makes m'blood boil."

"I wouldn't caution you so strongly if it were any wee village body, but this girl Chrystie is, according to my information and my observations, extraordinary clever."

"Blast her to hell."

"Quite. Play your cards carefully. Your strongest weapon is the children. The Duke adores them."

"Aye, the bairns. Well," the Duchess said, picking up the mirror and patting her hair, "I enjoy being the Duchess of Gordon and all the wealth and position that goes with it."

Tissy rose to her feet. "Keep a still tongue." If you can, she thought.

The Duchess winked at her in the mirror. "We'll see. I've never been beaten yet."

Alexander smelt the bonfire and rich meats cooking in the village square as he came through the new and imposing gates at the entrance to the castle. He walked as far as Jean's house and fitted the key into the side door. She was singing in a low, melodious voice. It stopped immediately and she came running towards him.

"I thought you might be in the square," he said, smiling tiredly.

She took one look at his face and held out her hand. "Come in and rest."

A peat fire was burning in the hearth and there was a smell of roses and lavender. On the low table her needlework lay where she had placed it hastily. He sat down on the chair and thought, this is what I need, the tranquillity of this lovely room. She brought him a drink without asking; it tasted of whisky and herbs. Not entirely to his liking, but he drank it obediently, knowing that she was trying to heal his body in her own way. He smiled wearily and thanked her, then listened as she talked in answer to his questions.

No, she had decided not to travel when the sickness struck the village. Strangely, she had no regrets now, for life in the village was back on its old footing. "To tell you the truth, Alexander, it's even better than before, for folk are not running to me every time they have a pain in their toe, now that most families have seen or experienced a real illness. And another thing, they've become cleaner in their ways."

"The standard of hygiene has risen?"

She nodded her head. "The new houses have made it easier for people to manage, they were able to be sick with a bit of comfort." She looked at him. "Are you mending well?"

"Yes," he said briefly. And she knew by the look on his face that he did not want to discuss his injury—later, perhaps.

"—'Tis a pity the English won't accept the American Declaration of Independence and leave them be," she said quickly.

He looked surprised and slightly irritated. "We can't possibly do that. But," he added, "I have not been to the colonies or, as rumour had it, on my way there. My regiment is protecting the Northern coast against invasion. There is a lot of trouble out there."

She poked the fire and looked at him out of the side of her eyes. Suddenly he smiled, ruffled her hair and said: "I think you are a Highland rebel."

"Aye, maybe. You are a divided man, though, Alexander. One half is English and the other, a Scot."

## The Forgotten Duchess

"Politically, I am all English. But my heart is in Scotland." He shut his eyes and said: "Dear heaven, how unprepared our navy was. One hundred and nineteen ships were supposed to be ready for service and only half were fit to go to sea." He shook his head. "Come and sit by me, darling. How good it is to be here." He sighed. "I feel like an elderly gentleman—stiff and weary."

"I'll give you some lubrication. Perhaps the Duchess would apply it; a woman's touch is best."

He looked away.

"Is something wrong?" Then she remembered how she had called out his name on the village green. Feeling guilty and dismayed, she said, "The Duchess knows about me?"

"We have discussed it," he replied, frowning at the understatement.

She rose and went to the still-room and returned with a lotion. "Don't throw it away."

"Not if you have made it."

"It is good to have some exercise," she said anxiously, "but I think you have overdone it today."

When he returned to the castle, the Duchess was as usual, holding everyone's attention. The minute she saw the Duke entering the room she rose to her feet and held out her hand. "Come and sit here, Alex. Move over dearest," she said to her daughter. "Give Papa plenty of space." Jane Gordon linked her arm in her husband's and smiled at the children, who were happy to see their parents on such close terms again.

For their sake, Alexander thought, it is best to make a pretence of being contented with each other. After a reasonable time he excused himself from the company, and went to bed early.

Some hours later he was awakened by the sound of his bedroom door opening, then he felt the bodily weight of his wife burrowing into the bed beside him. Uneasily, he moved away. But Jane Gordon was determined that the full act of reconciliation would be completed.

## Chapter 18

"Alexander, you look like some poor ghost that has wandered from a battlefield." Jean walked up the little slope to the summer-house and kissed his cheek, glad that he was home for good after the last few years with his regiment, now disbanded. "Welcome home, my love. Come inside and sit down while I brew you a refreshing drink of mint-tea for I think you need some God-given minerals inside you."

The Duke suddenly felt the tension that held him melt away, and he began to laugh, then he drew her to him.

"Be cautious with your loving," she said gently, withdrawing from his arms. "I caught a sight of Mr Marshall down yonder."

"I'll be content to gaze at you after such a long time," he said as they entered the summer-house.

"Aye, for a whiley... Here's the tinder-box, put a light to the cones and I'll pick some mint. I should have brought some with me for the soil in the Quarry garden is not as good as in my garden."

He watched her preparing the brew, youthful and lovely in lemon- sprigged muslin.

"It's all over then?" Though she felt that she had to make some comment, it was not her intention to ask any question, realizing that the British defeat in the colonies was a bitter blow to him. She was surprised when he replied: "Thank God, the British fleet has been able to raise its head proudly again."

"What do you mean?"

"After the disastrous siege at Yorktown Peninsula, when Cornwallis had to surrender, Rodney sailed to the West Indies and met the victorious De Grasse and his fleet of thirty-five ships off the island of Dominica. He broke the French fleet in two."

Aye, but the English had to clear out of America, she thought, pleased.

When they had their drinks, Alexander said, "Is your gown too fine to go walking in the hills? I have a great longing to look down on my peaceful kingdom."

They walked until they came to a green glade where they rested and talked, and watched a pair of greenshanks changing over nesting duties. He felt relaxed after the strain and work during the past few years with his regiment. Thank goodness he would be able to rest for a while and then begin work on his estates. Jean, too, felt suddenly released from the nagging regret that had filled her mind over the past few years, of not being happily wed and raising a family like other girls of her age.

He kissed her lightly on the lips, as though frightened to show the feeling rising in his body at her closeness; he felt as though the age of battle was leaving his limbs, that this beautiful girl was giving him back his youth.

She put her hands on each side of his face, and watched the smile slowly touching the strong, perfectly shaped mouth. "What are you thinking?"

"How can I wait until this evening to hold you in my arms?"

"Mr Marshall?"

"He's gone home and the factor is in Elgin." His eyes went to a tunnel of low-sweeping branches. He rose and held out his hand.

The next occasion for a bonfire to be lit in the village square was to celebrate the birthday of Alexander's eldest son, George, Marquis of Huntly. The Duchess crowded the castle with servants, friends and artists. Jean knew by the look in her cousin's eye that Robert Burns was going to be one of the guests.

On the night of the bonfire, the bard and Sheena were together most of the time. Jean wondered what the Duchess of Gordon thought of it for, according to Claire Gubbay, tongues had been wagging in far-off London about the number of times Burns had accompanied Jane Gordon to balls and functions in Edinburgh.

The following morning, Jean was over in the inn helping Sheena to fold some linen. "I saw you with that Robert Burns last evening in the square."

"And what if you did?" her cousin answered defiantly.

"Sheena, he's not for you. He'll have you in the hay and breeding as likely as not."

Colour flamed in her cousin's cheeks. She tossed her head and said: "Look who's talking!"

"I know," Jean said gently, "but you and he are like ships that pass in the night. He's got an awful reputation, fathering bairns from here to Ayrshire, I'm told."

"He'll not father mine 'till I've a ring on my finger."

"There's some who say he's wed already. Sheena, I'm only speaking for your own good. Have a care, that Rabbie Burns would lure a scarecrow out of a field. You'll never be able to handle him."

Her cousin picked up the pile of linen. "Thanks for your help, Jean. I'm no more anxious to discuss Robert Burns than you are to discuss the Duke of Gordon."

Jean was thinking about the poet farmer as she walked from the inn to the post office. And there he was, talking to the post-mistress whose face was melting like butter on a hot tattie.

Burns was feeling on top of the world. He was no longer a shy young man who had attracted the Duchess of Gordon's attention by his wit and talent. Now he was a highly successful poet and the toast of Edinburgh society. He liked Jane Gordon and enjoyed her company. She was that rare thing in a woman of her class: bawdy in speech and out-spoken in her political opinions. He was looking forward to several days of the Gordons' hospitality at the castle, and the good company. He liked the Duke too, who was quietly humorous, with no mean talent himself but not in the class of his clerk, William Marshall. He frowned for a second; though he was lionised by all these society people he could not earn enough to rid himself of the debts which constantly clouded his life. Still, best to put them out of his thoughts for now. There was something else about this visit to Fochabers, something that sent the blood pumping through his veins: the lovely fair lassie who lived at the inn—Sheena.

The postmistress touched his arm. "Mr Burns, may I introduce you to our minister?"

Robert turned and looked at the dour-faced man. God's truth, clerics were an awful pain in the belly to him.

"I've heard about you," the minister said loftily.

"Oh aye," the bard replied with a twinkle in his eye. "I hope it was to my credit."

Jean and Elsie Chalmers were surprised when the minister said bluntly: "Some things, sir, were *not* to your credit."

Robert Burns's eyes darkened. "I have done my stint on the Stool of Repentance, so I'll have no preaching from you, please, if you don't mind."

"I can tell you, sir, that I disapprove of your lewd verses and," the minister banged the counter, "I hope, Mr Burns, you will leave no pain in this village. I think you know what I mean." And with those words, he walked out of the post office.

The outburst silenced everyone. The minister must have seen Sheena with the bard, Jean decided. But what lewd verses? She remembered the lovely words Alexander had recited to her from one of Burns's poems:

"It is na, Jean, thy bonnie face
Nor shape that I admire
Altho' thy beauty and thy grace
Might weel awauk desire.
Something, in alka parts o' thee,
To praise, to love, I find,
But dear as is thy form to me,
Still dearer is thy mind..."

Robert Burns, with the impish grin of a small boy, shrugged away the uncomfortable scene, paid for his purchases and went out of the post office, leaving a trail of charm behind him. A few days later, Big Annie told Jean that the bard had left the castle sooner than the Gordons had been expecting.

"What do you think happened?" she enquired.

Annie explained that she had been delivering meat at the castle and had listened to the gossip in the kitchen. The Duchess had been overheard rebuking Lady Charlotte, telling her to "keep her big orbs off the bard. He's not for the likes of you. Colonel Lennox will be asking papa for your hand any day now". "What do ye think of that, Jean?"

Lady Charlotte will be all right, she thought, but what about poor Sheena? Surely the minister's warning had not frightened away anyone as worldly as Burns? She went across to the inn, making the excuse of enquiring about her aunt, who was ailing.

Uncle John rolled his eyes. "She'll no' see you, lass. She says she'd rather die in peace than be touched by sin! Go in and see Sheena, she's wilting these days too and I dinna ken what's ailing her either. You lassies."

Jean went into the kitchen and sat down. "I hear Rabbie Burns has left the castle," she said carefully.

"Has he?" Sheena replied without lifting her eyes. "Did the Duke tell you?"

"No, he never discusses the guests at the castle. You don't seem all that surprised, Sheena."

Her cousin chopped an onion and put it in the stock pot. "I don't want to end up like you, Jean, breaking my heart over a man who can never wed me but for all that, would like to bed me."

Jean rose and put her hand sympathetically on Sheena's arm. She didn't know what to say. The minister must have preached at her. He would have a lot of influence on someone like her cousin. Still, whatever happened, the bard had shown great strength of character by taking himself off, if that had been the reason for his departure. She looked closely at Sheena and was sad to see how her delicate colouring seemed to have a faded look already. Jean dreaded that her cousin might end her days with this far-away expression in her eyes.

The picture that Claire Gubbay had painted all those years about the life Jean should expect if she became the mistress of the Duke of Gordon, did not turn out to be entirely accurate. Although Alexander had to be away for a certain amount of time, because he held many important offices, including Lord Keeper of the Great Seal of Scotland, and Lord Lieutenant of Aberdeenshire, he always hurried back to Fochabers. He was still passionately in love with Jean.

In his absence she continually read the pieces she had cut out from the news-sheet about him. Lord Keines had called him "The greatest subject in Britain, not only in the extent of his rent-roll, but of the number of persons depending on his rule and protection". When they climbed the hills, or crept silently through the woods to watch the wildlife, Jean found it difficult to think that this gay, casually-dressed man was so important.

With all her happiness, a cloud remained in her life: the constant yearning to have a child. Then suddenly, after all those years of longing, she became pregnant again and remained in that state long past the time when she usually miscarried.

She was sitting sewing in the garden one afternoon when Claire Gubbay called, accompanied by Tessa, who now worked for Claire all the time. Fiona carried out a tea tray, then she and her mother went to the kitchen to chat about family affairs. Tessa had never married again, but had devoted her life to her family and to the church. Jamie, who was the image of his father, had leased land from the Duke and ran a successful farm down in Dallachy.

"Have you told him yet?" Claire asked, accepting a piece of shortcake.

Jean smiled. "When he returned from London he thought I looked bonny with my increase in weight!"

Claire smiled to hide her concern. Jane Gordon will go wild if there is a child of this union. "Tell him, my dear. It is not a burden you should bear alone."

A burden, Jean thought ...a very precious one. After Claire and Tessa left, she strolled down to the burn and sat on the bank by a cluster of harebells and watched the clear water chattering merrily to the stones as it hurried on to the river. It was the scent of broom, carried by a soft wind, that made her feel restless. She wondered if she dare walk towards Bogmore. Perhaps a walk would do her good after weeks of resting.

When she was on the high ground, she noticed one of the castle gillies waving his hands to another figure standing higher up. Alexander had explained to her how he had introduced semaphore on the estate to give notice of the movements of the deer. She realized it would be unwise to return the way she had come in case she interfered with the effectiveness of the signal. But her body was beginning to need rest. Perhaps it would be a good idea to walk on to the Quarry garden, which was not all that far off now. The minute Jean stretched out on the couch in the summer-house, she was aware of how foolish she had been to walk so far.

The day was drawing in when she was disturbed from a long, deep sleep. "Jean–" Alexander crossed quickly to her side. "Are you ill?" he asked in alarm.

"Nae, love, not ill," she said sleepily, "just cautious."

"What do you mean, darling?"

"I mean," she said deliberately, "if I hadn't rested a bit, I might have lost the child I'm carrying." She shut her eyes. Now he knows. I can't be bothered if he's put out or not. When he didn't say anything, she said sharply: "I can breed as well as the Duchess, and I'll tell you something, Alexander Gordon, I've got as much right to whether you like it or not. My bairn was conceived out of love. I've got everything else in life... I've been wanting a bairn for years." Tears began to run down her cheeks. He put a finger on her lips, then slipped his arm around her shoulders and said: "I really am delighted, my love. I don't think anyone will begrudge you this happiness."

Oh dear heart, she thought wearily, they'll not like it. It's one thing to be the Duke's mistress but to set up in opposition to the Duchess is a step in the wrong direction, even though Jane Gordon must be past child-bearing. "Alexander, I'll have to bide here for a while. You see–" Then she told him about all her fruitless pregnancies and her great fear that she would lose this child, too.

Horrified, he stared at her. "All those times and you never told me."

"You wouldn't have been so pleased when you were younger, but as things worked out you seemed to be away at...convenient times."

He jumped to his feet. "You're not to put a foot on the ground," he said sternly. "I'm sending a gillie back to the castle for a carriage. I'll carry you down to the road."

"Och, Alexander..."

"Stay here," he commanded, moving towards the door. Then he turned and putting his hands around her face said: "It is my child too. I can't think of anything more beautiful than having a child of our own."

Some months later, Jean and Alexander's son, Adam Gordon, was born; a fine strong child who bore a remarkable resemblance to his father. Right through the remaining months of her pregnancy, and afterwards, the Duke took Jean out driving in his carriage. When the Duchess heard about it she wrote a long, bitter letter to her husband. "It is one thing to air your strumpet in *our* carriage, but I must ask you not to air your bastards as well."

The years passed and once again, Jean was overjoyed when her daughter, Charlotte, was born. Sadly, the child was frail from birth and did not live for long. I was too old, she thought, feeling heart-broken at the death of her baby daughter. For the first time in her life, she began to feel envious of the woman who had borne Alexander daughters and sons.

Down through the years, Claire Gubbay had kept her informed about the Duchess's activities. Often, Jean found herself secretly admiring the extraordinary woman who was Alexander's wife. Particularly when she presented her son, the Marquis of Huntly, at court in his kilt while she herself wore a gown made of tartan which afterwards became the rage of London. The incident delighted Jean's Jacobean heart when she heard that the action had infuriated the Duchess of Cumberland, whose uncle had been responsible for debarring the kilt and tartan as symbols of disloyalty after his victory at Culloden. The entire countryside was filled with admiration when the Duchess took to the roads on horseback to raise a Highland regiment–the Gordon Highlanders–by offering a kiss with the King's shilling.

Some of the Duchess's exploits annoyed Alexander and one day, for the first time, he complained bitterly to Jean about his wife's extravagances. He was angered that she had made a trip to France where she had tried to make a match between his youngest daughter, Georgiana, and Eugene de Beauharais, Napoleon's stepson. Jean remembered the stories Claire had told her about the Duchess's ambition to marry all her daughters to dukes or better, and the extravagant parties she had held to make her ambitions succeed.

The Duchess's continual absence from the castle troubled her. It was more noticeable than before, for Jane Gordon seemed to have made a complete break with her life in Fochabers.

"She has taken too many of my affairs into her hands and mismanaged them," Alexander said angrily one day. "I will not tolerate any longer this vast drain on my resources."

If only, she thought, he had taken a firmer line years ago, for now there was this continual trouble between them. She could not help but feel guilty, even though she had read in the news-sheet that the Duchess and Mr Pitt had been inseparable for years. Surely, though, the Prime Minister was years younger than Jane Gordon?

The Duke was away from Fochabers when news reached the village of his wife's illness. Then, some weeks later, there came word of her death. Claire Gubbay was very distressed and, though she suffered from rheumatism, she made the long journey to Kinrara where Jane Gordon was buried. Though the Duchess had not visited the village for several years, everyone was saddened by her death.

When Alexander eventually returned, he and Adam went out walking together while Jean kept quietly in the background, performing her customary duties about the village. One evening, some months later, she and Adam were sitting by the fire. He was reading, and she was entering notes in her herbal book. Suddenly he looked at her and said: "Mother, will my father marry you now that the Duchess has died?"

Startled, she stared at him, unable to speak for a moment. "What sort of daftie are you, Adam," she said sharply. "You know that is not possible."

"But you are so close, Mother. Sometimes you sit down here for hours, talking. I can hear your laughter when I am working up in the study. Fiona thinks that Father might–"

"I'm surprised that Fiona has aired her opinion on the matter. Indeed if it is as daft as yours, I'll not hear it." Agitatedly, Jean bent over her work. Several times Alexander had approached the subject. At first she had been horrified, now if he brought it up she would say quietly: "I am content as I am." It was unthinkable, a woman of her station marrying into the great house of Gordon. She could just imagine the horror of Alexander's heir, the Marquis of Huntly, and his daughters, who were married into the most important families in the land. Jean loved her son dearly and felt troubled that he was cherishing a dream that his parents would marry one day.

"How are you getting on with your studies, Adam?" she asked to change the subject.

"I don't know why Father insists on my studying Latin. What good is it when all I want is to be a farmer?"

"He wants you to be well educated, dear. I wish I had been. If I wasn't so old I'd be up in the study beside you, taking heed of your tutor."

At that moment Fiona came through the door carrying the supper tray. "Fiona," Adam said, "my mother is thinking of coming up to the study to work with me and my tutor."

Fiona put down the tray and began to giggle. "Och, the poor wee mannie will no' ken whether he's coming or going. He falls o'er himself every time he sees your mother. He's right taken wi' her." And no wonder, she thought, she's still as bonny as ever, not a grey hair in that magnificent head of hair and her eyes as clear as a young girl's.

Out in the kitchen, Fiona put some fuel on the fire and prepared to leave to go to her own home where she lived with Dobson. She smiled; after all the time they had been married, she still thought of him by that name. The castle servants called him Dobbie, but his first name was Tim.

It was strange how they had become friends, the shy Englishman— years older than herself—and the awkward young girl. Fiona let her mind drift back to the day when she had been outside her mother's house trampling blankets in the wooden tub. Tim had come along and greeted her, then had looked away quickly, for her skirts had been rolled up above her knees. She had been so intent on gazing at his back that she had slipped and tumbled out on the grass. She giggled every time she thought of his embarrassment when he helped to pick her up. After that they had become friends.

She had needed friends then, particularly a lad of her own.

Village boys had not been anxious to take up with Tessa's illegitimate daughter. Through Tim Dobson's eyes, and Jean's help, Fiona had made a rapid change from the unattractive self-conscious girl, who had been plagued with spots on her skin. Jean used to scold her for thinking so little of herself, but it was Tim who had brought about the miracle when he told her one day that she had the most beautiful eyes he had ever seen, like pools of dark brown velvet. Och, he was daft at times!

When she and Tim Dobson were wed, the Duke had given them a house down at Burnside. Now she was as happy as the day was long.

Jean spent a restless night. She was glad that Alexander was calling in the morning, though they had not planned to drive far, just down to Dallachy to look at some land.

"Bring out my best bonnet and gown," she told Fiona when she was dressing.

"To go to Dallachy? Are ye calling anywhere?"

"No."

"Well, if ye want to dress up for the cow's..."

"For the Duke!"

"But ye know fine well, Jean, he likes you in your second best gown."

Jean smiled. "I fancy giving my best one an airing."

As the three of them were driving past Bellie churchyard, Alexander said, "Did you know, Adam, that the eldest son of the great Montrose was buried somewhere over there in the churchyard?"

"Really? Can we look, father?"

The carriage was stopped and they alighted. As they drew near the church grounds, Jean hesitated. There seemed to be a garden party going on. At that moment Mr Rennie, the minster, came towards them and insisted that the Duke and his guests should take some refreshments. As they approached the crowd of people, all smartly dressed in bright colours, Jean recognised a few of them. The minister explained that the garden party had been organized by Lord and Lady Derwent for the church funds.

"Derwent?" Alexander said. "I haven't seen him for some time."

Mr Rennie led them across to where the gentry were gathered, and presented the Duke of Gordon and Mistress Chrystie. Adam hung back, not knowing what to do; at the same time, he understood the minister's awkwardness about presenting him.

Lady Derwent swept a curtsey to the Duke. "How delightful to meet you, your Grace." Then deliberately, she turned her back on Jean and Adam, took Alexander's arm, and went to lead him towards her friends.

Jean felt as though someone had thrown a bucketful of icy cold water in her face. Adam flushed, and to her dismay, she saw his head drop in deep embarrassment. It all happened in a second. The Duke withdrew slightly from the clutching woman and said in a loud voice. "Pardon me, Lady Derwent, but first may I present to you, Jean Chrystie, the future Duchess of Gordon, and my son, Adam Gordon." A silence fell over the crowd, then the minister with a delighted expression turned to Jean with his congratulations. Adam raised his head and smiled happily at his parents.

Back in the carriage, Alexander said with a mischievous grin: "Now you cannot very well get out of it, my darling, can you?"

Speechless, she shook her head, as a feeling of happiness rose in her. Alexander kissed her hand and Adam hugged her.

It was a beautiful hot day in July when Jean Chrystie became the Fifth Duchess of Gordon. They were married by the Reverend Rennie in the church of Bellie. The villagers, carrying armfuls of flowers, flocked to the church to wish them happiness. That evening, in the village square of Fochabers, there was a bonfire and a banquet on the village green where roast ox, game and Spey salmon were served to the villagers.

Later, when Fiona was helping Jean to prepare for bed, she put her hand to her mouth and said "Och, I canna get it out."

"What's the matter?" She looked anxiously at Fiona. "Has something got stuck in your tooth?"

Fiona shook her head. "Your Grace...the Duchess of Gordon."

Their eyes met in the looking-glass and then they both began to laugh helplessly, as they had done so often down through the years.